THE RIDDLE AT GIPSY'S MILE

An Angela Marchmont Mystery Book 4

CLARA BENSON

MOUNT STREET PRESS

Copyright

© 2014 Clara Benson

All rights reserved

ClaraBenson.com

Cover concept by Yang Liu
WaterPaperInk.com

Cover typography and interior book design by Colleen Sheehan
WDRBookDesign.com

Print spine and back cover design by Shayne Rutherford
DarkMoonGraphics.com

CHAPTER ONE

THE ROMNEY MARSH in Kent is famous for its stark, flat beauty, and its vast expanses of landscape. A thousand years ago it belonged to the sea, but over the centuries the enterprising local populace slowly began to drain the land and claim it for their own. Today, it is a quiet, sparsely-inhabited place: an area of grazing land bounded by a criss-crossing of drainage ditches and narrow lanes in which it is easy for the unwary traveller to lose his way. It is so deserted that one might travel for miles without seeing a soul.

It was along one of these lanes on a chilly September day that Lucy Syms rode her chestnut mare at a gentle trot. The morning had been fine—sunny with just that hint of crispness in the air which betokened the arrival of autumn—but after lunch, when she had set out again, the clouds had descended suddenly and the mist had begun to roll in across the marsh. Soon it would be impossible to see anything. Lucy gave an impatient click of her tongue. Her horse, Castana, was a skittish, nervy type who disliked the fog and needed only the slightest excuse to become restive.

'Don't worry, girl,' said Lucy soothingly, as the mare tossed her head and snorted. She patted Castana's neck. 'We'll turn back in a moment. It's just our bad luck that this mist decided to come down now.'

She straightened up and looked about her, hoping that the sun would burn through the mist quickly. But no: even as she looked, the grey dampness extended its arms and enfolded them both in its clammy embrace. The horse pranced and huffed.

'Bother,' said Lucy. She nudged Castana. 'Come on, then. We'll have to try again when the fog lifts.'

Just then she heard the familiar sound of a motor-engine in the distance, and paused to listen. The sound grew louder. She tugged on the reins gently and managed to persuade Castana to leave the road and stand on the grass verge. Presently, the outline of a large motor-car could be distinguished through the mist. It approached slowly and came to a halt by Lucy, its engine purring gently. A window opened.

'Hallo,' said a voice cheerfully. 'I'm awfully sorry to trouble you, but we seem to have lost our way.'

The voice belonged to a woman with dark hair and a smiling expression. She was dressed fashionably and elegantly and appeared to be somewhere in the middle thirties.

'Where do you want to go?' asked Lucy.

'It's a house called Gipsy's Mile, just outside Littlechurch,' said the woman. 'The signposts are rather confusing around here and I fear we may have taken a wrong turning a little way back.'

'Yes, you did,' agreed Lucy. 'I know Gipsy's Mile very well. You must go back the way you came, then turn left. Carry on for five hundred yards or so then turn right at the crossroads. The house is on your right about a mile farther on.'

'Thank you,' said the woman, then to Lucy's surprise turned and said something that sounded like, 'Two bob!' to her driver.

'Are you a friend of the Harrisons?' asked Lucy curiously.

'Yes,' replied the woman. 'Do you know them?'

'Yes—at least, my fiancé is a friend of Miles's.'

'Oh? Then perhaps we'll see each other again. I'm Angela Marchmont, by the way.'

'Lucy Syms,' said Lucy. Castana was getting restless and showing signs of wanting to throw herself in front of the car. 'I must take my horse home now. She doesn't like the mist. Goodbye, and good luck!'

She nudged the mare and set off back the way she had come. A little way down the road she looked back and saw the car turning with some difficulty. After a few minutes it was successful and roared off into the fog. Lucy patted her horse's neck and they started home at a trot.

In the car, Mrs. Marchmont was engaged in an animated debate with her American driver, William.

'You agreed two bob,' she said.

William shook his head.

'I think you must have misheard me, ma'am,' he said. 'I merely said that if I were a betting man, I would bet you two shillings that this was the right road.'

Angela assumed a mock-stern expression.

'I am shocked, William, shocked, that you should attempt to use such a shabby excuse to worm out of your responsibilities. I distinctly heard you promise to pay me money if you were wrong.'

'Well, that's as may be,' said William. 'It would be impertinent of me to contradict you directly, ma'am. But I'd like to remind you—respectfully, of course—that you still owe me half a crown from the last time we had a bet.'

'What? Do you mean the boat race? But surely I paid up?'

William shook his head.

'Nope,' he said.

'Are you quite certain?'

'Perfectly certain.'

'Oh!' said Angela, and paused. 'Then I suppose that means I am in your debt for sixpence.'

'It would seem so, ma'am,' agreed William, abandoning all pretence about the existence or otherwise of the two-shilling bet.

'We shall have to do something about that,' said Angela. 'Now, let me see, what have we got? There's the Autumn Double coming up. That ought to be worth a flutter. Terms to be agreed upon.'

'You're on,' said William. 'I want my sixpence, at the very least. Now then, that must be the turning there.'

He guided the Bentley carefully around the sharp bend, and almost immediately the car plunged into a dense patch of fog, rendering the countryside around them almost completely invisible—so much so that it was barely possible to see more than a yard or two in any direction.

'Dear me!' said Mrs. Marchmont. 'How inconvenient. Should we stop and wait for the fog to clear, do you think?'

'I don't know, ma'am. How long does it generally last around these parts?' said William doubtfully. 'Days, or only hours?'

'I was thinking rather in terms of minutes,' said Angela, 'but since I have no desire to sit in the middle of a field until Sunday, perhaps we had better press on. Be careful, though.'

William switched on the head-lamps and advanced cautiously. The road was wide enough to admit only one vehicle, and was bounded on both sides by deep drainage channels which were almost entirely screened off by thick hedgerow. One careless move and the car could career off the road and into the ditch. After a hundred yards or so, the fog thinned and William accelerated a little. He was too precipitate, however, for almost immediately they plunged into another fog patch, causing him to slow again—luckily for the flock of sheep which happened at that moment to be wandering in the lane just ahead of them. There was a thump and a chorus of bleats, and William gave a yell of surprise and swerved to the right. He was briefly aware of a horde of startled woolly faces caught in the beam of the head-lamps, before the Bentley hurtled through the hedgerow, tipped forwards and screeched to a stop on a muddy bank, just inches from the water.

There was a moment of silence.

'Are we there yet?' said Angela sweetly.

William drew a deep breath and wiped his brow.

'I'm deeply sorry about that, ma'am. You're not hurt, I hope?' he said.

'I don't think so,' said Angela. 'What about you?'

'I'm fine—I think,' he said.

'Can we get out, do you imagine?'

William opened the door and stepped out carefully. Angela, fearful that the alteration in the car's weight might cause it to slide further into the ditch, did likewise without waiting for him. They gazed at the Bentley, which sat at a crazy angle and seemed to glare back at them reproachfully.

'I don't suppose there's any use in trying to back it out,' said Angela. 'The sides of this ditch are far too steep. We shall need some horses, or a mechanic, or something. Do you think there's much damage?'

William rubbed his chin and bent to examine the front wheels.

'I don't know,' he said. 'There was a mighty big thump as we went down. I wonder about the front axle.'

'Well, there's nothing we can do at present,' said Angela. 'Suppose we get the luggage out and carry it up the bank. I'll help you.'

William unloaded the suitcases while Angela examined the muddy sides of the ditch, trying to decide upon the best and least dirty spot from which to climb up to the road. During its header, the Bentley had torn a gap in the hedgerow, and the bank there was slippery, with deep tyre tracks, and impossible to climb. Angela picked her way gingerly along the water's edge to where the undergrowth was thicker and the slope less steep and muddy.

'I believe we might be able to get up here,' she called to William. The young man joined her and she pointed out the spot she meant. 'You see?' she said. 'There, to the left of that blue rag. We can use these branches as handholds.'

William nodded.

'All right,' he said, and picked up the biggest suitcase, which was awkward but fortunately not heavy.

Angela picked up a smaller bag.

'No need to do that, ma'am,' said William.

'Don't be silly,' said Angela, and motioned to him impatiently to start.

They scrambled with difficulty up the steep bank, fighting their way through the thick undergrowth and using tree roots as stairs, then finally emerged from the thicket and stopped to catch their breath. The sheep were still milling about on the road. One seemed to be limping.

'Look, that must be the one you hit,' said Angela.

'Blasted animals,' said William with feeling. 'Begging your pardon, ma'am.'

'Is that everything?' said Angela.

'There's just my own things to fetch,' said William, and half-swung, half-jumped back down the slope with a great cracking of twigs. Angela regarded the sheep. The sheep regarded Angela. Then one of them bleated and received a chorus of bleats in reply. It was almost as though they were laughing at her. She felt quite uncomfortable and turned away. The mist had thinned again and the sun was making feeble attempts to appear. Gipsy's Mile was still some way away, but if they started soon they would arrive in time for tea, at any rate.

At that moment, there was a cry from behind her, and she heard a crack of branches and a thud. She turned and peered through the vegetation to find that William had dropped his suitcase, which had fallen and landed in the ditch. He was holding tightly onto the trunk of a tree, staring at something, pale in the face.

'What on earth—' began Angela, then followed his gaze and saw what he was looking at. Her eyes opened in surprise and she started forward, back down the bank.

'Get away, ma'am,' said William. 'Get away.'

But it was too late. The two of them stared, open-mouthed, at the sight before them. Angela wondered how she could possibly have missed it, for the blue rag which she had seen before was not a blue rag at all. It was a woman's coat. She was still wearing it, and she was quite, quite dead.

CHAPTER TWO

WILLIAM SWALLOWED. HE was still very pale.
'Go and fetch your suitcase,' said Angela grimly.
'We must call the police as soon as possible.'

'Do—do you think it could have been an accident?' said
William.

'I doubt it,' said Angela. She moved a little closer. The dead
woman was lying on her side, one arm thrown out above her
head and the other wrapped about her own waist. It looked
as though she had been thrown down the slope at the point
where the undergrowth was thickest. Had William not swerved off the road, she might never have been discovered.

'Perhaps we ought to carry her to the top of the bank,' said
William, although he did not look as though he relished the
prospect.

'No,' said Angela firmly. 'She must be left here. The police
will want to examine the scene. We've already disturbed enough as it is. Go and get your things. We had better start off
immediately.'

William did as he was instructed and returned, unable to stop himself from glancing at the dead woman as he passed again.

'We shall get on quicker if we leave our things here,' said Angela. 'We can send someone back to get them later. Now, which way was it? I believe we carry on to the end here then turn right and walk for another mile.'

They set off along the road at a brisk pace. Lucy's directions proved correct, and about twenty minutes later they arrived at the house and turned in at the gate. Gipsy's Mile was a low, rambling farm-house which was set well back from the lane and was surrounded by grazing land. The house was named after a nearby field that had once been the site of illegal horse-racing, and it suited its name perfectly, given its ramshackle exterior and peeling paint. The Harrisons had moved to Kent from London on a whim a year or two ago, and Angela had been surprised at first, knowing Marguerite Harrison, who was not the sort of person to hide herself away from society. However, Marguerite had soon surrounded herself with a regular coterie of friends and hangers-on from London and elsewhere and, she assured Angela, had never been happier.

'Darling! What on *earth* have you been doing to yourself?' came a dramatic voice from a downstairs window as Angela and William walked up the front path with torn clothes and muddy shoes. 'Don't move an inch!' the voice continued.

The window slammed and shortly afterwards the front door was flung open to reveal a tall, angular woman wearing an extraordinary head-dress and a gorgeous array of silk scarves and shawls. She ran out and engulfed Angela in a perfumed embrace, then stood back and examined her from head to toe in an attitude of exaggerated horror.

'But where *have* you been?' she said. 'We were expecting you hours ago!'

'I—' began Angela, but Marguerite had caught sight of William, who had removed his chauffeur's cap in order to brush the dirt off it.

'And *who* is this?' she said. 'Why, Angela, you sly thing! You never said a word.'

William's face turned a splendid shade of pink and he immediately clapped the hat back on his head.

'This is my driver,' said Angela hurriedly. 'We had a bit of an accident on the way here.'

'An accident? Why, you poor darling! You're not hurt?'

'No, just rather muddy. But Marguerite—'

'Then we must get you cleaned up. Come in, darling, come in!' She ushered them both into the house. 'Miles! Miles! Angela has been in a terrible accident.'

'Oh, no, it was nothing like that,' said Angela as William escaped thankfully to the kitchen.

Miles Harrison emerged from somewhere and looked at Angela vaguely. He was even taller and thinner than his wife, with a long, mournful face and the air of a man who had long since given up the fight.

'What's that?' he said to Marguerite. 'Who's had an accident?'

'Angela, of course. Can't you see the state of her?'

'Oh, hallo, Angela,' said Miles, seeming to recognize her at last. 'What's all this?'

'We had an unexpected encounter with some sheep and ran into the ditch,' said Angela. 'We had to leave the car and our luggage and walk the rest of the way here. But listen, that's not important—'

'Miles, are those people at the garage in Littlechurch on the telephone? You must call them immediately,' said Marguerite. 'No—I have a better idea. Miles shall go and get your things and I'll call the garage—or would it perhaps be better if we sent your driver? Let me think, now—'

Angela turned her eyes beseechingly to Miles Harrison, who perfectly understood.

'I think Angela wants to tell us something, old girl,' he said to his wife, who had grabbed the telephone and was gabbling urgently into the receiver, asking to be put through to the garage.

'We must call the police immediately,' said Angela. 'You see, when we were climbing out of the ditch I'm afraid we found something rather unpleasant.'

Something in her tone caused both the Harrisons to turn their full attention to her.

'What was it?' said Marguerite, the receiver suspended in her hand.

'It was the body of a woman.'

The Harrisons looked at each other. Even Marguerite was briefly silenced.

'How awful,' she said at last. 'Did she fall into the ditch?'

'No,' said Angela. 'I'm very much afraid that she was murdered.'

'Why do you say that?' asked Miles, just as Marguerite cried, 'Murdered!'

'Because her face was all smashed in,' said Angela. She felt a little sick at the memory. 'I don't think she could have done that simply by falling.'

Marguerite turned back to the telephone.

'I've changed my mind,' she said. 'Put me through to the police, please. What do you mean, you can't put me through? Oh, I see. Is that Mr. Turner? Hallo, Mr. Turner, it's Mrs. Harrison here. I shall need you to send your men along to pull a car out of a ditch presently, but not just now. No, nobody has been murdered. Are you sure you can't put me through to the police? Oh, very well. I shall call you again in a while.'

She rattled the hook and spoke to the operator again.

'Perhaps you had better talk to them,' she said to Angela.

Angela took the receiver and found herself speaking to a young police constable who perked up immediately at the prospect of a real murder case. He listened carefully as she told him what had happened, then asked her to describe exactly where they had found the body. No, there was no need for Mrs. Marchmont to show them where it was—he knew the spot perfectly. He would speak to the sergeant immediately and they would take some men along to investigate. In the meantime, please would Mrs. Marchmont be so kind as to remain in the area until tomorrow? Mrs. Marchmont said she was more than happy to do so, and hung up.

'You look as though you could do with a brandy,' said Miles. 'Come and sit down and I'll fix you up.'

Angela acquiesced gladly and followed him into a large, comfortable sitting-room that bore all the signs of Marguerite's eclectic taste in furnishings. None of the chairs matched: some were low and overstuffed, others rigid and high-backed. Occasional tables were placed about the room, some of them displaying odd items from Marguerite's collection of ornaments and sculptures produced by her artistic protégés, many more scattered with books and newspapers. The walls were draped in brightly-coloured tapestries, most of them produced by Marguerite herself during a brief passion for the art a few years earlier. The overall effect was very characteristic and not unattractive.

Angela sat down thankfully on a sofa and accepted the glass of brandy that Miles had poured her. After a sip or two she felt much better, and capable of replying to Marguerite's barrage of questions. The Harrisons were most concerned at the idea of there having been a murder nearby, but both agreed that it was most likely the work of someone who was merely passing through—probably a man who had rowed with his girl and ended up by killing her. No doubt he had disfigured her face in a panic, in the hope that it would prevent anybody from identifying her.

Angela was wondering whether it would be a good idea to accept a second glass of brandy when the sitting-room door opened and a loud voice said, 'Hallo, hallo, what?'

The voice belonged to a large, red-cheeked man in shabby tweeds, who was accompanied by a bird-like woman with sharp eyes that missed nothing. The woman caught sight of Angela and the sharp eyes gleamed.

'Angela, *darling!*' she cried.

'Cynthia, *darling!*' said Marguerite, descending on the newcomers in a cloud of scent and kisses.

'Marguerite, *darling!*' said Cynthia Pilkington-Soames. She flung off her coat and hat and threw herself into a chair. 'Get me a drink, Herbert,' she said to her husband, then went on, 'What a simply *awful* time we've had getting here! Why, we must have got lost at least ten times, I'm sure. What on *earth* made you move to such a God-forsaken part of the world? I'll bet there isn't a decent butcher for miles around! Oh, but of course you needed to save money, didn't you, after that sculpture exhibition of yours did so terribly badly. *Such* a shame nobody wanted to see it.'

'Yes, but it's so refreshing too, to shake off the cares of the world and return to a simpler life,' said Marguerite. 'Why, I find that living here, one is completely removed from the lures and temptations of the city. Perhaps you should try it, darling. It must be so tiresome for you, to be continually reminded of all those debts. Chemmy, isn't it?'

The two women smiled sweetly at each other as Herbert Pilkington-Soames retreated to the safety of the drinks cabinet. Angela and Miles exchanged glances and Angela decided to accept the brandy after all.

'I'm so glad to have caught you at last!' said Cynthia, leaning forward and patting Angela's knee. 'We still haven't done that interview for the *Clarion*, have we? Not since you cancelled your visit here in July to go to Cornwall and recover from your nervous breakdown.'

'I did *not* have a nervous breakdown!' exclaimed Angela, more emphatically than she had intended.

'Well, I can see you're much better now, at any rate—why, you're positively blooming. The sea air must have agreed with you. And of course, Mr. Bickerstaffe is still frightfully keen to get you. We shall have a cosy chat tomorrow, just you and I.'

'Not if I can help it,' thought Angela.

'Is Freddy here?' said Cynthia, looking around.

'Not yet,' replied Miles.

'He promised so faithfully that he would be punctual this time,' said Cynthia with a sigh. 'I swear, darlings, I have simply no idea what to do with that boy. He can't seem to settle down at all. But then twenty-one is such a difficult age.'

'I seem to recall that eighteen, nineteen and twenty were difficult ages for him too,' said Marguerite. Cynthia bridled.

'Not at all,' she said. 'He's just naturally delicate and can't stick at things in the same way others can.' She smiled complacently. 'But I've found him just the thing. They have been looking for a smart young man at the *Clarion*, and I have put Freddy's name forward. I think he'd make a perfectly marvellous reporter, don't you?'

Angela privately thought that the Pilkington-Soameses' indulged only son and child would most likely get the sack after less than a week, but forbore to say so.

'He's already missed a story by being late,' said Marguerite. 'Hasn't he, Angela?'

Angela would far rather have kept the matter quiet, and so merely nodded.

'What's that? Has something happened?' said Herbert, who had made himself at home and was regaling himself with a large whisky.

'Oh yes,' said Marguerite. 'Angela crashed her car on the way here and ran over a woman.'

'That's not quite what happ—' began Angela, but Cynthia's eyes were glittering with excitement.

'You *ran over* a woman?' she said.

'Of course not,' said Angela. 'We ran into the ditch and found a dead body there, that's all.' She added the 'that's all' in the hope of making the thing seem less sensational, but immediately realized to her annoyance that it merely made her sound unfeeling.

'It wasn't *just* a dead body, though, was it?' said Marguerite. 'Angela seems to think she had been murdered. Her head was quite bashed in, you see.'

'No!' breathed Cynthia, thrilled. 'Who did it? Was it a jealous lover, do you suppose?'

'I have no idea,' said Angela. She saw the prospects of escaping Cynthia and her sharp pen receding rapidly, and her heart sank.

'Have the police been here?'

'Not yet,' said Miles. 'I imagine they will come along later, or perhaps tomorrow.'

'And in the meantime I suppose they've told you not to leave the country, Angela, what?' said Herbert with a great guffaw. 'Will they pin it on you, do you think?'

'I hope not,' said Angela politely. Her head was starting to spin from the brandy, and she put down the glass. The events of the past hour were starting to catch up with her. 'If you don't mind, I think I'd like to go and wash, and perhaps have a little rest,' she said.

'Certainly you shall,' said Marguerite. 'Why, you look completely done in, you poor thing. It must have been more of a shock than you thought. Go and lie down for a while, and in the meantime Miles will go and fetch your bags.'

'Oh, certainly,' said Miles in surprise.

'Thank you, I shall,' said Angela, and went out.

CHAPTER THREE

A N HOUR OR two later Mrs. Marchmont emerged
from her room, feeling much refreshed, and went downstairs and into the sitting-room. It was empty apart from a
bored-looking young man who was lounging carelessly in an
easy chair, smoking and yawning. He brightened when he saw
Angela.

'Hallo, Mrs. M,' he said. 'I gather you've been finding dead
bodies all over the place again.'

'Just the one,' said Angela. 'Hallo, Freddy. Where are the
others?'

Freddy Pilkington-Soames gave a shrug expressive of
splendid ennui.

'They *said* they were going to get your things,' he said.

'What, everyone at once? I didn't bring that much.'

'Well, of course, your suitcases are just an excuse, aren't
they? It means they can go and watch all the fun,' he said.

'Oh, *no*,' said Angela.

'I don't think Miles and Father were terribly keen,' he said, 'but you know Mother. She hates to miss out on anything, and of course Marguerite is never one to be outdone.'

Angela could picture it only too well.

'I don't suppose the police will be any too pleased to have a crowd of onlookers,' she said.

'Oh, I dare say they'll all be back in a few minutes, having received a flea in their collective ear,' agreed Freddy. 'Let us hope at least that they remember to bring your bags. Would you be a dear and pour me a glass of whisky? It's taken me half an hour to get this comfortable and I fear that if I got up I should have to start over again.'

Angela raised her eyebrows but poured the drink without comment and handed it to him. He took one or two sips and settled back with every indication of great contentment.

'I should have thought cocktails were more your line,' said Angela.

'Oh, I am too old for such things nowadays,' he said grandly.

'What? At twenty?' said Angela, laughing.

'Twenty-one, if you please,' he said. 'When one reaches man's estate one starts to take life a little more seriously.'

'Oh yes?'

'Yes,' said Freddy sententiously. 'I have been living the life of a mere child up to now, but I think it is time that I accepted my responsibilities and grew up a little.'

'Ah, yes,' said Angela. 'I understand your mother has found you a job.'

Freddy waved his hand.

'Yes,' he said. 'You see before you the new star reporter at the *Clarion*. I am going to shake them up and make them understand that things have changed. No longer can they be content with doing things the old way. We youngsters know a thing or two and we shall show the Old Guard how it's done. I expect I shall be promoted to editor in a year or two. Old Bickerstaffe can't carry on for much longer. Why, he must be forty, at least. I shall pension him off and give him a well-deserved rest.'

He wriggled more comfortably into the cushions.

'Oughtn't you to have gone with the others, then?' said Angela. 'Surely the finding of a dead body is a story worth having?'

He gave a *moue* of distaste.

'Oh, but it's terribly sordid, don't you think? Hardly worth bothering with. Some rough fellow bashes his girl over the head in a fit of anger and throws her out of the car—why, things like that happen a hundred times a day. No, I shall be concentrating my attention on the really important stories.'

'But what could be more important than a murder?'

Freddy hesitated for a moment.

'Well, I suppose that from a certain point of view one *could* say that murder is interesting to the public,' he admitted finally, 'but I am more concerned with the really sensational stories—you know, the ones where Lady So-And-So shoots her lover in a jealous rage and is blackmailed by her maid. They sound so much better when written down.'

'Yes, but you don't get cases like that every day,' said Angela. 'You can't expect Lady So-And-So to go around shooting her lovers all the time just for your benefit.'

'I suppose not,' said Freddy. 'At any rate, though, I mean to show them all how it is done. Not for me the life of a lowly sleuth-hound, sniffing out a scent and running off anxiously to Chelmsford, or Maidenhead, or Huddersfield, to question hundreds of slack-jawed representatives of the local populace. No, I shall merely stand quietly apart from the scene and observe. Then, once I have taken in all the information I require and applied my exceptional powers of the brain to the matter, I shall fasten unerringly on the salient facts of the thing, scribble a note or two and then go home and throw forth a thousand words of such elegant and affecting prose that my colleagues will be moved to tears of joy and envy and Mr. Bickerstaffe will resign on the spot.'

He paused to dwell pleasurably on this enticing prospect and took another sip of whisky.

'If that is the case, then I shall look out with interest for your first piece,' said Angela.

'Do,' he said. 'I assure you, you won't be disappointed. Oh, they're back.'

They looked out of the window and saw Miles's old motor-car turning into the drive. It came to a halt, and shortly afterwards the sound of voices was heard in the hall and Cynthia came breezing in.

'Oh, you're up, Angela,' she said. 'We've been to fetch your bags.'

Freddy said, with an eagerness that belied his earlier apparent lack of curiosity:

'Well, then? What news? Were the police there? Did you see the body?'

Cynthia grimaced and shook her head.

'No, more's the pity. The police would have none of it, even though I told them I represented the *Clarion*. To hear them, one would have thought that we had merely gone along to gawp. Imagine that! Why, we'd never dream of doing anything so vulgar!'

'Quite, darling,' said Marguerite, who had just come in. 'I was most offended. Why, the sergeant even had the impudence to suggest that we had no right to take your luggage, Angela, and that he might have to withhold it as vital evidence.'

'He didn't!' said Angela in alarm.

'Oh, don't worry: Miles convinced him to hand it over in the end. I rather think we'll be receiving a visit from them tomorrow, though.'

'Yes,' said Herbert with a laugh. 'I hope you've a good story ready, Angela.'

'I don't know what I can tell them, other than what they've already seen for themselves,' said Angela.

'Did you spot any clues at all?' asked Miles. 'Anything that might have suggested who did it?'

Angela shook her head.

'Hardly,' she said. 'As soon as we saw what it was we got away as quickly as possible. It wasn't exactly the most pleasant sight, poor thing. That reminds me—I must go and see that William is all right.'

'Your handsome chauffeur?' said Marguerite. 'I gave him to Hannah to look after. She was overjoyed. I saw them flirting in the kitchen just now when we came in. It will be a wonder if we get any dinner this evening.'

'Oh, I am glad,' said Angela, but whether she was relieved at William's well-being or the prospect of being deprived of Hannah's indifferent cooking was unclear.

At that moment the telephone rang shrilly, and Marguerite went to answer it.

'That was Gilbert,' she said when she returned. 'He's heard about our little bit of excitement here, and wants to know whether the police have decided which of us did it.'

'Good gracious,' said Angela. 'How quickly news travels around here! I wonder how he found out.'

'I don't know, but he sounded positively eaten up with curiosity. He and Lucy are going to come over after dinner.'

'Lucy?' said Angela. 'Do you mean Lucy Syms? I met her in the lane on the way here, shortly before we went off the road. We were lost in the fog and she gave us directions. She was on horseback.'

'That would be Lucy,' said Miles. 'Never off a horse. She's engaged to Gilbert Blakeney. Terribly sensible girl. She'll be good for him.'

'I think I've heard you mention Gilbert before. Is he the old army pal you used to talk about?'

'That's the one. He and Herbert and I were together at Passchendaele. Poor Gil: he rather took to the military life. He loved the travelling, and the marching—I even believe he liked the rough digs and awful food—but then just after the war ended his father died, and he found that everyone was expecting him to settle down and take over the old place like a good boy.'

'Which old place is that?'

'Blakeney Park, over towards Hazlett St. Peter. It's an enormous estate—been in his family for centuries, I believe, and every last blade of grass in it belongs to Gil—although he'd far rather it didn't!'

'Oh?' said Angela.

'Yes,' said Miles. 'He'd be the first to admit that he's not the most business-minded fellow. As a matter of fact, there was a period, when he first inherited the estate, during which everybody despaired of him—especially his mother. He couldn't seem to buckle to his responsibilities at all—kept disappearing for weeks on end and then returning, looking very much the worse for wear and refusing to get out of bed for days.'

'The war hit a lot of chaps hard, of course,' said Herbert soberly.

'True,' said Miles, 'but I always thought that in Gil's case it was the *end* of the war that did for him. The task of running the Park was a little too daunting for him. He hasn't the kind of brain that's needed.'

'No, he's not at all bright, is he?' said Cynthia unfeelingly. 'Quite frankly, I'm surprised Lady Alice was prepared to let him loose on the place. He's the sort of person to do all kinds of well-meaning but stupid things. Knowing him, I half-expected the estate to be bankrupt within three years.'

Miles winced.

'At any rate,' he went on, 'he's engaged to Lucy now. They've known each other since they were kids. She has a good head on her shoulders and she'll see him right. I shouldn't be surprised if she were to take the running of the estate upon herself, as a matter of fact.'

'I wonder how she and Gilbert's mother are getting on,' said Cynthia. 'I don't believe Lady Alice ever liked her much. Lucy's far too much the type to take over and start ordering her dear son around. Such a blow to the family pride!'

'Oh, didn't you know, darling?' said Marguerite. 'The engagement was Lady Alice's idea in the first place.'

'No!' said Cynthia.

'Oh, but yes. It's true enough that she and Lucy can't stand each other, but Lady Alice was shrewd enough to see that Lucy was the ideal wife for Gil. After all, she herself is not getting any younger, and she hated the thought of dying without first seeing the estate secure. Lucy is from one of these old families, you know,' went on Marguerite to Angela. 'Some people attach great importance to that kind of thing, although I don't myself—personally, I think a dash of mongrel blood improves a line—but Lady Alice wanted only the finest pedigree stock for the Blakeney estate.'

'Are the Blakeneys a titled family, then?' said Angela.

'No,' said Marguerite, 'although Lady Alice was a daughter of the Duke of Stoke. There were six daughters, I believe, and none of them had a penny to their names as their father was a dreadful old profligate who spent all his money and his wife's and died in debt. Lady Alice was cast out upon the world to make her own way, and had the good fortune to attach herself to Gilbert Blakeney *père*, who was much older than she. Gil was their only child. In recent years, though, she seems to have developed a kind of mania for carrying on the family and seeing to it that the Park is passed on to the next in the Blakeney line. It's odd, really, since the place is only really hers by marriage.'

'Perhaps it is a kind of vicarious interest,' said Angela, 'since her father lost his own property.'

'And people do tend to go a bit dotty when they get old,' said Cynthia.

'I should hardly call Lady Alice dotty,' said Miles. 'Why, she seems perfectly sane to me.'

'Oh those ones are often the worst,' said Herbert darkly. 'The ones who seem the sanest are quite often complete lunatics when you dig beneath the surface.'

'Is Gilbert as keen on making a good marriage as his mother is for him?' asked Angela.

'Well, he and Lucy are coming over later, so you shall ask him for yourself,' said Miles.

CHAPTER FOUR

GILBERT BLAKENEY WAS a large, fair man of about thirty-five whom nobody would ever accuse of being too clever for his own good. What he lacked in brains, however, he made up for in geniality and eagerness to please. On being introduced to Mrs. Marchmont he clasped her hand in an iron grip and wrung it energetically, beaming and blushing as though he had wanted nothing more in life than to meet her and could now die happy.

'I've read all about you in the newspapers, of course,' he said. 'I must say, this detecting thing all sounds very exciting. How do you go about it? Do the police call you in?'

Angela patiently explained, as she had many times before, that she was not a detective and that, far from the police calling her in, they were much more likely to view her as a tremendous nuisance. He nodded, but she saw that he was not listening. People rarely did.

'Will you be investigating this latest one?' he asked, sure enough. 'It was you who found the body, wasn't it?'

'Yes—or rather, it was my driver who saw her first.'

'I gather she was completely unidentifiable,' said Lucy. 'Who did that, do you suppose?'

'Presumably the same person who killed her,' said Angela.

'Rather careless of him to leave her where she would be found so quickly.'

'He wasn't really careless,' said Angela. 'As a matter of fact, it was pure chance that she was ever found at all. The undergrowth grows thickly on both sides of the ditch at that spot, so she couldn't be seen either from the road or from the field on the other side of it. Why, if we hadn't gone off the road she might well have lain there forever, completely undiscovered.'

'It's jolly bad luck for the murderer,' observed Freddy, 'especially now Angela is looking into it.'

'I'm not looking into it,' said Angela. 'It's nothing to do with me—I just happened to stumble upon the body. I dare say the police will catch the fellow who did it quickly enough, once they identify the woman. I wonder who she was.'

She could not help picturing the crumpled heap of clothing and limbs that had once been a person. The smart but cheap blue coat and the worn shoes. The battered mess that had once been a face, surrounded by a halo of golden hair. What had she been like in life? Had she been beautiful? Who had loved her? Loved her and then presumably tired of her and conveniently disposed of her? No doubt it was the usual story, and the man who had killed her would soon feature in a few sorry paragraphs in the *Clarion* when he went on trial. It was all terribly sad.

The two visitors stayed for drinks and the party became rather silly and noisy, and the household did not retire until well past midnight. Angela slept badly that night and came down late the next morning to find the others having breakfast, all apart from Freddy, who was presumably still in bed.

'Hallo, darling,' said Marguerite. 'Do help yourself to coffee and eggs. Herbert has eaten all the muffins, I'm afraid.'

'Sorry, Angela,' said Herbert. 'You'll just have to get up earlier tomorrow.'

'Sergeant Spillett telephoned a few minutes ago,' said Miles, who was buttering some toast. 'He is coming here to talk to you about the woman in the ditch. I dare say he'll want to speak to your man too.'

'But you must tell us all about it,' said Cynthia. 'It will give marvellous colour to my piece for the *Clarion*.'

Angela's heart sank at the thought. It was clear that she would not be able to escape Cynthia's clutches, but she was determined to give as little away as possible. Indeed, the mere thought of having her life history spread all over the papers filled her with horror. She said nothing, but helped herself to coffee and began idly to concoct a few useful lies which would be suitable for consumption by the public and which, she hoped, would spare her too much embarrassment.

She was just finishing breakfast when she was informed that the police had arrived and would like to speak to her at her earliest convenience. She rose immediately.

'See what you can find out!' hissed Cynthia as she went out.

When Angela entered the little parlour she found William already there, looking uncomfortable in a stiff-backed chair, together with two policemen in uniform: a grey-haired sergeant with a bushy moustache and a pimpled youth brandishing a notebook as though not quite sure what to do with it. The three of them rose as she came in.

'Mrs. Marchmont, I believe?' said the elder of the two policemen. 'I am Sergeant Spillett, and this here is P. C. Bass.'

P. C. Bass gave a strangled utterance that might have meant anything, and they all sat down.

'I understand you have come to ask us about the poor woman in the ditch,' said Angela. 'I'm not sure we can tell you anything useful, however.'

'P'r'aps not,' said Spillett comfortably. 'We've still got to ascertain all the facts about the matter, though, and you never know—you might have seen something you didn't think was important but might turn out to be an important clue.'

'I take it the body has been removed?'

The sergeant nodded.

'Yes. We did that straightaway. Wouldn't have done to have left her there overnight, now, would it? It wouldn't have been respectful. She's in the mortuary at Littlechurch.'

'Had she been lying there long? From the glimpse I had of her it looked as though she had been placed there quite recently—perhaps even that same day.'

'Yes,' said Spillett. 'She can't have been there too long, to judge by the condition of her. Her clothes were in a decent state too, always allowing for the mud she collected on her tumble down the bank.' He took out his own notebook and consulted it. 'Now, then, I'd like you to tell me under exactly what circumstances you found the dead woman. I gather from Mr. Harrison that you had a bit of a mishap on your way here yesterday.'

He looked up at them both inquiringly. Angela nodded to William, who described, with some embarrassment, the incident with the sheep in the fog and the discovery of the body.

Spillett nodded sympathetically.

'So that's how you ended up in the ditch. You have to watch out for the fog in these parts—it's a treacherous beast. Nobody hurt, I hope?' he said.

'Not at all,' said Angela. 'We just got a shock.'

'Well, that's all clear enough,' said the sergeant. 'Have you found anybody to come and fetch your car?'

'Mr. Harrison has spoken to a Mr. Turner in Littlechurch, I believe.'

'That's your man,' agreed Spillett. 'He'll see you right.'

''S my uncle,' put in the young constable, then blushed.

'Now then,' went on the sergeant, 'do you remember whether you met or saw anybody on your way here? Another car, for example? Or perhaps a man walking along the road?'

'No,' replied Angela. 'The only person we met along the way was Miss Syms on her horse. We took a wrong turning and she gave us directions.'

'Miss Syms, eh? Make a note of that, Sam. We'll have to speak to her. Maybe she saw somebody. Now,' he continued, 'you say you just had a glimpse of the dead woman, and that's as may be, but I will say that people in general are curious by nature, and there's not a few would have gone up close and taken a good long look—for the best of motives, mind you. Are you quite certain that neither of you touched her at all? Perhaps you wanted to take her pulse to make sure in your mind that she was dead, for example—and I'm sure nobody would think the worse of you if you did.'

Angela shook her head firmly.

'Oh, no,' she said. 'It was quite clear that she was dead as soon as we saw her.'

William nodded in agreement.

'It did occur to me to wonder whether we ought to carry her up to the road,' he said. 'I didn't like leaving her there. But Mrs. Marchmont said that we must leave her where she was, so as not to disturb any evidence.'

'And she was quite right,' said Spillett approvingly.

'I did look at her for a moment or two, wondering who she was,' said Angela, 'but I should hardly call it "taking a good long look," since it wasn't the pleasantest of sights, all told.'

'Then you didn't recognize her at all?'

'No. I have no idea who she was.'

'Me neither,' said William.

'Whoever did it certainly took care to make sure she was unrecognizable,' said Spillett, 'presumably because her identity would lead us straight to him.'

'Didn't she have a handbag with her?' asked Angela.

'No handbag that we could find, and nothing in her pockets,' said Spillett. 'She wasn't even wearing a hat.'

'No, she wasn't, was she?' said Angela thoughtfully. 'I wonder why.'

'Perhaps her killer took it. At any rate, all we have to do now is find out who she was, and then I dare say we'll have our man.'

'Do you know how she died?' asked Angela. 'There wasn't much blood, so I guess she must have been dead already when the murderer smashed her face.'

'We can't say yet,' said the sergeant, 'but the police surgeon will be able to tell us something shortly, no doubt. Did you get all that down, Sam?' he said to the young constable. P. C. Bass nodded.

'Well, then, I think that's all we need for the present,' said his superior. 'We'll be off now, but you will let us know if you think of anything that might help us, won't you?'

'Of course,' said Angela.

She returned to the sitting-room and found the others all there waiting for her.

'Well?' said Cynthia as soon as she entered the room. 'What did they say? Did you get any dirt out of them?'

'None at all,' said Angela. 'It looks as though it's exactly what we thought. The police still don't know who she is, but they seem to think that once they have discovered her identity it will be easy enough to trace the culprit.'

'Oh yes,' said Marguerite. 'No doubt there's a husband or a jilted lover behind the whole thing. Now then, darlings, we all drank a *little* too much last night, so I propose a walk in the fresh air to blow away the cobwebs. What do you say to that?'

The proposal was agreed to and they all went off to change into their outdoor things. Angela was just about to follow them when Freddy drifted into the room, having been finally roused from his bed by the advancing sun.

'I say, what the devil is all this noise?' he said, stifling a yawn. 'How on earth is a chap supposed to get any sleep?'

'It's nearly eleven o'clock,' said Angela.

'Exactly,' he said. 'Far too early to be getting up. I must say, I don't think much of this country life if it requires one to rise before noon. By the way, was that the police I just saw out of the window?' Angela replied in the affirmative, and he went on, 'What active fellows they are. I suppose they came to ask you lots of terribly impertinent questions, did they?'

'Not at all,' said Angela. 'They were very polite.'

'Well, I must say that this whole affair is disrupting my weekend, rather,' he said, 'although I imagine Mother is absolutely thrilled at finding a dead body on her doorstep, so to speak. One doesn't wish to speak disrespectfully of one's parents, but she is rather vulgar, don't you think?'

'She seems to have a good nose for a story,' said Angela pointedly, 'which is a very useful thing to have in the newspaper business.'

'She's a mere amateur,' said Freddy grandly, 'but she's certainly got her hooks into you, hasn't she? She's simply dying to write about you and prove to old Bickerstaffe that she's got the talent to be a real reporter.'

'I don't know why,' said Angela. 'I'm not at all interesting.'

'Oh, come now!' said Freddy. 'Why, everybody knows you have a dark and thrilling past that you have sworn to keep hidden until your dying day.'

'Do they, indeed?' said Angela.

'Of course. You still haven't told anyone what you were doing in America all those years. Mother is convinced it was something shady.'

'Shady? Do you mean drug-running, organized murder, something of that sort?' said Angela with a laugh. She was intrigued, wondering what rumours had been flying around about her.

'Well, perhaps not as shady as that,' said Freddy uncomfortably, 'but something jolly mysterious all the same. She's sworn to worm it out of you, so you had better watch your step.'

'There's nothing to worm,' said Angela. 'My life in the States was very dull and ordinary, for the most part. I shall tell her about all the Committees of Good Works I sat upon in New York. Then she will regret ever having asked me for an interview.'

She went to change into a pair of stout shoes, then returned downstairs to find the others waiting for her.

'Aren't you coming, Freddy?' asked his father.

'Good gracious, no,' said Freddy in horror. 'I haven't had breakfast yet. I can't face the day until I've had two cups of coffee and three cigarettes at the very least. No, you go on, and I shall stay here to receive any callers.'

'Angela, darling,' said Cynthia as they went out. 'You simply must talk to me as we go. Our readers want to know all about your life in America. I've heard you carry a gun. Tell me, is it true that Buffalo Bill wanted you to join his show?'

She grasped Angela's arm firmly. Angela glanced back to see Freddy smirking on the doorstep. He gave her an ironic salute and shut the front door.

Chapter Five

INSPECTOR ALEC JAMESON sat at his desk and frowned. He was writing a report about a case which he had recently brought to a successful conclusion and feeling rather grumpy about it, since he disliked paper-work in general. Still, he had done rather well in this latest case, he reflected—well enough even to bring a smile to the face of his bad-tempered superintendent, perhaps, so he supposed the report-writing would be worth it in the end, even if he had had to give up his Saturday morning for it.

He finished the report and signed his name with a flourish, then read through it carefully. It was only then that he noticed to his annoyance that he had mixed up the name of the gang leader and that of the chief witness throughout the report, which was a long one. He swore to himself, then began laboriously scratching out each name and replacing it with the correct one, but after a paragraph or two it was starting to look very messy. The super would not be pleased. Jameson sighed, pulled a blank sheet of paper towards him and began copying out the report again, this time with the right names.

He had almost finished the first page when the telephone on his desk rang. He picked it up.

'Jameson speaking,' he said. His sergeant, Willis, had just entered the room to deliver a file, and Jameson motioned to him to remain as he listened. Willis hovered politely.

'Where's that? Littlechurch?' said the inspector. 'Can't they deal with it there? It doesn't sound as though it's in our line. Oh, I see. Really? *Who* found it, did you say? Well, I'll be—no, no, it was nothing. Very well, then. Willis and I shall start immediately. We'll be there as soon as we can.'

He put down the receiver and swung round to the sergeant, whose eyebrows had been rising gradually up his forehead during this conversation.

'We've got to go down to Kent,' said Jameson. 'Do you know the Romney Marsh at all?'

'I've been to Hastings once or twice,' said Willis, 'but that's about it. What's the story?'

'They've found a woman in a ditch with her head bashed in.'

'Not our usual sort of thing, is it?' said the sergeant.

'There seems to be some mystery as to how she died,' said Jameson. 'The blow to the head was done after death.'

'Strangulation?' suggested Willis.

'Apparently not. They're doing a full post-mortem today, but in the meantime they want us to go down and take a look. There's one other thing,' he went on.

'What's that?'

'The body was found by Angela Marchmont, who happened to be visiting friends in the area.'

Sergeant Willis pursed up his lips and whistled.

'Mrs. Marchmont, eh? She seems to have a knack of tripping over a crime everywhere she goes.'

'So it seems,' Jameson agreed. 'If I didn't know better, I should say we had a female homicidal maniac on our hands, but I think she's just been unlucky enough to get caught up in some rather notorious cases lately.'

'Or lucky enough, sir.'

'What's that?'

'Well, she gets her name in the papers, doesn't she? Perhaps she likes all the attention.'

'She doesn't strike me that way,' said Jameson, considering.

'Nor me, sir,' said Willis. 'I was just trying a theory out loud to see how it sounded, so to speak.'

'Well, you can ask her yourself,' said Jameson. 'Anyway, you'd better go and get the car. And find a map of the Romney Marsh. I was there a few years ago and I spent half my time going around in circles. It's a different country down there.'

A few minutes later they were heading out of London along the Kent road. There were few cars out, and in a shorter time than they expected they reached Ashford and turned off the main road.

'This is where it gets more difficult,' said Jameson. 'Keep your eyes peeled for sign-posts.'

But it was a clear day—much clearer than the day before, when Mrs. Marchmont and William had had to find their way blindly through the fog, and so, after stopping for directions once or twice, the Scotland Yard men reached the lane they were looking for without too much difficulty. It was easy to see that they had found the right place, for a small knot of people were gathered, talking and gesticulating, while two enormous cart-horses, escorted by a small boy, stood waiting patiently until they were called upon. A police constable pointed into the undergrowth that lined the side of the road and seemed to give directions to an elderly man, while a youth wearing oil-stained overalls uncoiled a length of stout rope and looked on doubtfully. Farther along, a motor-lorry blocked the lane completely.

'This must be the place,' said the inspector, who had spotted Angela Marchmont immediately. She was standing a little apart with a young man Jameson recognized as her chauffeur, observing the proceedings with interest.

Willis stopped the car and they got out. The sergeant went to talk to the constable, while Jameson went to greet Mrs. Marchmont. Her face broke into a wide smile of pleasure as she saw him.

'Why, Inspector Jameson!' she said. 'I didn't expect to see you here.'

'Hallo, Mrs. Marchmont,' replied the inspector. 'I understand you have another dead body for us.'

'Oh, have they called in Scotland Yard?' said Angela in surprise. 'I thought it was meant to be quite a simple case. Yes,' she went on, 'we found the poor woman yesterday when we took an unexpected detour into this ditch.'

Jameson looked over the edge and saw the Bentley sitting askew and forlorn in the mud at the bottom of the bank.

'Good Lord,' he said. 'You're lucky you didn't go into the water.'

'Quite,' said Angela. 'We were very fortunate not to be hurt. But while we were down there, we found rather more than we had bargained for.'

'Indeed,' said the inspector. Willis and P. C. Bass approached them. Introductions were made, then the young constable said:

'We've got the garage along to get this lady's car out of the ditch. Shouldn't take too long, once they've got the horses hitched up.'

'I hope the area has been swept thoroughly for evidence,' said Jameson.

Bass blushed.

'Oh no, sir, I mean yes, sir. You can ask Sergeant Spillett. It was all done properly yesterday. We never found nothing. Well, nothing apart from a dead body, of course. But then, we already knew it was there. But there was nothing else that we could see.'

He broke off in confusion, and the inspector smiled sympathetically.

'I'm sorry to say that William and I rather disturbed the scene of the crime ourselves,' said Angela. 'You see, we climbed out of the ditch very close to where she was lying and so may possibly have covered over any tracks that the murderer might have left. Of course, we should have found another place to climb up had we had any idea that she was there, but we didn't spot her until we'd already got out.'

'That's a pity, but it can't be helped,' said Jameson.

'Why are you here, inspector?' asked Angela curiously. 'I didn't think Scotland Yard were called in for straightforward crimes such as this.'

'I haven't spoken to the sergeant yet, but I gather there are one or two unusual features about this case,' replied the inspector. 'We may or may not be needed in the end, but they wanted us to come down and take a look. They are pretty sure the dead woman was not local—at least, they've had no reports of missing women—and so they think we may be able to help in finding out who she was. We have more resources at our disposal in London, you know,' he said.

'I see,' said Angela.

While they were talking, Mr. Turner and his assistant had succeeded in hitching the Bentley to the horses, and it looked as though the fun were about to begin.

'Stand back, everyone,' commanded Turner. They all obeyed and there began a great stamping and a heaving and a snorting, as the horses strained to pull the car up the bank. Presently the Bentley appeared at the top of the slope and was pulled safely onto the road, spattered with mud and with a highly offended air. Mr. Turner crouched down stiffly and examined the front wheel.

'She's got a bent axle, right enough,' he said to William. 'Want us to take her away and put her right for you?'

'Oh yes, do, please,' said Angela. 'Will it take long, do you think?'

'We can have her back for you by Monday, if you like,' said the old man.

'That will be perfect, thank you,' said Angela.

He nodded.

'Back the lorry up, Bob,' he shouted to his mate.

'You'd better move the car, Willis. There's not room for all of us in the lane,' said Jameson.

'They're expecting me back at the station, so I'd best get off, if you don't mind, sir,' said P. C. Bass as the sergeant went off to do as he was bid.

'No, carry on,' said Jameson. 'Willis and I shall follow you shortly. We are going to scout about here for a few minutes, but then I shall want to talk to Sergeant Spillett and the inspector, if he's there.'

P. C. Bass retrieved his bicycle from where he had leant it against a tree and rode off with a wave. The small boy, who had shown signs of wanting to stay until the end, was remunerated and dismissed. He led the horses away, but stopped some distance down the road to observe the proceedings.

Angela, William and Inspector Jameson watched as the car was hitched to the lorry and towed away in great state.

'I hope she's going to be all right,' said William mournfully. He was very fond of the Bentley and was suffering severe pangs of guilt for having run it and his mistress off the road.

'I'm sure she will,' said Angela. 'And anyway,' she added as an afterthought, 'we can always buy another one if she's not.'

William brightened up immediately at the thought.

'How are you going to get back to your friends' house?' asked Jameson.

'Oh, we'll walk,' said Angela. 'It's not far—not more than a mile and a quarter, I should think.'

'Willis can give you a lift, if you like. I am going to stay here and look for clues—always assuming they haven't all been destroyed by a Bentley, its passengers and two cart-horses.'

'Don't make me feel worse than I already do,' said Angela.

'I'm sorry—I was just teasing,' he replied. 'If it weren't for you, we'd never have found her in the first place.'

'I suppose not,' she said.

Angela looked down at the tracks left by her car as it came up the bank. The deep grooves at the bottom of the slope had begun to fill with a muddy ooze as the water from the ditch seeped into them.

'Look,' she said suddenly.

'What is it?' said Jameson.

She pointed at the depression that had until a few minutes ago been occupied by the Bentley's near side back wheel. There, squashed and filthy and ground into the mud, was something that might once have been blue.

The inspector whistled in surprise and called over Sergeant Willis. William came to look too. They all gazed at it.

'Well, someone's going to have to get it,' said Jameson at last.

'I'll do it, sir,' said Willis, but Jameson waved him away.

'No,' he said resignedly. 'It shall never be said that we Jamesons quailed in the face of a bit of mud. Wish me luck,' he said to Angela.

'I shall wave my handkerchief,' she said solemnly. 'However, if you want to get down without sliding all the way I suggest you take the same route we did yesterday. Those bushes provide plenty of handholds.'

'Ah, yes,' he said, and did as she advised, reaching the bottom of the bank without too much difficulty. He made his way back along the water's edge to where the thing was and bent to retrieve it.

'Why, it's a hat!' said Angela. 'So she was wearing one after all. We must have landed on top of it and squashed it flat.'

'Is there anything else, sir?' asked Willis.

'I don't think so,' said Jameson after looking around. 'I'm going to come back up.'

He did so, and arrived at the top safely, holding his prize. They all looked at it. It was in a sorry state—battered, filthy, sodden and practically unrecognizable, but it was most certainly a hat.

'Pity it's not a handbag,' said Jameson. 'If it were, we might be able to find out something about her.'

'I wonder,' said Angela, 'might I have a look, inspector?'

He handed it to her. She took it gingerly, pulled the squashed edges apart and peered into it. Then she put her hand in, as though feeling for something.

'Ah!' she said, and brought something out carefully.

'Why, it's a ticket for the cloak room at Charing Cross!' said Inspector Jameson, taking it. It was wet, but quite clean. 'Where was it? In the inner hat band? Why on earth did she keep it there?'

'Oh, I've often kept things in my hat band, myself,' said Angela. 'I'm dreadful for losing bits of paper and it's a jolly good way of keeping them safe.'

'Then she must have come down from London,' he said, 'possibly in the company of the fellow who killed her. We'll have to start inquiring at the railway stations hereabouts if the local police haven't done that already. Hastings is the most obvious one, I imagine. We want to know whether they saw a blonde woman wearing a blue coat and hat arrive in the last few days, and if so, whether she was with a man. It's a long shot but somebody might remember something. I wonder if they hired a car?'

'She might have come down alone, of course,' said Angela. 'Perhaps she was visiting someone here in the area.'

'Yes—we'll have to look into that too. But the first step will be to go and get whatever it was she left at Charing Cross. With any luck it'll be a suitcase with her name on it!'

'Yes, that would be helpful,' agreed Angela. Her curiosity was fully aroused now, and she was just about to make some more suggestions when she remembered that by rights all this had nothing to do with her. She bit back her intended remark and resolved to leave it all to the police, who presumably knew what they were doing.

'We'd better get over to Littlechurch, Willis,' said Jameson. 'Can we offer you a lift?'

'No, you go and do your duty, inspector,' said Angela. 'We shall be quite all right. It's not far.'

'Just as a matter of interest,' said Jameson, 'why are you here? I mean, why didn't you leave William to see to the removal of your car?'

There was a pause. Angela blushed slightly.

'Oh, very well, I'll admit it,' she said all in a rush. 'I was curious to see the scene of the crime again. I can't help it—I think murder has got into my blood.'

'I thought as much,' he said. 'Yes, it can take one that way. Be careful, Mrs. Marchmont. Remember that curiosity killed the cat.'

'Thank you,' she replied. 'I know that only too well.'

She and William watched as the two men drove away, then set off themselves in the direction of Gipsy's Mile.

'It sure seems a queer business, ma'am,' remarked William as they walked. 'I don't like to think of that poor woman lying there in the dirt for hours or even days.'

'No,' agreed Angela soberly. 'I hope the police can find her killer soon. I hate to think of him getting away with it.'

'It's a funny coincidence that they called Inspector Jameson in on the job, of all people.'

'Yes,' said Angela. 'He must be quite tired of tripping over me everywhere he turns. But he's a very capable man, and if anyone can solve the case, he can. I wonder, though—'

She paused, and William glanced at her sideways.

'What?' he asked.

'Oh, it's nothing,' she said. 'I just wondered what Inspector Jameson was not telling us.'

CHAPTER SIX

THE TREES GREW black and thickly, stretching their arms skywards and entwining one with another to form an arched roof of green leaves and yellow moss. Angela walked along the woody tunnel, feeling rather as though she were in a church, except that the floor beneath her feet was of dirt, and the pews were tree-roots. The nave of this place of worship appeared to go on for miles and the walk was beginning to tire her out, but she was determined to reach the altar far ahead of her, which was formed of a silver birch tree that extended its branches gracefully upwards to the heavens. She wanted to reach it, but the faster she walked the farther it seemed to recede. Eventually, it disappeared altogether and she clasped her hands together in desperation. As she looked about her, however, she suddenly noticed that the dirt path branched off to her left, and ended in a little glade a short way away. Almost of their own accord, her feet followed the new path, and soon Angela saw ahead of her something blue, lying slumped on the ground, bathed in a beam of sunlight that had found its way in through the verdant canopy. As she came closer, she saw it was a woman in a blue coat, lying on her back, her face completely hidden by a covering of moss and mud. She knelt down next to the corpse, then suddenly everything changed and she saw that it was not a woman at all, but the body of a man dressed in a smartly-tailored suit and a straw hat. Something glittered at the corner of her vision, and when she looked to see what it was, she saw to her surprise that his hand was clutching what appeared to be a diamond necklace. She felt something stir in her memory and peered more closely at the dead man. His face was quite obscured, and yet she was sure she recognized him from somewhere. Her heart thumped. Could it perhaps be—?

'Goodness me!' exclaimed Angela, waking up and sitting bolt upright in bed, her hand to her throat. She looked about her wildly, then slumped back against the pillows in relief as she realized that it had just been a dream. She was in her bedroom at Gipsy's Mile, and they were going to have Sunday lunch at Blakeney Park, and she was going to spend much of the day avoiding Cynthia Pilkington-Soames and laughing at Freddy. Yes, that was it. It was all quite clear now. She waited until her breathing had slowed, then groped for her cigarette-case and lit one, feeling extremely disconcerted and not a little betrayed by her treacherous subconscious.

It was still early, but there was no getting back to sleep after such a dream, so Angela rose and dressed, then went downstairs. She expected to be the first one up, and so she was surprised to find Miles and Herbert sitting in close conference over cold meat and coffee. They looked up guiltily as she entered, and then greeted her so heartily that Angela was sure they had been talking about her. Perhaps they had been discussing the shady past she was supposed to have had, if one were to believe Freddy. She pretended not to have noticed anything, and helped herself to coffee and toast.

'What time are we expected at Blakeney Park?' she asked.

Miles attacked a slice of ham.

'Noonish, I think,' he said. 'Gil's not a stickler for time-keeping himself, but one has to arrive reasonably punctually in order to stay in Lady Alice's good books. You shall meet her today, Angela.'

'Is she as formidable as she sounds?' asked Angela.

'Oh, she's not a bad old stick once you get to know her,' said Herbert with a guffaw. 'Rather formal and stuffy, perhaps, but easy enough to get around.'

'She gives Gil plenty of headaches, though,' said Miles. 'She won't let him rest, poor fellow. And he'll be kept just as busy once he's married, too.'

'It'll do him good,' said Herbert. 'The rest of us have to put up with being browbeaten by our womenfolk, so I don't see why he should get out of it.'

'Shall they be happy, do you think?' asked Angela curiously.

Miles hesitated.

'Yes, I believe they shall,' he said. 'Lucy is a fine girl, and Gilbert—well, you've met him, haven't you? He's an excellent chap—brave, and loyal and great-hearted, and all that—but he's never going to set the world alight. And he's the only one left to run that enormous estate of his. He needs Lucy. I've no doubt she'll be the making of him.'

Herbert was nodding vigorously in agreement.

'You're both very fond of him, aren't you?' said Angela, smiling.

'Difficult not to be fond of a chap when you've been through Hell with him,' said Herbert gruffly. 'He saved my life, you know. If it weren't for him I should have taken a sniper's bullet through the heart. Shouldn't be here today, in fact.'

'It's a great shame he wasn't put forward for a medal,' said Miles. 'There was no-one to match his bravery in the face of the enemy. He ought to have stayed in the army, really.'

Herbert gave a sudden roar of laughter.

'I say, Miles,' he said. 'Do you remember those two days we spent in Paris?'

Miles raised his eyebrows humorously.

'If they're the two days I think you mean, I'm not sure Angela ought to hear about them,' he said.

'Oh—ah—perhaps you're right,' said Herbert, suddenly embarrassed.

'I'm simply dying to know, now,' said Angela.

'Ah, well, now, you see, the fact of the matter is—' said Herbert.

'Yes?' said Angela innocently.

'Stop teasing him, Angela,' said Miles. 'Our behaviour while on leave was perhaps not the most dignified, but in those dark days one had to take one's fun in whatever way it presented itself.'

'I know that very well,' said Angela. 'I lived through it too, of course.'

'But I thought you were safe in America then.'

'Not all the time,' said Angela, and turned the subject.

Soon afterwards, Marguerite breezed in in her usual dramatic fashion. She was wearing a glorious orange kaftan with gold stripes, and a gold turban.

'Good morning, darlings,' she said. 'How early you all are today! Angela, I have just been talking to your young man. What a delightful boy he is! Wherever did you find him?'

'Why, in the States of course.'

'And so handsome, too! Americans are so good-looking, I always find.'

'As a matter of fact, he was born in England,' said Angela.

'Really?'

'Yes. He has led a most interesting life. He was born into a family of acrobats who moved to the States when he was very young. He grew up performing with the family troupe, and then went on to star in vaudeville.'

'How thrilling!' said Marguerite, clasping her hands together. 'But however did he end up working as your chauffeur?'

'It's rather a long story,' said Angela, 'but I happened to render him a service on a particular occasion—quite by chance, as it happened. We rather took to each other, so I asked if he would care to come and work for me, since I was looking for a driver and man-of-all-work at the time, and he had already mentioned that he was tired of his life on the road. He's awfully impertinent and familiar—not at all like an English servant—but I don't mind that, and he's terribly loyal, so we get along famously.'

'I see,' said Marguerite. There was a gleam in her eyes, and Angela, who knew her friend well, wondered whether she ought perhaps to give William a warning, although he was surely old enough to look after himself.

At a quarter to twelve, Angela found herself sitting with Freddy Pilkington-Soames in his little two-seater as they drove along the narrow lanes towards Blakeney Park. When not affecting incurable boredom, Freddy was rather good company, and Angela laughed—guiltily, it is true—at some of his more acerbic remarks about the party.

'I see Marguerite has got her hooks on your driver,' he said slyly, somewhat to Angela's surprise. Before she could determine whether or not to admit to having noticed the same thing, he went on, 'I shouldn't worry, though—she'll lose interest quickly enough. She did in me.'

At that, Angela opened her eyes wide and turned to him sharply.

'Freddy!' she exclaimed. He nodded and she hardly knew whether or not to laugh at his complacent expression. 'But— did you—?' she said hesitantly.

'I shall say no more, for I am the very model of discretion,' he said.

'Oh!' she said, disappointed.

'But rest assured, William will soon be yours alone once more.'

'Don't be absurd, Freddy,' she said. 'I don't make a habit of dallying with the servants.'

'Then perhaps you ought,' he said, wagging his eyebrows significantly. This was too much, and Angela burst out laughing.

'But what about Miles?' she asked finally.

'Miles is a jolly good egg,' said Freddy, 'and I won't hear a word said against him. They're very happy, you know, the two of them. You wouldn't think so, would you? After all, they are such different characters. And then, of course, she is rather older than he. But they understand each other. She is a woman of enthusiasms, as you well know, and he—well, he likes a quiet life. He is quite prepared to turn a blind eye to her peccadilloes provided she lets him have that. It was his idea to move to Kent, you know. London was too much for him, I believe. But Marguerite still goes up to town for her art exhibitions, and always has a protégé or two hanging about down here, so they rub along quite contentedly.'

There was a silence as Angela absorbed this information. She was a little startled at Freddy's perspicacity, and began to see him in a new light. She glanced at him sideways as he drove. She had always supposed him to be rather empty-headed, but she wondered whether she had not perhaps done him an injustice. Shallow and lazy he certainly was, but he seemed to be more observant than she thought.

'You're wondering now whether I won't make rather a good reporter, aren't you?' he said, to her surprise. 'I can see it.'

'If you can read minds like that, then I should say you certainly shall,' said Angela.

'It's just a knack,' he said modestly.

'I see I shall have to watch my thoughts.'

'If you have no secrets, then you have nothing to fear from me,' he said. 'Or from anyone, in fact,' he added.

'That's very reassuring,' said Angela dryly.

CHAPTER SEVEN

T HEY HAD NOW turned in through the great gates of
Blakeney Park, and Angela turned her attention to their
surroundings. They drove up a long avenue of trees, and finally emerged into the open, where they got their first view
of the house. Blakeney was a large, stately pile built in the
Jacobean style, in red brick with mullioned windows and
tall chimneys. It was situated overlooking a formal garden
and lake, from the centre of which sprang a magnificently
florid fountain depicting an uncomfortable intertwining of
nymphs, cherubs, mermaids and sea-creatures various. The
grand walk up to the house was lined with statues, and an
arched loggia ran along the front of the building. It was all
very fine.

'Here we are,' said Freddy. 'Watch out for fireworks!'

'What do you mean?' said Angela.

'Why, between Lucy and Lady Alice, of course,' he said.
'Oh, they're very genteel about it and put on a show of unity,

but that's only because of Gil and the estate. Everyone knows that in actual fact they can't stand each other.'

The car drew up before the grand entrance and they alighted. The others had already arrived and were just entering the house. Gilbert Blakeney was there to welcome them.

'Hallo! Hallo! How marvellous to see you again!' he said, greeting Angela in delight as though she were an old friend he had not seen in years, instead of a new acquaintance he had met only two days ago. Freddy received a similarly rapturous welcome, with a bone-crushing hand-shake and a clap on the shoulder. Gil was rather like an eager puppy, Angela thought. There was something very appealing about his child-like simplicity and undisguised friendliness.

'Shall we go and have drinks?' said Lucy, who was standing beside him to greet the guests. They were about to move off, when she suddenly said, 'Oh, I almost forgot—Gil, you must speak to Hardesty about the broken fence in the bottom field. I've told him about it before, but yesterday the cows got through to the nursery and broke a window-pane in one of the greenhouses. It's really too bad. You shall have to reprimand him.'

An expression of panic passed briefly across Gil's face.

'Oh—ah—yes,' he said. 'You told me about it last week, didn't you? I meant to do it, but it must have slipped from my mind somehow. I'll do it tomorrow.'

He looked sheepish and apologetic, almost as though he were afraid that he was going to be made to sit in the corner and write out a hundred lines, but Lucy smiled indulgently up at him and patted his arm affectionately, and his expression changed to one of relief.

They made an odd couple, Lucy and Gilbert: he tall, fair and loping, and she compact with brown hair and an evident firmness of purpose. Lucy was not a beauty by any means, but she had the rosy cheeks and clear skin that spoke of a life lived in the open air, and this, together with her calm, sensible manner, rendered her not unattractive. There was something rather touching about the way she took Gil gently in hand and guided him. She was already acting the part of the chatelaine of Blakeney Park, Angela noticed, even though she was not yet Gil's wife and so did not live at the house but in Littlechurch, where she looked after the family home left to her by her parents.

The guests were shown into a large saloon which could not have contrasted more strongly with the darkness of the panelled entrance-hall, being light and airy, with long windows that presented a delightful view over the lake and the fountain. The room was furnished elegantly and comfortably, and had clearly been in the hands of someone with an eye for such things. A tall, silent manservant held a tray of drinks, and they all took one with varying degrees of alacrity.

'Mother did all this a few years ago, just before the Governor died,' said Gil, in reply to Angela's complimentary remarks. 'She always took great pride in the house. She will be sorry to have to give it up. Oh, there you are, Mother. Angela was just saying how much she admires your taste.'

The last remark was addressed to a woman who had just entered the room. This was Lady Alice. She nodded to the assembled company, then approached Gil and Angela and introduced herself to the latter. Her manner was somewhat distant but gracious enough, and Angela regarded her with discreet curiosity. Lady Alice Blakeney had evidently once been a great beauty, for there were traces of it still in her face. She was small, with dainty hands and ankles, and although a little on the plump side, still had a narrow waist which she took care to accentuate in her tailoring, even though it went against the dictates of current fashion. Her face was almost unlined and her skin was fair and so uniform in texture that Angela strongly suspected her of resorting in some measure to cosmetic preparations. She looked nothing like her son, who presumably took after his father.

Marguerite descended on them, waving her arms and looking rather like a giant and exotic bird. She kissed Lady Alice, who looked somewhat startled.

'Darlings, so kind of you to invite us all,' said Marguerite. 'Angela was simply *dying* to see Blakeney Park. Isn't it the most beautiful house you've ever seen, Angela?' She did not wait for a reply, but went on in the same breath, 'My, but aren't we having an exciting weekend, with all these dead bodies turning up all over the place!'

Gil looked astonished.

'Have they found another one?' he asked.

'I was exaggerating just a little, of course,' said Marguerite. 'No, we just have the one up to now. Lady Alice, I ought to warn you that Angela simply can't go anywhere without falling over a dead body. She has *quite* a knack for it! Murderers and criminals seem to follow her about everywhere.'

'Indeed?' said Lady Alice, with polite interest. 'That must be most inconvenient, my dear.'

Angela laughed.

'I have had rather an eventful time of it lately, it's true,' she said, 'but I expect it will all calm down sooner or later. It's not as though I seek it out deliberately.'

'And now we even have Scotland Yard down here,' said Marguerite. 'I expect they'll want to ask us questions about what we've all been doing this week. I do hope you have a good alibi, Gil.'

'Scotland Yard?' said Gil blankly. 'But whatever for? What have they to do with all this?'

'I guess it's just a matter of routine,' said Miles, who had heard the conversation and now came over to join them. 'But I dare say Angela will be able to tell us more about it, since she's great pals with the inspector who came down yesterday.'

'I don't know much,' said Angela, 'but I think there is some uncertainty as to how the woman died.' She said nothing about the cloak room ticket, unsure as to how much information she ought to give away and deciding to err on the side of caution.

'You'll be investigating, of course, won't you, Angela?' said Cynthia.

'Good gracious, no!' said Angela. 'I've already told you—it's nothing to do with me. I've told the police everything I know, and now they will have to make what they can of it.'

'Have they found out who she was, yet?' asked Lucy.

'I don't believe so,' said Angela.

'But how on earth did she get into the ditch? It's all most odd. I simply can't understand it. How did her face get all smashed up like that?'

'Better not think about it, my dear,' said Lady Alice. 'The whole thing sounds most unpleasant. Perhaps one should be asking what she was doing running about the countryside alone. A woman like that is bound to get herself murdered, or worse.'

'I don't think there's any suggestion that she was alone,' said Angela. 'I believe the police are assuming that she came here with someone.'

'Alone or not, I am certain that she was no better than she should be,' said Lady Alice with finality, and began to talk determinedly about an exhibition of sculpture that Marguerite was planning to hold in Littlechurch. It was clear that she did not wish to pursue the subject of the dead woman, and so the conversation passed on to other things.

At one o'clock luncheon was served and they were conducted into a large, stately dining-room. Angela found herself sitting next to Freddy, who distracted her at frequent intervals by nudging her significantly whenever anybody said something he considered to be of note.

Herbert and Gil began to talk about shooting, while Miles put in a remark now and again. Marguerite declaimed loudly about her exhibition to anyone who would listen, while Cynthia, curious as ever, said to Lucy:

'And so next year is the wedding! You must be looking forward to it very much. When is it, exactly?'

'It's to be in August,' said Lucy. 'The engagement was announced in the *Times* last July.'

'August! And then Blakeney Park will be all yours! How marvellous!' said Cynthia, with her usual lack of tact.

Freddy nudged Angela so hard that she almost spilt her soup, and nodded surreptitiously towards Lady Alice, who wore a furious expression.

'And shall you take a honeymoon?' went on Cynthia. 'I understand Italy is supposed to be delightful. The Knowleses went to Venice last year after their wedding—you remember them, don't you, Freddy?'

'Oh, certainly,' replied Freddy. 'As a matter of fact I spoke to Rupert only a week or two ago. He was rather down, I must say, although he is convinced that the separation is just a temporary fancy on Diana's part.'

Cynthia glared at her son, and Angela looked hard at her soup as she fought the urge to laugh.

'No, I don't think we shall have time to go away,' said Lucy. 'August is a busy time on the estate and we shall probably be needed to see to things.'

'Oh, I am sure the Park can manage without you both for a week or two,' said Lady Alice. 'As a matter of fact, I am almost certain that Gilbert has been away at that time of year many times before. And I shall still be here. I can take care of it all quite well.'

'But they will be making the hay then,' said Lucy, 'and I— Gil was planning to start work on having the boundary fences repaired, weren't you, Gil? They've needed it for such a long time.'

Gilbert looked up in alarm at the mention of his name.

'But that can be done at any time,' said Lady Alice, and there was a steely note in her voice. 'Why, if you start earlier it can even be finished by the time of the wedding.'

Freddy was nudging Angela so often that in deference to her frock she quite gave up any attempt to finish her soup.

'Well, perhaps we shall think about it,' said Lucy reluctantly.

'Oh, yes,' said Gil, who had evidently not been listening fully to their conversation. 'I should like to go away after the wedding, shouldn't you, Lucy?'

Lucy smiled tightly and tacitly admitted defeat on this occasion. Angela wondered which of the two women came out on top most often. It looked as though Lady Alice had the upper hand at present, although once Gil and Lucy were married it was inevitable that her influence would wane. It was clear that Gil would be caught in the middle of the two of them. Would they be able to forget their differences and rub along together for Gil's sake, or would the enmity continue after the marriage? Odd that the engagement had apparently been Lady Alice's idea. Angela wondered very much how it would all turn out.

CHAPTER EIGHT

SERGEANT WILLIS ENTERED the room and dumped a battered suitcase on his superior's desk.

'Here we are, sir,' he said. 'One suitcase, retrieved from Charing Cross cloak room, as instructed. It was left on Wednesday.'

Jameson pushed aside his report, which was nearly finished and this time contained the correct names, and stood up.

'So that's where our mystery woman left her belongings,' he said. 'Still no handbag though, I take it.'

'No, sir.'

'Have you heard from the Littlechurch police yet? Do you know whether they've had any luck in finding a trace of her at the stations?'

'I spoke to them this morning, sir. They've had no luck yet. Nobody remembers seeing the woman at all, either by herself or with a man.'

'Hmm, that's hardly conclusive, at any rate,' said Jameson. 'Just because no-one saw her doesn't mean she wasn't there.

Now, since you say her belongings were left in the cloak room on Wednesday, I think we can assume she went there on that day, left her suitcase and then got on a train shortly afterwards—unless, that is, our murderer is more subtle than we have given him credit for, and left her things there himself and put the ticket in her hat. That doesn't seem very likely, however. The train down to—where, though? Ashford or Hastings? Or somewhere smaller, perhaps. Appledore?'

'Could have been any of those, sir,' said Willis. 'If anybody saw her I'm sure the Kent chaps will find them sooner or later.'

'I suppose so,' said Jameson. 'Very well, then, let's see what we've got.'

Willis opened the case and they peered inside.

'Pretty much as you'd expect,' remarked Willis. 'Just clothes.'

'Yes,' said Jameson. He lifted something out. It was a pale pink evening-frock of cheap satin, a little stained and crumpled, and smelling of cigarette smoke. 'Evening things,' he said. 'Recently worn, too, I should say.'

He put it to one side and brought out the other things one by one. Two more evening-dresses and a pair of satin gloves. A slightly moth-eaten fur stole. One or two plain skirts and jerseys. One pair of satin evening-shoes, but no day-shoes. Underthings. A number of items of cheap jewellery. Cosmetics.

'Do you notice anything, Willis?' said Jameson.

'She seems to have had rather a lot of evening clothes,' said Willis.

'Hmm,' said Jameson. He regarded the sorry collection of things that had once been owned and perhaps prized by the dead woman, and wondered, not for the first time, what she would have thought had she known that a stranger was rifling through her belongings. In his years as a detective, he had learned that it was unwise to allow himself to be too deeply affected by the fates of those who had met an unfortunate end, but he had never quite managed to shake off that twinge of sadness he always felt when first confronted with their possessions—the only thing that remained of them, and a permanent reminder that they had once been people too, with loves and hates, desires, faults and virtues. He welcomed the feeling, for it reassured him that, in spite of all the unpleasant things he had seen, he was still human.

'Where was she from, do you think?' he said to the sergeant. 'Somewhere outside London, in which case was she just passing through on her way to Kent? Or was she a Londoner? Either way, I wonder why she left the suitcase. She can't have been leaving for good, since she would have had to come back for it.'

'Perhaps she was going away for a few days with the mystery man,' said Willis, thinking. 'No, that's no good, is it? If she was she'd have taken her suitcase with her. Presumably she didn't plan to be away long, then. It's a pity nobody saw her, or whom she was with.'

'It's possible, of course, that she wasn't with anyone when she got on the train,' said the inspector. 'It may be that she had arranged to meet someone when she got down there.'

'That's always assuming she was killed by someone she knew,' said the sergeant. 'We still can't be certain that she wasn't attacked and thrown in that ditch by a passing madman.'

'Oh, I think we can,' said Jameson, 'if what the police surgeon in Littlechurch says is correct.'

'Ah yes, I'd forgotten about that.'

'They are sending the body up here tomorrow. Let's see what our lot make of it.'

Willis picked up a satin dress and examined it.

'Why so many evening clothes?' he said.

'I rather think they are her work clothes,' said Jameson. 'I shouldn't be surprised to find out that she worked as a dance hostess or something of that kind.'

'That makes sense,' agreed Willis. 'Is there anything else in the suitcase?'

'No,' said Jameson. 'Ah, just a second, though—there's a little pocket here.'

He felt inside it and brought out a piece of paper, which had been folded over several times. He unfolded it and glanced at it, then whistled.

Willis craned his neck to see what it was.

'It's a handbill of some sort,' he said. 'What does it say?'

Jameson handed him the paper. Printed on it in large characters were the words:

COME FOR THE MUSIC
COME FOR THE DANCING
COME EARLY AND STAY LATE!
ALVIE BERTEAU AND HIS JAZZ ORCHESTRA
THEY'RE THE CAT'S PYJAMAS!

'What's this symbol here?' said Willis, peering at some-thing in puzzlement. 'It looks like the sun, but what's that meant to be? The moon?'

'The earth, I think,' said Jameson. 'Don't you recognize it? It's a handbill for the Copernicus Club.' Willis looked momentari-ly blank, and he went on, 'You remember the Copernicus, don't you? It's just off Brewer Street. Mrs. Chang's place.'

'Oh, that place,' said Willis. 'Didn't it get shut down?'

'Yes, briefly. It's been closed a few times, as a matter of fact. Every so often we raid it, and Mrs. Chang gets brought up before the magistrate and fined. Then we all shake hands and off she goes and opens up again. It's become rather a game, I think.'

'Waste of time, if you ask me,' said Willis in disgust. 'We could be out catching real criminals.' His expression made it quite clear what he thought of the current licensing laws.

'This handbill does give some credence to our theory about the woman's job, though,' said Jameson.

'A dance hostess,' said Willis. 'If that's all there was to it, of course.'

'Well, that's the thing, isn't it? There's been some suspicion that more goes on at the Copernicus than just unlicensed drinking, but we've never been able to prove it. And if our dead woman was engaging in—er—less salubrious activities, shall we say, then we may have the devil of a job to find out who her man friend was. It looks as though the next step will be to go and pay a visit to Brewer Street and speak to Mrs. Chang. Perhaps she'll be willing to give us some information in return for a good word from us the next time she is raided.'

'Let's hope so,' said Willis. He had been poking about inside the suitcase pocket. 'Look!' he said, and brought out something else. 'You missed this. It was stuck right down in the corner.'

Jameson took it, and saw that it was a small photograph of an infant of perhaps two or three years old.

'I wonder if this child is hers,' he said.

'Very sad if it is, sir,' said Sergeant Willis. 'I don't like to think of a child without its mother.'

'It's rather an unusual face,' observed Jameson, gazing at the picture. 'I might almost say a foreign face. There's a Latin quality to it—Italian, or Spanish, perhaps. If this child is the woman's, I wonder whether he resembles his mother. Perhaps she was foreign.'

'She might have been,' said Willis, 'but she'd been here long enough if so, to judge by her clothes. Nothing foreign about them.'

'No, you're right,' said Jameson. 'Her clothes are recognizably English. I shall put the men onto tracing them, if possible, although I don't suppose they'll have much luck. This is all the sort of stuff one can find in any cheap dress-shop in England.'

'True enough,' said Willis.

'And have a look at the missing persons reports. We may find our woman on there. If not, we shall have to advertise in the newspapers. Someone must surely be missing a young, blonde woman in a blue coat. Young women tend to have friends. Somebody must know who she is.'

'It's a queer story,' said the sergeant. 'At first glance I'd've said it was straightforward—chap rows with his girl then bangs her on the head and dumps her in a panic. We get three or four cases like that every year. But this is something different.'

'Yes,' agreed Jameson. 'We'll know more in the next few days, of course, once our medical man has made his report, but there's no reason to suppose the Littlechurch surgeon has made a mistake.'

'Arsenic, wasn't it?'

'That's what he seems to think.'

Willis shook his head.

'That's premeditation, that is. Strangling, now, or a blow to the head: either of those might have happened on the spur of the moment. But arsenic is a different matter.'

'It certainly is,' said the inspector. 'And if somebody did poison her it makes things that much more complicated.'

CHAPTER NINE

THE SUN WAS sinking low when the Gipsy's Mile party returned home. This time Mrs. Marchmont travelled with Herbert Pilkington-Soames, since Cynthia wanted to go with Freddy—in order to pump him about what he and Angela had been talking about, Angela suspected.

Herbert was a stout, hearty man of forty-five whose lack of hair on his shining pate was more than made up for by a luxuriant moustache. He both admired and was terrified of his wife, despite his size, and freely admitted that he did whatever she told him to.

'The woman's a menace,' he said as they drove. 'Since she took up cards she's been running through money as though it were water. I don't mind telling you that it's been a close thing once or twice, and I have had to put my foot down. "Cynthia," I said, "if you really must gamble then why on earth can't you do it with sixpences instead of guineas? No," I said, "this must stop." To her credit, she had the wit to see that we were plunging towards disaster, and so she promised to find a way of bringing some money in. That's how she ended up doing this scribbling business at the *Clarion*. Of course, it's all a heap of nonsense—Bickerstaffe only took her on because she swore to him that she had the telephone-number of every aristocrat who had ever been caught with someone they shouldn't be, and could get the low-down on all the latest scandals. I think he's regretting it now, though—why, the woman can barely spell her own name, for heaven's sake!'

He paused to navigate around a difficult bend. Angela, who was enjoying his indiscretions immensely, given the badgering she had had to put up with from Cynthia, said:

'Does it pay well, then?'

'It depends on what she produces,' he replied. 'She might get anything from fourpence a word to ninepence, depending on the story. I rather think you're ninepence, I'm afraid.'

'I feared as much,' said Angela. 'It's a pity—if I were cheaper, I might be able to get out of it. In spite of appearances, I am not exactly keen on having my name in the newspapers.'

'I can believe it,' Herbert assured her. 'You're not the type to seek attention—why, anyone can see that. But that won't stop Cynthia. If I were you, I should probably tell her a pack of lies. I do that all the time. It makes life so much easier.'

Angela laughed at his shameless confession.

'It had crossed my mind,' she admitted.

'I sometimes think things would be easier if we left London,' he went on, returning to his original train of thought. 'Town is so expensive, and of course all her friends are there—that awful Nancy Beasley in particular. Do you know her?'

'No.'

'Ghastly old harpy,' he said. 'She'd sell her grandmother to pay for one more night at the tables. Cynthia has never been the same since she fell into her company. If we lived down here, now, things would be so much quieter and there'd be fewer temptations.'

'And you'd be able to see Miles and Marguerite much more often. And Gil.'

'Yes, I should like that very much. I rather miss my pals,' he said.

Angela was curious.

'Isn't Gil much younger than you and Miles? Doesn't it ever seem like rather an odd friendship?'

Herbert nodded.

'Yes, it's true—I am the oldest of the three. I already had a wife and son when I was called up, while Miles wasn't married and Gil was practically a boy. But war does funny things to people—it can drive them apart or it can bring them together, and in our case it did the latter. I owe my life to Gil, and Miles was a good friend too. He bucked me up once or twice when I was in a funk—I don't mind telling you that we were all terribly afraid at times. But it wasn't all hard work. We had fun together too.'

Angela smiled sympathetically at Herbert's sincerity. Despite his slightly crass exterior she found him rather likeable.

'Ah, yes,' she said. 'Your famous weekends in Paris.'

Herbert shifted uncomfortably, but underneath his moustache his mouth twitched in a smile.

'I should like to be young again,' he said. 'Youth lasts such a short time, and one is far too busy doing things to enjoy them—if you see what I mean.'

'I think I do,' said Angela, 'But sometimes I think the memory of a thing is better than the thing itself: we forget the worst bits and hold on to the good bits.'

'I wish I could forget the worst bits,' said Herbert gruffly. 'Here we are,' he said in a more cheerful tone as they arrived back at Gipsy's Mile. 'Poor Gil. I'll bet he wishes he could have left those two women fighting over him in that draughty mausoleum of his, and come back with us. I wouldn't change places with him for all the world, in spite of his money.'

Angela was inclined to agree. The simple, eager Gilbert Blakeney had looked somewhat incongruous set against the grand surroundings of the house that was his birthright and his destiny. Even Lucy, who had no business there yet, had looked far more at home in the place.

Miles's car was standing in front of the house; presumably the Harrisons had already arrived back home. Angela wanted something from her room, so went upstairs to fetch it. As she returned downstairs she thought she saw a flash of orange and gold disappearing round a corner. In the hall she found William waiting respectfully for her, slightly pink in the face.

'What is it?' she said.

'Mr. Turner sent a message to say that the Bentley has been fixed, ma'am. They're going to bring it over tomorrow.'

'Oh, good!' said Angela. 'That's a relief, at any rate. We shan't have to buy a new one after all.'

'No, ma'am,' agreed William, although he looked slightly wistful. Angela laughed.

'Come now, we don't want to waste money unnecessarily, do we?' she said. 'Don't be so downcast! Perhaps we shall have a new one next year instead. Wasn't it a Rolls-Royce you had your eye on the other week?'

'Why yes, it was, as a matter of fact,' said William, cheering up.

'Well, we shall see,' said Angela, and was about to move away when a thought struck her and she turned back to him. 'William,' she said, then stopped.

'Yes, ma'am?'

She moved a little closer in order to speak more quietly.

'Is everything quite all right?' she said. There was nothing in the words themselves, but her expression gave them meaning. William went pink again.

'Why, yes, thank you, ma'am,' he said.

Angela looked across to where she had seen the flash of orange.

'I think you know what I am referring to,' she said kindly. 'Naturally, I shouldn't dream of interfering in your personal affairs, but you will let me know if there is anything you'd like me to help with, won't you? I won't stand by if anybody is—bothering you in any way.'

William had quite recovered his self-possession.

'Thank you, ma'am,' he said. 'I understand. Nobody is—bothering me.'

Angela glanced at him sideways. They exchanged a knowing look. She smiled and went off. Well, she had done her best. What William got up to now was his own affair.

She went and joined the party in the sitting-room. The atmosphere was a little frosty and the men were all looking wary and uncomfortable, so she deduced that Marguerite and Cynthia had had one of their regular little blow-ups. These never amounted to more than a pointed remark or two, and the two ladies were invariably the best of friends again immediately afterwards.

'Darling, there you are!' said Marguerite. 'What *did* you think of Lady Alice?'

'She seemed pleasant enough,' replied Angela, 'although I see what you mean about her and Lucy. They do seem to clash, rather, don't they?'

'Oh, you simply can't imagine!' said Marguerite.

'Are you quite certain that Lady Alice encouraged the engagement?' asked Angela. 'I can't see it myself.'

'Oh yes, there's no doubt about it at all,' said Marguerite. 'All three of them swear it.'

Angela said nothing but thought that Lady Alice must be a remarkable character if she could encourage her son to marry a woman whom she herself strongly disliked, purely for the sake of carrying on the family name and assuring the future of their landed estate.

'Now, Angela,' said Cynthia, and Angela saw to her dismay that she had taken a dainty little notebook and pencil from her bag. 'We've just time to do this before dinner. Shall we go into the parlour?'

There was no escaping it now. Angela rose and followed Cynthia out of the sitting-room. She pulled a mock-terrified face at Herbert as she passed. Freddy was regarding her with a malicious grin and she narrowed her eyes.

'Here we are!' said Cynthia. 'Don't worry, this ought to be quite painless,' she said with a trilling laugh. 'Now, then, I've been watching you all weekend and taking notes—just for background detail, you know—' (Angela widened her eyes in alarm) '—but now I really want to *talk* to you—you know, to find out all the personal details that make you the celebrity you are. Your innermost thoughts and secrets. I still don't feel I've quite got to the bottom of the question: who is the *real* Angela Marchmont? Our readers are dying to know. Tell me, Angela, what is your motivation—your impetus? What really *stimulates* you?'

Angela bit back the urge to reply, 'A martini would do the trick nicely just now,' and made some vague and embarrassed response. She looked at the clock, but there was still half an hour until dinner and Cynthia was now asking questions about Angela's married life which Angela had very much rather not answer. She sighed inwardly and began to make use of some of the lies she had invented earlier. It would be too much to see the truth splashed across the popular pages.

After fifteen minutes or so she was rescued by Freddy, who had taken pity on her and brought in drinks.

'Thank you, Freddy, darling,' murmured Cynthia, who was scribbling away in her notebook. 'We shall just be a few more minutes.'

'I think it's time you let poor Angela go,' he said. 'I hate to see beauty in distress.'

'What on earth do you mean?' said his mother.

'Look at the poor creature,' he said, indicating Angela, who had been unaware of her pained expression. 'You'd much rather not do this at all, isn't that right, Mrs. M?'

'Don't be silly,' said Cynthia. 'Why, everybody loves talking about themselves.'

'Not Angela,' said Freddy. 'Let her alone now. You've had plenty of time to pry. And you can always make it up—that's what you usually do, anyway.'

'I do not,' said Cynthia indignantly.

'All right—let's agree to call it "creative embellishment",' said Freddy.

Fortunately, dinner was announced before a row could develop, and Angela flashed Freddy a grateful smile and escaped thankfully. For the rest of the evening she took great care to keep out of Cynthia's way, and went to bed early, hoping that she had got off lightly.

The Bentley arrived the next morning as they were having breakfast, and Angela went out to see it.

'How is the patient, Mr. Turner?' she said.

'Good as new,' said the old man. 'Nothing wrong with her that a few whacks with a hammer wouldn't put right. You'll have no more trouble with her. Leastways, as long as you don't go driving off the road again.'

William was inspecting the car joyfully. It was polished and gleaming, and he stroked the paint-work with pleasure.

'I don't need to ask whether you are glad to have it back,' said Angela. 'We shall be leaving after breakfast, so you'd better put the luggage in.'

'Sure thing, ma'am,' he said, and went off to do as instructed. Angela returned to the house to finish her coffee.

At half-past ten they were ready to leave. Miles saluted Angela amicably, but Marguerite was nowhere to be seen. Cynthia and Herbert had left earlier, as Herbert had to get up to town.

'Do look out for my piece in the *Clarion*,' said Mrs. Pilkington-Soames as they left. 'I expect it will be in on Friday. *Can't* I change your mind about having your photograph taken, darling?'

'I'm afraid not,' said Angela, happy that she had been able to put her foot down on that, at any rate. She was relieved that the whole thing was over and done with, although still nervous at the thought of what Cynthia might take it into her head to write.

Freddy walked her out to the car.

'Cheer up,' he said. 'You can always move to Siberia if it all gets too embarrassing.'

'Oh, don't! I have no idea why on earth I agreed to do it at all.'

'Mother can be very persuasive when she likes,' said Freddy.

'I'm more inclined to blame those cocktails we had on Friday,' said Angela. 'They were rather strong. I believe she took advantage of it.'

'Beware the demon drink,' said Freddy. 'The ruination of women throughout history.'

'And men,' said Angela. 'Now, where on earth has William got to?'

'I can make a jolly good guess,' said Freddy significantly.

'Nonsense,' said Angela.

Just then, William appeared in a hurry. He muttered a jumbled apology for keeping Mrs. Marchmont waiting and opened the door for her. Angela was just about to step in when Marguerite descended and kissed her enthusiastically.

'Simply enchanting to see you again, darling,' she said. 'You must come again for my Littlechurch exhibition.'

'I'll see what I can do,' promised Angela, ignoring the malicious grin on Freddy's face.

They set off. Angela waved until they were out of sight then turned around and sighed.

'Well, that was an eventful visit,' she said. She settled back into her seat, but not before she had noticed a red smudge on William's cheek. 'Wipe your face, William,' she said.

He understood her immediately and scrubbed at his cheek in horror. The car swerved slightly.

'But don't put us in the ditch again,' said Angela.

'I'm sorry, ma'am,' said William.

Angela shook her head, then looked out of the window and covered her mouth to hide her smile.

CHAPTER TEN

'THAT ALL SEEMS clear enough,' said Inspector Jameson.

'Oh yes,' said Dr. Ingleby. 'The body contained a large dose of arsenic. Quite enough to kill her, there's no doubt about that.' He adjusted his spectacles and glanced at his notes. 'She had eaten a few hours before death, but her stomach was empty. That, together with certain traces on her clothes, indicates that she'd had an acute gastric attack.'

Jameson and Willis wrinkled their noses in sympathy.

'Yes,' went on Ingleby, 'I'm afraid she was probably quite ill for some hours. The symptoms of arsenic poisoning are very unpleasant, and can include anything from a burning pain in the throat, diarrhoea and vomiting of blood to convulsions and coma.'

'Poor woman,' remarked Willis.

'However,' said the little doctor. 'It doesn't look as though the gastric attack was the immediate cause of death, although of course the poison was the ultimate cause. By the state of the intestines—which I won't go into so soon after lunch—I should judge that she survived the initial attack. She may even have begun to feel a little better. That can happen with arsenic, you know—you can recover from the original symptoms of poisoning, but then be struck down by the after-effects. In this case it looks as though she died of cardiac failure. There was some congenital weakness there—signs of mitral stenosis and so forth, and I can only assume that the arsenic proved too much for her heart.'

'What about the injuries to the face?' said Jameson.

'They were inflicted some time after death, that's certain,' said Ingleby. 'Clearly, the purpose was to disguise her identity.'

'Presumably that means whoever killed her knew there wouldn't be too much hue and cry about her disappearance,' said the inspector. 'We've certainly had no luck in tracing her up to now. No-one fitting her description has been reported missing.'

'What have you been looking for?' said Ingleby. 'A blonde? You do know her hair was dyed, don't you?'

'Was it?'

'Oh yes. One almost never sees that light shade of blonde on a grown woman. Yes, she was a natural brunette. Almost black, in fact. It's a colour that's quite rare in England.'

Jameson remembered the photograph of the infant which they had found in her suitcase, and his impression that the little boy had been foreign.

'Yes, that makes sense,' he said. 'How stupid of me not to think that her hair might have been dyed.'

'Comes from not being married, sir,' said Willis comfortably.

'You're married, though. Why didn't you think of it?'

'Mrs. Willis's hair has always been a very fine shade of auburn, sir,' said the sergeant. 'No artificial colour required.'

'Certainly not,' agreed the doctor. 'I must say I prefer a woman to wear the hair colour that God gave her.'

'Mrs. Willis's hair was the first thing I noticed about her,' said Willis. 'That and her ankles. Very narrow ankles, she had.'

'I hate to interrupt your romantic reminiscences,' said Jameson, 'but we have work to be getting on with. You had better take another look at the missing persons register and see if any dark-haired women matching her description have gone astray. It might be that she dyed her hair after she went missing.'

'Right-oh, sir,' said Willis.

'But before you do that, we are going to pay a visit to an old friend of ours.'

Mrs. Chang lived in a flat on the top floor of her night-club premises in Brewer Street. She was a tiny Chinese woman who might have been aged anywhere between fifty and seventy. Her hair was long and still jet black, and she wore it pinned in a tight bun on the top of her head. She was dressed smartly and soberly, and would have looked the very epitome of respectability were it not for the mischievous look in her glittering eyes, and her tendency to assume a calculating expression whenever she was asked a direct question.

She greeted Jameson and Willis fulsomely, as though they were old friends.

'Hallo, hallo, Inspector Jameson! And this Sergeant Willis. Yes, yes, I remember very well. We have talk together six months ago, yes? We have talk together when you come and raid my club. Very polite policemen, both. Not like other one, what his name? He very rude. I respectable business-woman, I tell him, but he not polite at all. Why you here today, then? You come to shut me down again? You not find anything here today. Everything above the board. You see? Three o'clock now and we shut. We open later but all very above the board. Fine music and dancing, but no illegal drinking. We have very fine Negro orchestra. Famous all over America. Pay generous, too—we not cheap like other places that hire Negroes. Dukes and princes and film-stars come from all around to see them.'

When Jameson could speak, he assured her that they were not there to shut her down, and she clapped her hands and beamed.

'Well, well! Then why you come? Maybe you speak to my son, Johnny. He take over business soon when I too old. No good to rely on daughter—she just got married to very respectable man. You don't trust daughter, inspector. She run off and get married instead of help with business.'

'I congratulate you,' said the inspector politely. 'Now, we have come about a rather delicate matter.'

The smile immediately disappeared from Mrs. Chang's face and she sat up, her attention caught.

'Yes?' she said.

'Yes. I don't know whether you have read the newspapers lately, but if you have you may have seen reports about a dead woman, who was found in a ditch in Kent.'

The calculating expression appeared and Mrs. Chang said, 'Yes? Yes? Maybe I remember. Woman with her head crashed, yes? I think I read the story. Very sad.'

'That's the one,' said Jameson. 'Now, we are trying to find out who she was. She had no identification on her when she was found, but she did leave a suitcase, which contained a handbill for the Copernicus Club.'

Mrs. Chang nodded.

'Yes, many people come to my club. Very fashionable with the upper classes. Also many foreign princes and ladies.'

'I don't think she was upper class,' said Jameson, 'but we did wonder whether she mightn't have worked here as a dance hostess.'

'Ah, yes, my girls,' said Mrs. Chang. 'Very good girls. They dance with foreign princes. Only dance, though. We are re-spectable business. Nothing—how you say—below the belt here.'

'Er, quite,' said Jameson.

'I fetch Johnny,' she said. 'He know all the girls. He tell you what you want to know.'

She sprang up with a surprisingly youthful energy and hur-ried through the door to the top of the stairs. From there, she leant forward over the banister and yelled piercingly in Chi-nese. Willis winced. Presently, they heard a door open on the floor below and a man's voice reply. The two exchanged rapid words and then the man made a huffing sound and ascended the creaky stairs.

'This my son, Johnny,' announced Mrs. Chang. 'He tell you what you need to know. Johnny, you answer policemen's ques-tion.'

Johnny Chang was a stocky, serious-looking young man in shirt-sleeves. Although not particularly tall, he towered over his mother, who gazed at him impatiently.

'How may I help you, inspector?' he said, in a surprisingly educated voice.

'My son go to Oxford,' put in Mrs. Chang proudly. 'Graduate first-class. He the clever one of the family. He look after his mother like a good boy.'

Johnny said something impatiently to her in Chinese, and she snapped back at him then smiled once more at the two policemen.

'Johnny say I interfere. Perhaps so. I leave you to talk.'

She went into a back room and pushed the door to. Jameson was almost certain she was listening through the crack. Johnny Chang turned to them inquiringly and Jameson explained what they were looking for and why they had come.

'Given the handbill, we wondered whether she might have worked here,' he finished. He observed Johnny carefully as he spoke, but the young man's expression was unfathomable.

'Yes, we have girls here,' he said. 'Their job is to dance with the men and entertain them.'

'And to encourage them to buy drinks?' said Jameson gently.

Johnny permitted himself a smile.

'If one of our clients wants to buy a pretty girl a drink— why, there's nothing wrong with that, is there, inspector?'

'Nothing at all,' said Jameson.

'It's all completely harmless,' said Johnny, 'and I assure you that we select our hostesses very carefully. Only respectable girls are allowed here. If we caught the slightest whiff of anything untoward going on, they know perfectly well that they'd be out. Our clientele is what you might call rather top-drawer, you see, and we can't afford to get a bad reputation.'

Jameson forbore to remind him of the Copernicus Club's intermittent adherence to the licensing laws as evidenced by his mother's frequent appearances before the magistrates.

'Oh, there's absolutely no suggestion that this woman was up to anything she oughtn't to have been,' he said mendaciously. 'We are just anxious to find out who she was, and this is the only clue we have.'

'I see,' said Johnny Chang.

'*Have* any of your girls gone missing recently?' said Jameson. Johnny shook his head.

'No,' he said. 'I can assure you that all our girls are accounted for. I'm sorry, inspector, but I'm afraid I can't help you.'

He spoke with finality. Jameson saw that there was no use in questioning him further, and he and Willis rose to leave. Mrs. Chang returned and beamed at them.

'You come here whenever you like,' she said, 'but in dinner-suit next time, please, and without warrant-card. We have fine music and beautiful girls. You have a good time, yes? We like the police. They very good drinkers.'

Jameson thanked her and they went out, Johnny Chang following them down the stairs. They reached the entrance-hall just as the front door opened and there entered a group of men carrying instruments whom Jameson guessed to be the Negro orchestra, presumably come to rehearse. The arrivers and the departers ran into each other and there was some confusion and many apologies as they all disentangled themselves.

'Goodbye, inspector,' said Johnny Chang, then turned to one of the band, a gangling young fellow who was carrying a trumpet-case. 'Just a minute, Alvie,' he said. 'I want to speak to you.'

'Inspector?' drawled Alvie, looking at Jameson in surprise. 'We got the cops here again already, Mr. Chang?'

'It's nothing,' said Johnny. 'They're just looking for a missing girl. We can't help them, of course. Now, let's go upstairs.'

Alvie glanced back at the two policemen as he followed Johnny up the stairs, but said nothing.

'It's no use,' said Jameson as he and Willis emerged into the street. 'They've closed ranks. They aren't going to give us any more information than they can help.'

'Hardly surprising,' said Willis. 'They know—or at least suspect—exactly what their girls get up to, but they can't admit it or they'll be pulled up for running a disorderly house, and that's the last thing they want just now.'

'Yes,' said Jameson, 'but that presents rather a problem for us if they won't tell us anything. We shall have to send a chap in under-cover, to see what he can discover. I want to find out who this poor girl was.'

CHAPTER ELEVEN

'I THOUGHT POLICEMEN never had time for lunch,' said Mrs. Marchmont as the waiter pulled out her chair for her.

'I don't, normally,' said Inspector Jameson, 'but I happened to be in the area and thought I'd look you up, just on the off-chance.'

'I'm very glad you did,' said Angela. 'I found myself unaccountably at a loose end today and was getting rather bored, but now I have someone interesting to talk to. I do hope you're going to be indiscreet.'

Jameson laughed.

'Only up to a point,' he said.

'Then I shall have to be content with that.' She paused as the waiter fussed about her, then said, 'Are you allowed to tell me how you are getting on with the case of that poor woman in the ditch?'

'I don't see why not,' he replied. 'The facts will all come out sooner or later anyway.'

'How splendid,' she said. 'I thought you might have to keep it all under your hat, since I'm not involved in any way.'

'Of course you're involved. Had it not been for you the body would never have been found, and besides, I should be interested to hear your perspective on things. You have that clarity of thought which is essential in a good detective, and may well be able to spot something that we have missed.'

'Oh,' said Angela, flattered.

'But it must remain between ourselves. I don't want to see it all in the *Clarion* tomorrow,' he went on, half-teasingly.

Angela felt herself going red.

'Oh!' she said again. 'I was rather hoping you didn't read that dreadful rag. I shall have something to say to Cynthia Pilkington-Soames when I see her. I never said half those things she wrote, and I only agreed to do it in the first place because she practically pinned me into a corner.'

'I must admit, I didn't recognize you from her portrayal,' he said.

'Well, that's a comfort, at any rate,' she said. 'But of course you know that I should never dream of allowing things told to me in confidence to get into the papers.'

'I know it,' he said.

'Then let's not talk about that stupid story any more, or I shall never live down the embarrassment,' she said.

He saw that she was rather ruffled by the whole thing and tactfully changed the subject.

The waiter came and hovered politely, and the important matter of the food occupied the next few minutes. Then they returned to the case at hand. Jameson told her about Dr. Ingleby's findings, and she was surprised.

'That is very interesting and rather odd,' she said. 'Yes, I can see why the Littlechurch police called you in. This is not an ordinary, everyday sort of murder, is it?'

'Not when poison is thrown in as an ingredient,' he agreed.

'But where was she given the arsenic, and how?' said Angela. 'I had rather thought that the whole thing happened on the spur of the moment. I assumed she had probably been strangled—perhaps even in a car—and then thrown down the bank. But it's difficult to poison someone in a car, I imagine. Presumably, in that case, she must have spent some time in a house or a hotel and been given the poison there, perhaps in a meal or a drink.'

The inspector nodded.

'Yes,' he said. 'And according to Dr. Ingleby, she didn't die immediately. She had a gastric attack, as one would expect from arsenical poisoning, but seems to have survived that. It was heart failure that killed her, caused by the after-effects of the poison. After she was dead, someone took care to disfigure her face and then disposed of the body, but it must have taken her quite a while to die before that.'

Angela looked sober, thinking of the unfortunate woman and her violent end.

'What about the cloak room ticket?' she said. 'Have you had any luck with that?'

He told her about the handbill and the photograph that had been found in the suitcase.

'Then she had a child?' said Angela.

'Not necessarily,' he said. 'Perhaps the picture is of a nephew or other relative.'

'It's possible, I suppose,' she said. 'I wonder, though. It will be very sad if a child has been deprived of his mother because of this. And what about the handbill?'

'I have it here,' he said, feeling in an inside pocket. 'Ah, yes.' He brought out the much-folded scrap of paper and handed it to her, and she read it curiously.

'The Copernicus Club? I believe I've heard of it,' she said. 'Isn't it owned by Mrs. Chang? I've read about her in the newspapers. She keeps getting arrested for serving alcohol after hours, I seem to remember.'

'That's her,' he said. 'She's a clever soul. The Copernicus is rather a haunt of the upper classes and the bright young people, you see, and the police raids and the arrests make the clientele feel terribly rakish and daring. I'm sure it's deliberate on her part—all part of the club's public image, one might say. She can easily afford the fines, and every time she is arrested the story gets into the papers and increases her notoriety.'

'And you think our mysterious woman may have worked at the Copernicus as a dance hostess?'

'I think it's entirely possible. She had several well-worn evening-frocks in her suitcase in addition to the handbill. But I've spoken to Mrs. Chang and her son, and either they could not or they would not tell me anything. It was impossible to get anything out of her, in particular—she's an old hand and knows exactly what she's doing. Her clashes with the licensing authorities have become a bit of a joke, but there are rumours that the girls who work at the Copernicus do more than just dance with the male clients, and if Mrs. Chang were to be found guilty of running a disorderly house—well, that would be a much more serious risk to her business. Johnny Chang, though—he's younger and less experienced, and perhaps less hardened than his mother. I got the impression that he knew something, although obviously he wouldn't admit to it, so we had to come away none the wiser. After that we sent in a plain-clothes chap to mingle with the throng for a few nights, but they must have been on the lookout for him and spotted him immediately, since he got nothing out of anyone. Evidently they'd all been warned not to talk, because they simply "clammed up", as I believe our American friends say, whenever he tried to broach the subject.'

'I see,' said Angela, gazing at the advertisement thoughtfully. 'Then you are no further forward in your search for our dead woman.'

'I wouldn't quite say that,' said Jameson. 'We are checking the missing persons lists, and of course the story has been published in most of the newspapers, so something might come of that. The Littlechurch police are making exhaustive inquiries at their end, in case anybody saw her there. And don't think we've given up on the Copernicus Club either— it's the only real clue we have up to now. We shall get someone to talk by fair means or foul, you'll see.'

Just then, their food arrived and they were silent for some minutes. Angela was thinking about what she had just heard.

So the dead woman had been deliberately poisoned, had she? That certainly put a different aspect on the matter. No longer did it look like a sordid but unpremeditated tragedy—no, somebody had actually taken the trouble to administer a deadly poison with deliberate intent, and then, once the woman was dead, had struck blow after blow to her face with terrible violence and cast her corpse aside to lie undiscovered forever. Except Angela and William had discovered it not long afterwards. How unlucky for the killer, Angela thought. She wondered whether he was anxiously reading the newspapers every day for fresh developments in the case, listening and starting at every knock on the door. A thought struck her.

'I wonder,' she said hesitantly. 'Might it have been suicide?'

Jameson looked sceptical.

'Do you mean she killed herself, but then someone else found her and disfigured her face? Why should anyone do that?'

'I don't know,' said Angela. 'I was just looking at possibilities.'

'Well, until we know who she was it's going to be difficult to make any deductions,' said the inspector.

'That's true enough,' said Angela.

They talked of other matters until the end of lunch, then Jameson looked at his watch regretfully.

'No peace to the wicked,' he said. 'I must go, I'm afraid. The superintendent is expecting me at three o'clock. I dare say he wants to complain about something.'

'Thank you so much for lunch,' said Angela, 'and good luck with your murder hunt. I only wish there were something I might do to help.'

'Unless you can tell me who she was, I don't suppose there is.'

'Well, if I think of anything useful, I shall telephone you,' said Angela. 'No, it's quite all right—there's no need to come back with me. I can see you're in a hurry and I'm only around the corner. You had better go and see your superintendent.'

He smiled briefly then glanced at his watch again and bade her goodbye. Angela watched him hurry off down the street then turned her steps towards home. She had just reached the corner of Mount Street when she hesitated and appeared to change her mind. She crossed the road and walked on, then turned into a little mews a few hundred yards farther on, where the Bentley and William lived.

She found the car standing in the street, its bonnet wide open, and William sitting on the pavement, smoking a cigarette and enjoying the early autumn sunshine. He ground out the cigarette and stood up hurriedly when he saw her.

'Any trouble?' she asked.

'No, ma'am,' he replied. 'Everything is fine. I just thought I'd give her a once-over. Do you want to go somewhere? I can go and get my jacket if you'll give me a moment.'

'No, no, it's quite all right. As a matter of fact, I came to ask you something. What was the name of your band-leader friend back in New York? Albie or Alvie something.'

If William was surprised he did not show it.

'Do you mean Alvie Berteau?' he said.

'That's the one I mean, yes. Is he in London now?'

'Yes, ma'am. He got an engagement in some night-club or other—I can't remember the name.'

'The Copernicus Club,' said Angela.

'Yes, I believe it is,' he said. 'Have you seen him there?'

'No, but I should like to speak to him. Can you introduce me to him?'

'Sure,' said William. 'Any time you like. I'll go look him up for you.'

'Thank you,' said Mrs. Marchmont.

William hesitated.

'Might I ask—' he began.

'I don't see why not,' said Angela. 'I think it is possible that he knows something about the woman we found in Kent.'

'You mean you think he killed her?' said William in astonishment.

'No, of course not. But the police seem to think that she worked at the Copernicus Club, and I wondered whether he knew her, that's all. I should like to find out who she was.'

'Don't the police know yet?'

'Apparently not, and nobody at the Copernicus will speak to them because they are all worried for their jobs. I thought perhaps I might be able to persuade him.'

'Maybe you can,' said William. 'I hope so. I don't like to think of that poor woman's not being claimed by anyone.'

'Nor do I,' said Angela.

Chapter Twelve

ANGELA LEFT WILLIAM to carry on tinkering with the Bentley, and decided to take a little walk to a hat shop near Regent Street of which she was rather fond. It was a fine afternoon and warm for September, and the streets were bustling and lively. Angela walked unhurriedly along Grosvenor Street, enjoying the sights and sounds of the city, the motor-cars and the wagons, the delivery-boys and the office-girls going about their business, and thought how pleasant it was to be in London at this time of year. A whinnying and snorting sound suddenly caught her attention, and she looked up to see a rag-and-bone man attempting to calm his horse, which had taken fright at the noise of a motor-cycle as it roared down the street. The horse was a mangy creature, and Angela could not help but compare it in her mind with Castana, Lucy Syms's well-fed mare. That train of thought led her back to the lunch at Blakeney Park the other week, when the clash of personalities between Lucy and Lady Alice had been plain for all to see. She wondered how the two women would get on after the wedding. Would Lady Alice retreat with a good grace into the background, or would she remain to assert her ascendancy over Blakeney Park? And how would Gil take it all? He did not seem to have the tact required to keep things rubbing along smoothly, but perhaps he had hidden qualities about which she knew nothing.

Angela was brought back to the present by a peal of church bells and a hubbub of voices before her. She looked up and saw that she had reached St. George's, and that a small crowd of people had gathered outside the church, including a number of reporters. Evidently somebody important was getting married inside, for a large, shiny limousine was waiting in the street, under the watchful eye of its driver and a policeman in uniform, who now and again shooed away various small groups of children that were hovering about.

Even as Angela watched, the crowd surged forward and she was just able to distinguish the happy couple as they emerged from the church. She was preparing to pass on, when she was accosted by a somewhat disreputable-looking young man who until a few moments previously had been leaning with bored nonchalance against some railings across the road, notebook and pencil in hand.

'Hallo, Mrs. M,' said Freddy Pilkington-Soames.

'Freddy!' exclaimed Angela. 'What are you doing here?'

'Earning an honest living, of course,' he replied. 'Society weddings are singularly dull, but it appears that the public appetite for them cannot be sated, and so here I am.'

'Oh, I see. The *Clarion* sent you, did it? And how do you like being a reporter?'

Freddy closed his eyes briefly and gave a little shudder.

'I don't think I can possibly describe to you in words how frightfully tiresome it is,' he said. 'To begin with, they force me to come in at half-past eight. Half-past eight! Have you any idea of the unearthly hour at which I have to get up? Then they send me out to stand in the streets for hours on end like a flower-girl, just because the public clamours to know the details of the wedding between some loathsome aristocrat and his shop-girl paramour. And they make me work in the evenings, too. Imagine that! I spent last Wednesday night attending a trade union meeting in a vile, damp, draughty hall in Bethnal Green, at which Mr. Rowbotham spent a good two hours holding forth—with quite execrable grammar, I might add—on the subject of The Working Man And His Future. Bethnal Green! I do believe I'd never been any further East than the Alhambra before that. I felt I was taking my life in my hands. Fortunately, as it happened, there was a chap there I knew at school, who has rather gone off his head and joined the Labour Party. He expects to stand at the next election, as a matter of fact. I suppose I shall write something flattering about him for the paper. One can't let down an old friend.'

Angela could not help laughing at the disgusted expression on his face during the greater part of this speech.

'And what shall you write about this wedding?' she said. 'Who are they, by the way?'

'He is Lord Blanchard, and she is a Miss Christabel Plunkett, whom nobody has ever heard of. He's forty-one years older than she and practically ga-ga. The Lord only knows how they got him to totter down the aisle without one or more of his limbs falling off. She—well, you can imagine what sort of a woman she is. I expect she wears an inventory of his possessions next to her heart at all times. I shan't say that in my piece, of course. I shall merely write about how the crowd cheered when the bride made her first blushing appearance with dewy cheek and eye, and all that rot. Then I suppose I shall put something about her fashionable bridal gown in rich white *broché*, cut daringly short at the front with pearl and *diamanté* embroidery about the *décolletage*.'

Angela stared at him in surprise.

'Was she wearing all that?' she said. 'How could you tell, from this distance?'

'Oh, I found out the name of her dressmakers, and asked them yesterday,' he said.

'I wonder you bothered turning up at all.'

'Well, you never know what might happen,' said Freddy. 'The bride might jilt the groom in favour of the vicar, or the bride's mother and the groom's sister might turn up in the same frock and have an unseemly tussle in the street. I should hate to miss that. However, it looks as though all has gone according to plan. Pity—I was half-hoping the old dodderer would drop dead just before the vows were exchanged. Can't you just imagine the to-do?'

'You are a very bad boy, Freddy,' said Angela.

'It's probably my mother's fault,' he said. 'Anyway, what are you doing here, vaunting your fame with brazen face by strolling through the centre of Mayfair in broad daylight?'

'As a matter of fact, I was going to buy a hat.'

Freddy gave a disapproving click of the tongue.

'The life of the idle rich,' he said. 'One day people like you will be put up against a wall and shot, or thrown to the wolves, or something. At least, that's what Mr. Rowbotham seemed to be saying.'

'But I need a new hat,' said Angela.

'You already have a hat. You're wearing it.'

'This old thing?' said Angela. 'Why, I should hardly call this a hat in the strict sense of the word. Besides, one can never have too many hats.'

'That is a particularly frivolous attitude. You ought to do something improving such as visiting a museum or helping in a charitable institution.'

'Is this the influence of your Labour Party friend?'

'Good Lord, no!' said Freddy. 'The whole thing was frightfully dull and earnest. And trades unionists wear the most utterly ghastly clothes, because nice ones would be awfully wasteful and they're not supposed to have fun, you see. Why, you ought to have seen the get-up my friend St. John was wearing. His tailoring was wholly beyond redemption. I felt quite sorry for him.'

'And you say *I* have a frivolous attitude,' said Angela.

Freddy grinned complacently. Angela regarded him search-ingly.

'I do believe you're rather enjoying your new job,' she said.

'"Enjoy" is a strong word,' he said. 'I don't enjoy *any* work. But I will admit it hasn't been quite as horrid as I was expect-ing. I am starting to understand what Mother sees in it.'

'Well, I hope you will stick more closely to the facts than she does. I don't know where she got half the things she put in that story about me.'

'Oh, that,' said Freddy. 'Yes, it was rather a work of fiction, wasn't it? It was your own fault, you know. If you won't give up the goods then people will be inclined to invent things about you.'

'But I don't like talking about myself,' said Angela.

'Don't you see, though? That's why everybody is so wild to know all about you. They think you must be hiding some terribly exciting secrets.'

'I'm not. I just don't particularly want the whole world to know every thought that goes through my head.'

'Then you will continue to attract attention,' said Freddy simply. He was gazing at the wedding-party, who looked as though they were about to depart. 'Now, I suppose I ought to pursue the thing to the bitter end and follow the happy couple to Claridge's. Perhaps the groom will expire face-down in the wedding-cake and make the day worth while after all.'

'Freddy,' said Angela, struck with a sudden idea. 'Do you know the Copernicus Club?'

'The Copernicus Club?' said Freddy. 'Why, of course I know it. It was the scene of many of the more regrettable occurrences of my youth.' He spoke grandly, as one who had reached a great and venerable age.

'What can you tell me about it?'

'Oh, lots of things,' he said. 'It's run by Mrs. Chang, of whom I'm sure you will have heard. I'm rather a favourite of hers, you know. It's full of rich young types and film-stars looking for the latest thrill. They do say—' he said, then lowered his voice mysteriously and recounted a scurrilous rumour about a minor member of the royal family.

'Good gracious!' said Angela.

'It was in a private room, though, and nobody will admit to having been there, so it must remain unproven.'

'Will you take me there?' said Angela.

Freddy was surprised.

'Why, I haven't been for months, but yes, I could take you if you like. Why this sudden interest in late-night revelry? I shouldn't have thought it was your thing.'

'I am very fond of late-night revelry,' said Angela with dignity. 'I'm not that old.'

'Of course you're not,' said Freddy. 'Then we shall go. When would suit you?'

'What about tomorrow?'

'Tomorrow? Why the haste?' He looked at her suspiciously. 'I believe there is something you are not telling me,' he said. 'Wherefore this sudden irresistible attraction for the Copernicus Club?'

'Somebody told me about it, that's all, and said it was great fun,' said Angela vaguely, but Freddy was not fooled for an instant.

'Rot,' he said. 'There's something, isn't there? Spit it out.'

'I can't,' said Angela. 'I promised not to say anything to the press—and especially not the *Clarion*.'

'I should think I know when to hold my tongue,' said Freddy, with a hurt air.

Angela sighed. It was clear that she would have to tell him sooner or later, since she could hardly spend the evening questioning the staff of the club without drawing his notice.

'Very well,' she said reluctantly. 'But this is not to be spread about. The police think there may be some connection between the Copernicus and the dead woman we found the other week.'

Freddy raised his eyebrows.

'I say,' he said. 'Now that's rather interesting. What makes them think that?'

Angela told him about her conversation with Inspector Jameson and the handbill which had been found in the woman's suitcase.

'Awfully convenient for you, having a friend in the police,' remarked Freddy. 'I ought to cultivate a useful acquaintance of that sort myself. And so they've had no luck in getting anyone to talk? I can't say I'm surprised. But what do you intend to do? Do you have something up your sleeve that gives you an advantage over the police?'

'Not exactly,' said Angela, 'but William has a friend who plays in the jazz orchestra there, and he's promised to give me an introduction. I thought I might begin with him. He's bound to know if any of the dance hostesses have gone missing.'

'This is starting to sound rather promising,' said Freddy. 'Old Bickerstaffe would lick his lips if he knew about it.'

'Mind,' warned Angela, 'I promised Inspector Jameson, so you mustn't tell anyone. If you do, I shall—I shall—' she cast about for a suitably awful threat, 'I shall tell your mother about you and Marguerite.'

Freddy paled visibly.

'You wouldn't!' he said, aghast.

'Oh, wouldn't I?'

'You're a cruel woman, Angela.'

'Then give me your word you won't say anything. If you're a good boy now, there's a chance that you might get an "in" on the story later.'

'You must introduce me to this inspector of yours.'

'Perhaps I shall.'

Freddy gave his word somewhat grumpily, then they parted, having agreed to meet again the following night.

Chapter Thirteen

IT WAS A damp, drizzly evening when Angela and Freddy emerged from a little restaurant that they had discovered was a great mutual favourite, and set off for the environs of Brewer Street. In spite of the late hour and the gloomy weather, Soho was full of noise and life, and the patrons of the various establishments enjoyed a roaring trade as the young and the not-so-young, the fashionable and the unfashionable, flocked to their doors to get a taste of London's gay and gaudy night-life.

They had just turned off Brewer Street when they saw ahead of them a little knot of people gathered outside a particular door.

'Here we are,' said Freddy as they approached the group. A young woman turned to see who the newcomers were, and her face broke into a smile of recognition.

'Hallo, Freddy, you ass,' she said amiably. 'I do believe it's been an age.'

'Hallo, Gertie,' said Freddy. 'Where have you been? Is your Governor still giving you trouble?'

'Yes,' said Gertie, who had a face and manner that promised nothing but mischief. 'Father has been a screaming bore ever since that business with the Cowboys and Indians party. I told him the damage to the car was nothing to do with me, and he said he didn't care about the car, but he wouldn't stand for any daughter of his riding a donkey through Covent Garden wearing only a poncho and a feather head-dress, and he confiscated my latch-key and stopped my allowance for simply weeks. I had to promise faithfully to behave myself before they'd let me out tonight. You'll take care of me, won't you, Walter?' she said to her companion. 'You'll make sure I stay on the straight and narrow path.'

'Y-y-yes,' stammered her young escort, who looked, as far as Angela could judge, quite incapable of preventing Gertie from doing anything she wanted if she was determined to misbehave.

Just then, the door opened and a solid-looking doorman stood back to let them all in.

'Hallo, Mr. Pilkington-Soames,' he said as they passed. 'We haven't seen you here in a while.'

'Jenkins,' said Freddy, nodding. 'Are the old crowd in tonight?'

'Some of them,' said the doorman. 'Mr. Doyle and Mr. Allison arrived earlier. They said they were expecting Mr. Bagley and young Viscount Delamere later on.'

'Delamere? But he's a frightful blister,' said Freddy. 'What on earth were they doing, letting him tag along?'

'I couldn't say, sir,' said Jenkins non-committally, and waved them in.

Angela had suddenly begun to feel rather old, and was wondering whether she ought not perhaps to have come with someone nearer to her own age. She had no time to indulge the feeling, however, for they were ushered to a door which opened to let out a blast of hot, damp air and deafening music. In through the door they went, and Angela's first impression was that they had entered Hell, for the whole place was clothed in a deep blood-red. The walls were red, the carpet was red, the chairs were upholstered in red velvet, and even the dim light seemed to wear a pinkish hue, thanks to the tasselled red lampshades that hung from the ceiling.

They were shown to a table, and Angela looked about her as her eyes grew used to the gloom. It was only ten o'clock, but the place was full of people. The tables were packed so tightly together that one could easily eavesdrop on nearby revellers— were it not for the loudness of the music, which in fact made it barely possible to conduct a conversation of one's own. The orchestra were in full swing, playing with great panache and humour, seemingly enjoying themselves as much as anyone, and the tiny dance floor was crammed with people, although there was not enough room to do much more than shuffle about. Angela looked towards the stage. The band-leader had launched into an intricate solo on the trumpet, which was rather impressive, especially since he appeared to be conducting the orchestra at the same time using his entire body.

A waiter came and Freddy ordered champagne, which arrived accompanied by a plate of stale bread and cold sausage. Freddy pushed the plate away and offered Angela a light for her cigarette. They sat companionably for a while, entertained by the comings and goings. Angela had already spotted, sitting in close conference, two film-stars who were married—although not to each other—as well as the titled wife of a rising politician, who was laughing affectedly as a dark man, who looked to be a foreigner, kissed her hand.

A young woman with unnaturally fair hair, red lips and a world-weary air passed their table and gave Freddy a brief wave. Angela watched as the girl spied a man sitting alone at a table and approached him, putting her hand on his shoulder in a familiar gesture. He motioned to a chair and she sat down. He summoned a waiter.

'So that's how it works,' thought Angela. 'Does she work here?' she said to Freddy, as soon as she could make herself heard.

'Yes,' he said. 'She's one of Mrs. Chang's girls. Their job is to relieve the male customers of any inconvenient spare cash they may have about their persons by encouraging them to buy drinks.'

'So I see,' said Angela. She rifled in her little beaded evening-bag, and brought out a tiny notebook and pencil. She scribbled a note, then signalled to a passing waiter and instructed him to give it to the band-leader as soon as he could.

'You ought to have given it to me to pass on,' said Freddy. 'Now the waiter will think you're trying to seduce a black man.'

'I doubt he'd blink an eye even if I were,' said Angela. 'I thought that kind of thing was all terribly normal nowadays in these circles. I doubt it would shock anyone for a second.'

The band had paused between numbers, and Angela watched as the waiter slipped her note to the man she had seen playing the trumpet earlier. He read it without apparent surprise but merely glanced inquiringly at the waiter, who pointed at Angela's table. The musician looked up, saw Angela and nodded at her, then gestured to indicate that he would join her as soon as possible.

'Suppose we dance,' suggested Freddy, as the next number began. 'He'll be busy for a while.'

'Why not?' said Angela, 'If we can find any room, that is.'

He led her to the floor and they essayed a rather cramped two-step. The girl called Gertie and her hapless escort were dancing too. Gertie flashed Freddy a wicked grin and looked at Angela curiously. The number finished and they went back to their table, a little breathless. Alvie Berteau put down his trumpet and nodded to a deputy, then came over to where they were sitting.

'Mrs. Marchmont?' he said.

'Mr. Berteau,' said Angela. 'I'm very pleased to meet you. William has told me so many things about you. Thank you for agreeing to see me. This is Freddy Pilkington-Soames.'

They all shook hands solemnly, and Angela invited Alvie to sit.

'Did William tell you why I wanted to speak to you?' she began.

A wary look came into Alvie's eye and he looked around cautiously.

'He did, ma'am,' he replied. 'But it's kind of difficult here, 'cause we're not supposed to talk about it. They'll throw me out if they find out I've been speaking to you.'

'Did you know—' began Angela, then stopped as Freddy shot her a warning glance. She looked up to see a young man of Chinese appearance standing before their table. He bowed genially to Angela and Freddy, then looked at the musician.

'Alvie,' he said, 'oughtn't you to be on stage?'

'Sorry, Mr. Chang,' said Alvie, and stood up, but Angela interrupted.

'I beg your pardon,' she said, 'I merely called him over because I wanted to tell him personally how delightfully talented he and his band are. Mr. Pilkington-Soames here works for the *Clarion*, and he was thinking of running a piece about the Copernicus and its jazz orchestra. I hope you don't object to the publicity.'

Johnny Chang hesitated.

'No, not at all,' he said affably. 'Alvie, you may speak to this lady and gentleman, but I should like you to be back on stage in ten minutes.'

He seemed inclined to hover, so Angela said, 'As a matter of fact, Mr. Berteau and I were just about to go and dance. You don't mind, I hope? Don't worry, I shall send him back to work as soon as the next number is over.'

Clearly supposing that Angela was a bored society matron in search of an illicit thrill, Johnny Chang bowed with the utmost politeness and stood back to let her and Alvie pass.

'I'm sorry for forcing you to dance, and I do hope I haven't got you into trouble,' said Angela as they stepped out onto the floor.

'No fear of that,' said Alvie in friendlier tones. 'You said the magic word "publicity". He'll be fine. They think a lot of their business, the Changs.'

He steered her around the floor carefully.

'I suppose we can talk now without being overheard,' said Angela. 'You know what I am looking for. A woman is dead and I want to find out who she was. It seems a great shame to let fear of the police get in the way of that.'

'Well, you know,' said Alvie cautiously, 'it may be that the girls here do just a little more than what they were hired for. I think you understand what I mean.'

He looked at her and Angela nodded.

'But the police don't like that one bit,' he went on. 'If it ever came out, this place could be closed down for good.'

'The policeman who is investigating this murder is not interested in closing the club down,' said Angela. 'And besides, all we need is a name. Whether or not she was doing anything illegal and whether it was sanctioned by the club is irrelevant.'

'I guess so,' said Alvie. 'How did she die?' he asked suddenly.

'She was poisoned with arsenic, then after she died someone smashed her face in so it was completely unrecognizable and disposed of her body in a ditch.' She said it quite deliberately, hoping to get a reaction.

Alvie bit his lip.

'Is there a girl missing from here, Alvie?' asked Angela gently.

He looked down at the floor for a moment, as though debating with himself.

'Lita,' he said finally. 'Her name was Lita.'

CHAPTER FOURTEEN

A NGELA WAS ABOUT to inquire further when she became aware of a sudden disturbance taking place across
the other side of the room. She turned, and her eyes opened
wide as she saw a group of twenty or thirty policemen in uniform pushing their way through the crowd.

'Not again,' said Alvie in resignation.

One of the policemen blew his whistle as he made his way
towards the stage. He motioned and shouted to the band to
stop playing. Some of them stopped at once, but others took
a little longer to notice. One by one, they gradually fell silent,
except for one poor trombonist who was lost in the music; he
carried on playing merrily and bobbing up and down in time
until a constable grabbed the instrument and pulled it out of
his hand. Alvie's look changed from consternation to amusement at the sight of his band-mate's astonished expression.

A police sergeant got up onto the stage and bellowed, 'Ladies and gentlemen, this club has been found to be in breach

of His Majesty's licensing laws and shall close immediately. Please collect your belongings and leave.'

There were groans, as well as several shrieks from some of the more excitable members of the audience, but most people rose obediently and made for the door. The exodus was proceeding in an orderly fashion when suddenly there was a loud screeching, and a tiny Chinese woman could be seen, struggling in the grip of two policemen. What happened next Angela was never entirely sure, but shortly afterwards there were screams and yells, and a group of people began scuffling on the floor. This set off something of a panic, and there was a general stampede for the exit. Angela felt herself buffeted from all sides as hundreds of people headed for the door at the same time, but before she could react she was knocked off her feet and almost fell to the floor. Fortunately, Alvie was still with her, and caught her just before she could be trampled in the rush, but there was no time to thank him as he pulled her out of the crowd and up onto the stage. From there she could see Mrs. Chang being borne away by the police. To Angela's astonishment, she also spotted Freddy, who was in the process of being subdued by two policemen with the aid of a truncheon.

'Good God!' she exclaimed. 'Whatever is going on?'

She hurried down from the stage, ignoring Alvie's warnings, and ran towards the disturbance.

'Freddy!' she cried, as she watched him being dragged away in handcuffs.

Freddy had no chance to reply before he was carried off. A policeman barred Angela's way.

'You can collect him in the morning,' he said. 'I dare say a night in the cells will do him a power of good.'

'But—' began Angela, but it was no good. The policeman shook his head and would not let her pass. Angela looked about her desperately as the sea of people surged towards the door, then hurried back to her table to collect her little bag. It was not there, but fortunately she found it on the floor after a brief hunt.

Another policeman came and chivvied her out of the place, and after a few uncomfortable minutes Angela found herself out in the cold street without her coat and hat. All about her were groups of people equally bereft and complaining loudly. She spotted Alvie standing with one or two of his bandmates, as well as a waiter and one of the hostesses. They were trying to persuade a policeman to let them back in to collect their things.

'No,' said the policeman firmly. 'Nobody is to come back in. I've had my orders. You can come back tomorrow and fetch them. Now, get along with you.'

Alvie turned away in disgust and walked off. Angela stopped him as he passed her.

'I haven't thanked you for saving me from being trampled to death,' she said.

He smiled.

'No problem,' he said. 'I guess William wouldn't have been too happy to find himself without a job.'

'Shall *you* be without one now?'

'Naw,' he drawled. 'Mrs. Chang will be out by tomorrow, and we'll open up again in a few days, busier than ever. It's happened before, and it'll happen again.'

'Rather an erratic way to earn a living, don't you think?'

He shrugged.

'It's a good place to work,' he said. 'They play fair—and pay fair.'

'Alvie, when can I talk to you again about Lita?'

He looked at her seriously, stroking his chin in thought.

'Listen,' he said finally. 'I don't know much about her myself, but she was friendly with a couple of the girls here. I'll see if I can get one of them to talk to you.'

'I'd be awfully grateful,' said Angela. The night air was chill and she wrapped her arms about herself. 'And now, I really ought to get home. I'm cold, and I've had rather more excitement this evening than I was expecting.'

Alvie laughed and helped her to find a taxi, which took some time given the number of people milling about in the street. They shook hands as she got in, and he promised to let her know as soon as possible when they could talk again. The taxi-driver looked surprised when Angela told him to take her to Mount Street, and she supposed she was looking rather disreputable, being without a coat or hat and having been handed into the taxi by a black man some years younger than herself. Her appearance was of little concern to her, however, since she was more worried about Freddy. Why had he been arrested?

The next morning she rose and breakfasted early. To her great disgust she felt a cold coming on, no doubt caused by her adventure of the night before. Her maid, Marthe, wanted her to remain at home and rest, but she refused with decision and called for William, who presented himself promptly.

'We must go to Bow Street magistrates' court this morning,' she said as he stood before her. William raised his eyebrows inquiringly and she went on, 'I have to go and—er—*spring* Mr. Pilkington-Soames.'

William's eyebrows rose further.

'Sounds like it was an interesting night, ma'am,' he said. 'What happened?'

'I'm not entirely sure,' said Mrs. Marchmont. 'It started with a police raid and ended with a stampede and in my losing my coat.'

'Did you talk to Alvie?' he asked eagerly. 'Did he tell you anything about the girl?'

'I spoke to him, but not for long, as the police rather interrupted things,' replied Angela. 'However, he knew her, and may be able to persuade one of the other girls to speak to me.'

'Let's hope so,' said William, and they went out.

Bow Street magistrates' court was filled with a raggle-taggle assortment of people who were waiting about for the various cases to be called. The crowd included several reporters, who were presumably waiting to see Mrs. Chang. Angela went in and sat through several cases of petty theft, public drunkenness and loitering with intent. It was all rather dull.

Finally, Freddy was brought in, as well as, to her astonishment, Gertie and her friend Walter. They were a sorry sight.

Freddy had a black eye, while Walter had a swollen lip. Gertie's make-up was smeared and she was carrying a crushed peacock feather, but she looked defiant. Angela caught Freddy's eye and waved. He raised a hand limply in reply, looking thoroughly fed up.

'Who are these people?' said the magistrate, eyeing them with disfavour. His clerk passed him the next case sheet and he applied his spectacles to his eyes. 'Frederick Herbert Pilkington-Soames, Walter Peregrine Anstruther, and—what's this? Gertie McAloon? Is that your full name, young lady?'

'No,' said Gertie shortly.

'Then what *is* your full name?'

Gertie glared at him for a second.

'Lady Gertrude Jacqueline Lucrèce Myrtle Sandford-Romilly-McAloon,' she said all in a rush.

Several reporters sat up with interest, and Freddy looked at her in surprise.

'Good heavens,' he said, 'that's rather a mouthful.'

'I'll say,' she said out of the corner of her mouth.

'Quiet!' said the magistrate, although he looked taken aback. 'Did you get that down?' he said to the clerk.

'I think so,' said the clerk.

'What are the charges against these—er—young people?' said the magistrate.

'Drunk and disorderly conduct and assaulting a police officer, m'lud,' said the clerk.

The defendants looked sulky.

'And how do you plead?' said the magistrate.

'Not guilty,' said Freddy.

'Not guilty,' said Gertie.

'N-not guilty,' said Walter.

The magistrate sighed in exasperation.

'Could somebody please tell me what happened?' he said.

A sergeant of police stepped up to the stand. He appeared to have a sore ear, for he kept on touching it and wincing. He took out a notebook and read:

'On the evening of Tuesday the 20th of September, we were carrying out our duties as members of His Majesty's Constabulary, to wit—'

'Yes, yes,' said the magistrate impatiently. 'I know what they are. Just tell me what happened.'

The sergeant gave him a pained look.

'Yes, m'lud,' he said, and turned a page in his notes. 'We were carrying out a raid on the night-club known as the Copernicus Club in Brewer Street, having been tipped off that they were serving alcohol outside licensing hours. We duly entered the premises and ordered all persons found therein to leave. The evacuation proceeded in an orderly fashion, except in the case of the accused, who had seemingly not heard the order to leave and who appeared to be playing some kind of game at their table. P. C. Grimshaw and I approached with the intention of speaking to them politely, but then this young lady suddenly and for no reason assaulted me with a dangerous weapon.' He paused uncomfortably.

'Indeed?' said the magistrate, looking at Gertie over his spectacles.

'I whacked him on the nose with a sausage,' said Gertie. 'It was an accident. I meant to hit Freddy.'

There was a shout of laughter from the court.

'Silence!' said the magistrate sternly. 'What happened then?' he asked the sergeant.

'I attempted to restrain the young lady, at which point this gentleman here' (he indicated Walter) 'leapt up and abused us using most unseemly language.'

Angela gazed at the prim Walter, trying and failing to picture it.

'He then attempted to punch P. C. Grimshaw in the face,' continued the sergeant. 'I let go of the young lady and intervened to restrain Mr. Anstruther, at which point the lady jumped up onto my back and began beating me about the head with the sausage again.'

There was more laughter from the court.

'You hit him!' cried Gertie. 'You oughtn't to hit people.'

'And why is this other young man here?' asked the magistrate tiredly.

'He got into a fight with Mr. Anstruther and then punched me on the ear,' said the sergeant.

'That's not how it happened at all,' began Freddy, but was immediately silenced by the magistrate.

'I've heard quite enough of this,' he said. 'I find you all guilty and fine you each ten pounds—except you,' he said to Gertie. 'I am fining you twenty pounds since you are a woman and ought to have known better. Next!'

The three of them were hustled off, protesting, and Angela rose to follow them into the lobby.

'But whatever shall I do?' Gertie was wailing. 'I lost all my money at the club. Walter, you must pay.'

The hapless Walter was patting his pockets and looking worried.

'There you are, Angela,' said Freddy when he caught sight of her. 'We're in rather a hole, I'm afraid. I don't suppose you could see your way clear—?'

'Of course,' said Angela. 'That's why I'm here. I feel rather responsible for this whole thing, although I hadn't realized that all three of you were involved.'

'I-I say,' stammered Walter. 'I'm aw-awfully sorry, Freddy. I've n-never been able to hold my drink very well.'

'So I see,' said Freddy, fingering his black eye gingerly.

'Why on earth did you hit a policeman?' said Angela.

'I was aiming for Walter,' said Freddy. 'I pulled him off the bobby and he took it rather amiss and gave me this shiner. Well, a chap can't take a thing like that lying down, so I had a go at him—landed him rather a splendid one on the kisser, as a matter of fact—sorry, old chap—but then he swung at me again and then ducked when I returned the blow, and I found my fist connecting with a policeman's fleshy ear instead.'

Angela shook her head but made no comment.

'I suppose we had better get the three of you out of here,' she said.

Fifteen minutes later they were standing outside the court and Angela was waving away their fulsome thanks.

'It's nothing,' she said. 'Now, let's get you all home. My car is waiting around the corner.'

William's face was impassive as he stood to let them into the car, but there was a pink tinge to the tips of his ears that spoke of great inner amusement.

'Now I have to go and confess to Father,' said Gertie. 'Or perhaps I shall just sneak into the house, collect my things and leave the country for a few months before he finds out. I hear Australia is very nice.'

'P-perhaps he won't f-find out,' said Walter.

Freddy laughed hollowly.

'No such luck!' he said. 'One of our chaps was there in court, looking as though it were his birthday. I'll be surprised if I still have a job by tomorrow.'

'Why don't you tell them you were doing research?' suggested Angela. 'You could say that you wanted to bring them the story of the seedy side of London's night-life, having experienced it for yourself.'

'Tell them I sacrificed myself deliberately, you mean?' said Freddy thoughtfully. 'That's an idea.'

'Just as long as you don't sacrifice me, too,' said Gertie. 'I'm in enough trouble as it is.'

Walter and Gertie were set down at their respective homes, leaving only Freddy in the car.

'I suppose there's no chance of Gertie staying out of the papers with a name and title like that,' remarked Angela. 'I wonder how she will explain it to her father. I feel rather sorry for her.'

'I shouldn't bother if I were you,' Freddy assured her. 'She is as tricky as a whole zoo-full of monkeys, and quite capable of getting around her old man. Oh, he plays the stern pater-familias all right, but really she can wind him round her little finger. She's quite safe.' He yawned. 'I have a beastly headache and should like nothing better than to go to bed for the rest of the day, but I suppose if I want to play the hero as you suggest, I had better go to work.'

'Oh,' said Angela, 'then we ought to have gone to Fleet Street first.'

'No, no,' said Freddy. 'I wanted to get rid of Gertie and Walter so we could talk about what this chap Alvie said to you.'

'He didn't have time to say much at all,' said Angela. 'All I have is the name Lita. I don't even know if it's the same girl. It might be somebody quite different, in fact. But Alvie said that one of the other hostesses might be willing to speak to me.'

'You will be sure and let me know whenever you hear, won't you?' said Freddy. 'I swore not to write anything, and I won't, but I still want to know who she was.'

Angela promised to tell him if she had any news, and they continued on to Fleet Street in a silence that was explained when Angela looked across and saw that Freddy had fallen asleep.

CHAPTER FIFTEEN

A NGELA DID NOT have to wait long before she heard from Alvie Berteau again. Two days later, William presented himself respectfully and said that if it were not inconvenient to Mrs. Marchmont, his friend Alvie would like to introduce her to someone who was willing to talk about the person they had discussed the other night at the Copernicus Club. Angela, who had been sniffling at home for two days with the cold she had caught that same night, was now feeling much better and was only too happy to get out of the house for a while.

Accordingly, on Saturday afternoon they sallied out to Soho in the Bentley. The place in which Alvie had suggested meeting was a little café of sorts—rather grubby, but home to the best coffee in that part of London, according to the large sign that hung in the window.

'You had better come in with me,' said Angela to William. 'I dare say you'd like to see your friend.'

William agreed with alacrity and sprang out of the car. He held the door open for her and they entered the dingy little establishment.

Alvie was sitting at a corner table with a young woman. She was dressed in ordinary day clothes, but Angela recognized her immediately as the hostess who had waved at Freddy on Tuesday night. Alvie stood up and greeted William with great affection, then introduced the girl as Geraldine.

'How do you do?' said Geraldine politely enough, but she looked uncomfortable. Angela saw that it would be difficult to speak confidentially to her in such a large group, so she turned to William and said:

'William, I'm sure you and Alvie have lots of things to talk about. Suppose you go and take a walk outside. You can come back in half an hour or so.'

The two young men went out obediently and Geraldine smiled gratefully. Angela summoned the waitress.

'What will you have?' she asked the girl. 'I should like to try this famous coffee of theirs.'

'I'll have one too,' said Geraldine. The waitress nodded and went off, and Geraldine said, 'Alvie says you want to know about Lita.'

'Yes,' said Angela. 'Did he also tell you why?'

'He says she's dead,' said Geraldine flatly.

'We don't know for certain,' said Angela, 'but a woman's body was found recently, and in her luggage was a handbill for the Copernicus Club, which indicates that she may have worked there at some time. When did you last see Lita?'

'I can't remember exactly,' said Geraldine. 'We don't always work the same nights, but it must have been about three weeks ago, I reckon. We shared a room, you see. I'd been out and got back and she wasn't there, but I didn't think too much to that at first, because it was quite normal for us not to see each other for several days. Anyway, I went to bed and when I got up again I suddenly noticed that she'd packed all her things and hopped it.'

'And did nobody remark upon her disappearance? Mrs. Chang, for example?'

Geraldine shook her head.

'No. Girls come and go in this business. One day they're here and the next they're not, and nobody ever asks where they went. I mean, it's hardly a steady job, is it? But I was friendly with Lita, and I would have expected her to mention something to me—give me her new address, at least—even if she said nothing to the Changs.'

'Tell me about her.'

'What do you want to know?'

'What did she look like, for example?' said Angela. 'Was she pretty?'

'Oh yes,' said Geraldine without hesitation. 'She was a beauty, right enough. All dark and exotic-looking, if you know what I mean. Lots of people thought she was Spanish or South American, but she was English through and through as far as I know. She called herself Lita de Marquez, but that wasn't her real name.'

'What was her real name?'

Geraldine shrugged.

'I don't know,' she said. 'She never told me.'

'You say she was dark,' said Angela. 'Did she dye her hair?'

'Yes,' said the girl. 'She did it a couple of months ago, just for a change, she said. I didn't think it suited her but she said she liked it. How do you know?'

'I was the one who found her body—if indeed it is she,' said Angela. 'The woman I saw had blonde hair and a blue coat, but I have since heard that the hair colour was not her own.'

'She did have a blue coat,' said Geraldine, thinking back. She looked sober. 'She really is dead, isn't she?'

'It looks like it,' said Angela.

'Who killed her?'

'I don't know, but I'd like to find out. Will you help me by telling me a little more about her?'

'Why, I don't know that there's much I can tell you,' said Geraldine. 'I liked her but we weren't what you might call close friends. I don't think she was the sort of girl to have close friends—not girls, anyhow. She liked to keep her own secrets. She didn't want to talk about what she'd done before she came to the Copernicus—there were things she wanted to forget, she said. I got the impression her home life wasn't a very happy one.'

'Did she have a child?'

'A child?' said Geraldine, surprised. 'If she did, she never mentioned it. Why do you ask?'

'There was a photograph of a little boy in her suitcase,' said Angela. 'I wondered whether he was hers.'

'Why, she never told me about it. Are you sure? I can't see her as the motherly type, myself. And she never said anything about a husband—although, of course, I s'pose she might not have had one. That would explain why she didn't like talking about herself.'

'Yes.' Angela hesitated, wondering exactly how to put her next question. 'Do you know anything about her men friends?' she said at last. 'I suppose she must have met quite a lot of men through her work. Do you think she might have—'

'Been tangled up with one of them?' finished Geraldine. She looked away, not meeting Angela's eye, and was silent for a moment. 'This job doesn't pay very much, you know,' she said at last. 'Sometimes a girl has to get along off her own bat.'

Angela understood her reply as an affirmative.

'Do you know of anyone in particular?' she said. 'I mean, anyone with whom she might have formed a closer association?'

Geraldine shook her head.

'No,' she said. 'I swear I don't know of anyone.'

Angela looked at her. Was the girl telling the truth?

'You understand, don't you, that we are looking for a murderer?' she said.

Geraldine nodded.

'Lita wasn't killed by a passing stranger,' Angela went on. 'She was murdered by someone she knew, and we need to find out about the events which led up to her death. We know, for example, that she packed her things and left them in the cloak room at Charing Cross station, then went down to

Kent—presumably by train—and never came back. What we don't know is: whom did she go with? Or, if she didn't go with someone, then whom did she go to meet? Are you quite sure you don't know where she was going? If you have any clue at all, then please tell me. Perhaps it will help us discover who did this to your friend.'

'Honestly, I don't know,' said Geraldine at last. 'She was friendly with lots of the men at the Copernicus—of course she was, that was her job—but she didn't tell me about anyone in particular. And her note never said anything about a man.'

'Her note?' said Angela. 'You didn't mention she'd left a note.'

'Didn't I?' said Geraldine. 'Of course she did. That's how I knew she'd hopped it.'

'What did it say?'

'I can't remember exactly. Something about how she was leaving because she had found better prospects somewhere else, and she was going after them. Then she wished me luck and all that and said she hoped we'd meet again some day. She left a week's rent in advance, too, which I must say was only fair on her part, as I had to find someone else in a hurry. She wasn't one to leave you in a hole, I'll say that for her.'

'She'd found better prospects and was going after them,' repeated Angela thoughtfully. 'Rather an odd way of putting it, don't you think? Are you sure that's what she said?'

'As sure as I can be.'

'You don't still have the note, I suppose?'

'No,' said Geraldine. 'I threw it away.'

'Have you any idea what she meant by "better prospects"?'

Geraldine shrugged.

'I thought she probably meant a new job that paid better,' she said. 'Oh,' she went on suddenly. 'I've just remembered. There was a man.'

Angela looked up.

'He came a day or two after she left, asking after her.'

'Came where? To the club?'

'To our digs. But I think he'd been asking at the club first and someone had given him our address.'

'Did he give his name?' said Angela.

'I think he did,' said Geraldine, 'but I can't remember what it was.'

'What did he look like?'

'Very dark. Young, I think. Foreign-looking. He wanted to know where she'd gone, and he seemed pretty upset when I said I didn't know. He said he'd been looking for her for ages—said he'd spent weeks asking around all the night-clubs, and was I sure? Well, of course, even if I had known where she'd gone I wouldn't just have told him like that, but I really didn't know where she was, so I said so. He said he needed to find her urgently, and if I heard from her to say that he'd been looking for her.'

'Did he leave an address?' said Angela, wondering who the young man could have been.

'Yes, I think he did as a matter of fact,' said Geraldine. 'I can have a look for it if you like. My digs are just round the corner.'

Angela assented and paid for the coffee, and they went out. Geraldine's lodgings were in a dingy side-street not far from the Copernicus Club itself. They climbed a grimy staircase up several floors until they reached the attic.

'This is it,' said Geraldine, taking out a key. Angela followed her in and gazed about her, marvelling that anybody could live in such a small space. The room was tiny, and was furnished with nothing but a worn rug, two beds and a little chest of drawers. Someone had rigged up a rail between the drawers and the window as a kind of wardrobe, and it was draped with all manner of cheap shiny satin frocks, fripperies, stockings and boas. The place was a mess, strewn with articles of clothing, magazines, cigarette-packets and shoes. Angela noticed a little spirit-stove on the floor in the corner, next to which stood a cup of some unidentifiable liquid that had been allowed to go cold. There was a cigarette-end floating in the cup.

'Sorry about the mess,' said Geraldine. 'I'm not exactly the tidiest of people.' She went on with some humour, 'Now you know why it took a while for me to notice that Lita had gone.'

'Is all this yours?'

'Most of it. I told the new girl she'd have to put up with it if she wanted to move in. She doesn't seem to mind, although she's a tidy one herself. Lita liked things neat and tidy, too.'

'Did she leave anything?' asked Angela.

'I don't think so,' said Geraldine. She was rummaging among her things with a frown. 'Now where on earth did I put it?' she said.

After some difficulty she finally unearthed a folded scrap of paper from the pocket of a skirt which had been kicked under the bed. Angela took it and read it. It bore the name 'Lew,' together with the address of a guest-house in Pentonville Road.

'Do you mind if I give this to the police?' she said.

'Suit yourself,' said Geraldine. 'But don't send them round here because I won't tell them anything. Mr. Chang has put his foot down and I want to keep my job.'

'Oh, is the club staying open, then?' said Angela. 'I heard that Mrs. Chang was given three months in prison after the latest raid.'

Geraldine laughed shortly.

'Yes, she was. I'll bet she didn't bank on that! But her son will keep running it and she'll be back. They're not too bad, those two, provided you don't cross them.'

'Well, good luck,' said Angela, taking out a card, 'and thank you. You've been very helpful. You will tell me if you hear from this man again, won't you? Here's my address, or you can reach me through Alvie, if you prefer.'

'I hope you find whoever did it,' said Geraldine. 'It's not right, what happened to her.'

'No,' agreed Angela. 'It's not.'

She left Geraldine standing thoughtfully among her jumbled possessions and returned to the street. William and Alvie were standing by the Bentley, laughing. William was holding something that Angela recognized immediately.

'My coat!' she exclaimed. 'And my hat! Why, thank you, William.'

'Thank Alvie,' said William. 'He fetched them.'

Alvie waved away her thanks and opened the car door for her.

'Back home now, ma'am?' said William.

Angela nodded and thanked Alvie once again, and they departed. As they drove through the busy streets, Angela thought about what she had learned from Geraldine. She was curious about the expression Lita had used in her goodbye note: what exactly had she meant by going after her prospects? It seemed an odd way of putting things if she were merely referring to a new job. And who was this Lew who had wanted to find her? Had he succeeded and then killed her? It was all most mysterious.

'At any rate, I have some evidence to give to Inspector Jameson,' she said to herself. 'Now I suppose I must withdraw gracefully and let him and Sergeant Willis do their jobs without any more interference from me.'

She felt a momentary twinge of regret, then shook it off and turned her attention to a prospective visit to the theatre that evening.

CHAPTER SIXTEEN

INSPECTOR JAMESON WAS most surprised when he heard about Angela's experiences at the Copernicus Club, but his astonishment soon turned to keen interest when she told him about her conversation with the girl Geraldine.

'So Lita de Marquez was her name,' he said thoughtfully. 'Spanish, was she?'

'Not according to her friend,' said Angela. 'Geraldine was certain she was English, and that her real name was something quite different.'

'Still, though, it's a start. And now we have a man in the picture, too. That is most interesting. We shall go to this hotel immediately and see what we can dig up about him. Now I suppose I ought to tell you off for interfering with the police in the execution of their duty, but of course I shan't. It would have been much more difficult for us to get the information out of any of them, given the edict they received from on high, so I shall thank you instead.'

'I gather Mrs. Chang is in prison at present. How is she?'

'Most indignant, from what I hear. I think she had started to consider herself to be above the law, but you know the Home Office is getting much more strict about that sort of thing nowadays. I fear she may not find it so easy to continue her business in future. Anyway, thank you again for all your help, Mrs. Marchmont. We shall go and pay a visit to this guest-house today.'

Angela hesitated.

'Would it be too much to ask that you let me know what you find out? I must confess to a terrible curiosity about the whole thing.'

'I shall if I can, certainly,' said Jameson, 'although it depends on what we discover. I mustn't prejudice the case, you know.'

'Of course, I quite understand,' said Angela, and with that she had to be content.

Fortunately for the relief of her curiosity, Inspector Jameson was able to inform her very soon of the results of his inquiry. He called her the very next day, but as might have been expected, he did not have much to report. The mysterious Lew had indeed stayed at the guest-house for several days, but had left the hotel a week or two earlier without mentioning where he was going. In fact, the staff had had difficulty in remembering him at all. This was not surprising: it was quite a large hotel, accustomed to receiving all manner of guests, from commercial travellers to foreign tourists, and Lew had not been one of their regular visitors, so nobody had paid much attention to him.

'Did you look at the register?' said Angela.

'Yes,' replied Jameson, but that was no go, as his signature was completely illegible. His surname might have begun with an M or an N, or even an H.

'Do you think he might be the man you are looking for?' said Angela.

'Well, he's the only man we've found so far who is known to have had a connection with her, apart from the people at the club, of course. That reminds me, we must make some discreet inquiries there. With Mrs. Chang out of the way at present, the staff may be more likely to talk. As for this other chap, I think we shall have to put an advertisement in the newspapers, asking for a man named Lew who was looking for a Lita de Marquez. The girl said Lita was English, you say? It's a pity we can't find out what her real name was.'

'Perhaps this Lew will know,' said Angela.

'If we can find him,' said the inspector with a sigh. 'This case is rather slow-going at present, I'm afraid.'

'I admire your doggedness,' said Angela. 'One always pictures the police swooping in on the suspect and arresting him immediately after the crime takes place, but it's not like that at all, is it? It's far more painstaking than the detective-novels would have us believe.'

'Yes,' said Jameson, 'it can be rather slow sometimes—very much a case of one step at a time—but there's a great deal of satisfaction to be had in bringing a case to a successful conclusion, so I don't mind it.'

'Well, I wish you luck,' said Angela, and rang off, as she had a luncheon engagement with Marguerite Harrison. She had been a little surprised to hear from Marguerite, but all was soon explained when her friend swept in, full of plans for her forthcoming sculpture exhibition in Littlechurch. She was looking very dashing and Bohemian as usual, swathed in gorgeous layers of deep purple and indigo edged with silver, and with a pair of enormous silver earrings dangling from her ears. She had come, she said, with the intention of drumming up some interest in the exhibition from several important artistic personages in London.

'Of course, Littlechurch is not exactly the centre of the art world, however much one might wish it were otherwise,' she declared, 'and so I thought written invitations wouldn't be *quite* enough. I have come, therefore, to solicit their interest *in prima persona*, as it were. You are coming to the exhibition too, aren't you, darling? You did promise, you know.'

Angela gave her assurance, since there was clearly no getting out of it—and indeed, she had no particular objection provided that she could keep away from Cynthia and her notebook as much as possible.

Marguerite had insisted on going to a little restaurant she knew on Charlotte Street, and so Angela summoned William—not without a certain mischievous curiosity to see what would happen. But William presented himself as respectfully as ever, wholly impassive and with no sign of consciousness that she could see. Angela was impressed despite herself. Marguerite, for her part, was as extravagantly friendly and flattering as always, and the three of them departed for Bloomsbury in the Bentley.

In the restaurant, Marguerite greeted the waiter familiarly by name and insisted on being moved to a more favourable table.

'I won't stand for being pushed into a corner,' she said to Angela. 'We women so often are, you know—which is ridiculous, because most of the time we are the only thing worth looking at. I much prefer to be on view, don't you?'

She then spotted someone she knew, and hailed him in her loud, carrying voice, causing everyone in the place to turn and look at them. The man—who, it transpired, was Luigi, the proprietor—came across and greeted her fulsomely. They kissed each other on both cheeks, and she asked after his wife. He replied at length and with great feeling.

'Poor Cara,' said Marguerite in a lower voice when he had gone. 'She was one of us, you know. Wonderfully talented— one of the most gifted girls at the Slade, as a matter of fact. Unfortunately, she was rather careless and got into a spot of trouble, and of course the man was long gone by the time she realized. But Luigi had been mooning after her for ages, and so she had to marry him in a hurry. Her parents were horrified at her marrying an Italian, but of course they don't know why she did it. Now they have five children and she has no time to paint, the poor thing.'

'Does Luigi know about the first child?' said Angela, startled.

'I have no idea,' said Marguerite, 'but it's probably best not to mention it. Is it too early for wine, do you think?'

She eventually decided against the wine, and went back to peering thoughtfully at the menu.

'How is Miles?' asked Angela.

'A little under the weather,' said Marguerite. 'Now, what do you say to oysters? They ought to be fresh at this time of year.'

'I'm sorry to hear that,' said Angela, referring to Miles rather than the oysters.

'Oh, he'll be quite all right,' said Marguerite. 'He gets these queer fits once in a while, you know—gets a little depressed and uneasy, but he usually recovers quickly enough. He snapped at me this morning when I asked him if he wanted another egg. *Quite* out of character, darling, as you know, so I left him to it and came out early.'

'I wonder,' said Angela, 'do these fits normally happen when you have an exhibition coming up, by any chance?'

She was teasing, but Marguerite opened her eyes wide and considered the suggestion seriously.

'Do you know, I believe they do!' she said. 'I hadn't thought about it before, but I think you must be right. Poor Miles. Perhaps I am just a *little* difficult to live with at times.' They laughed merrily, and Luigi came over to join in the joke and to take their order in person.

When he had gone, Marguerite became more serious and said, 'I wonder if Miles's bad mood has anything to do with concern for Gil. They have been putting their heads together a lot recently. I have the feeling that Gil is worrying about the wedding.'

'Why is that?' said Angela.

'Oh, just something he said when we saw him last,' said Marguerite. 'He said that he sometimes thought he wasn't good enough for Lucy, and that she deserved someone who wouldn't make such a mess of things as he did. He wasn't very good at this marriage stunt, he said. He was half-joking but I think he meant it seriously. Of course, Miles laughed at him and said he was getting cold feet and not to worry, everything would be quite all right. They went off and had a heart-to-heart later, and he *seemed* better, but I can't say I'm surprised. Lucy is a dear girl, and so capable, but I wonder if she doesn't rather frighten Gil sometimes with her competence.'

'Don't you think the whole situation is rather odd?' said Angela. 'I mean, that Gil has been chivvied into this marriage by his mother and Lucy. Do you really think he would marry Lucy if left to himself?'

Marguerite considered.

'Why, I don't know that he would, darling,' she said finally. 'To tell the truth, I'm not sure he would marry anyone at all if left to himself. He doesn't seem the type to do anything without being pushed into it by somebody.'

'But does he love Lucy? Does she love him?'

Marguerite made an expansive gesture.

'Who knows?' she said. 'Does it matter?'

'Perhaps it does to them.'

'Well, then, I think Lucy is fond of him, yes. But you must have seen for yourself that she's more of a motherly sort than a wife.'

'Rather awkward, when his real mother is still alive and re-fusing to relinquish the reins, don't you think?' said Angela. 'But from what I have seen, it is not Lady Alice and Lucy who stand between Gil and a happy life, but Blakeney Park itself. Without it, perhaps he wouldn't feel the need to marry well.'

'Oh, yes, it's an awfully big responsibility,' said Marguerite. 'I should hate it myself.'

They had their lunch and then rose to depart, not without ten minutes of ecstatic salutations to Luigi on Marguerite's part. Then they returned to the car, as Marguerite wanted to be dropped in Gower Street. She swept off in a whirl of scarves and scent, blowing kisses affectionately, then Angela instructed William to return home.

They arrived in Mount Street and William opened the car door for her.

'Oh,' said Angela suddenly. 'Marguerite has forgotten something.' She picked up the little package that lay on the seat next to her. 'It appears to be for you, William,' she said in some embarrassment. She handed it to him and was about to hurry discreetly away when she saw that he was holding it before him with an expression that was a mixture of puzzle-ment and dismay.

'Did Mrs. Harrison leave this?' he said finally.

'So it seems,' said Angela. Her curiosity overcame her. 'What is it?' she said.

He glanced at her, then opened it. Inside was a little box containing a watch. It looked rather expensive.

They stared at it in silence for a moment, then William turned a deep and furious red.

'I won't be kept, d'you hear?' he said fiercely, then without another word he got back into the Bentley, slammed the door and drove away with a screech of tyres, leaving Angela staring after him in astonishment.

Chapter Seventeen

Inspector Jameson and Sergeant Willis sat in the office formerly occupied by Mrs. Chang, but now, in her absence, employed by her son. Johnny Chang was regarding them with his usual polite but wary expression.

'So you see,' went on Jameson, 'our investigations elsewhere reveal that the dead woman was indeed employed here as a dance hostess.' He deliberately phrased it thus in order not to give away the fact that the staff had been talking without permission. 'According to our information, her name was Lita de Marquez.' He paused to see what reaction this got.

Johnny Chang's eyebrows rose in apparently genuine surprise and consternation.

'Lita de Marquez! She did work here, yes—but she left of her own accord. That is why I didn't mention her when you came here last time. I understood you were looking for someone who had gone missing, but as far as I was aware, Lita was alive and well and had merely gone to a new job.'

Jameson felt that this was splitting straws, but made no remark, and Johnny Chang went on, 'Is she really dead, then? That is most distressing.'

'We haven't formally identified the body yet, but we are working on the supposition that it was indeed Lita de Marquez,' said Jameson.

'Then I am very sorry,' said the young man, 'but I don't see how I can help you.'

This was clearly disingenuous, but again Jameson made no remark, and merely said, 'We shall need somebody to make a formal identification, at least. Unfortunately, her face has been disfigured beyond all recognition, but there are other distinguishing features that you or one of your employees might be able to identify. She had a rather distinctive birthmark on the inside of her left arm, for example. Somebody may perhaps have noticed it at one time or another.'

Johnny waved his hand.

'Yes, no doubt they did, if it is indeed she. I shall speak to them all and find out whether any of them are willing to identify her. I suppose they need not see her face.'

'No, that will not be necessary,' said Jameson.

'Very well,' said Johnny. 'Is there anything else?'

'We shall also need to speak to your staff,' said Jameson.

'But why?' said Johnny.

Willis shifted in his seat and Jameson sighed inwardly, seeing that the young man had determined to take refuge in polite but deliberate obtuseness.

'Because we believe she was killed by someone she knew,' he said, 'and possibly even by someone she knew from the Copernicus Club.'

'I can vouch for all my employees,' said Johnny Chang. 'I am not in the habit of employing murderers.'

'How do you know?' said Jameson with a slight touch of irritation. 'They don't exactly go about announcing the fact.'

'Naturally,' said Johnny uncomfortably, 'I know that. I merely meant that I only employ respectable people who come furnished with impeccable references.'

The inspector passed over this and continued, 'What about clients? Perhaps it occasionally happens that one of your girls becomes—shall we say attached—to a particular client? Please understand, Mr. Chang, that I am not in the slightest bit interested in anything your girls may or may not choose to do privately. That is not why I am here.'

But Johnny Chang was already shaking his head with decision.

'Absolutely not,' he said firmly. 'My mother and I do not allow anything of the sort. If a girl did happen to find herself—becoming attached—to a man, then we should ask her to leave, however honourable the association, since we run an honest establishment and do not wish to expose ourselves to charges of anything untoward.'

'Apart from breaking the licensing laws,' Jameson could not help saying.

Johnny Chang smiled in dry acknowledgment.

'There was some confusion over our licence,' he said. 'It was unintended on our part, naturally, and my mother is unfortunately paying the price for the misunderstanding. However, you will find that everything here is perfectly above-board now. You may come and raid us on any night you like, inspector. You won't find anything.'

'That is not my province,' said Jameson. 'I am concerned only with finding out who killed Lita de Marquez, and to do that I shall need to question your staff.'

'Certainly,' said Johnny Chang. 'I shall speak to them and instruct them to assist you as far as they can. I doubt very much whether any of them will be able to tell you anything, however.'

'Of course they won't, once he's spoken to them and told them in no uncertain terms to keep their mouths shut,' said Willis in disgust as they left the club afterwards.

'I think you're probably right,' said Inspector Jameson. 'The Changs have no intention of making things any easier for us, that's certain enough.'

The sergeant was right, of course. Two days later, Jameson sat in his office, sifting through various reports and his notes from the Copernicus. As he had suspected, there was not much to look at. Geraldine had been persuaded to identify the body and, red-eyed, had confirmed it as that of her former room-mate, Lita de Marquez. As for the staff, one or two of the waiters had been found to have criminal records for theft—although there was no history of violence in either case—and Jameson had received hints that a famous American gangster frequented the place, but since he had been on the run for years there was not much he could do about it except to keep an eye out. As for the rest of the clientele, many or most of them were well-known, or at least well-to-do, and it would be difficult to pin anything on any of them.

He was just about to call Sergeant Willis and set him on to the task of looking more deeply into the records of the known criminals, when he received a call from downstairs informing him that a reporter named Pilkington-Soames wanted to see him.

'Who?' he said impatiently. 'I don't want to speak to any reporters. Oh, he's a friend of Mrs. Marchmont, is he? I suppose you'd better send him up, then.'

A minute or two later, Freddy Pilkington-Soames swung insouciantly into the room, introduced himself and threw himself into a chair without being invited. Jameson regarded him with polite suspicion.

'How may I help you, Mr. Pilkington-Soames?' he said. 'I understand you are a friend of Mrs. Marchmont. Did she send you?'

'Good Lord, no,' said Freddy. 'I came off my own bat, but I guessed that my handsome face alone would not be enough to get me past the guard dogs at the entrance, so I thought I'd better send up her name.' He looked about him with mild interest. 'I say, I've never seen inside Scotland Yard before. It's all rather thrilling, isn't it? Do you have a prison here, or is it all offices? I had the misfortune to spend a night in the cells on Bow Street a few days ago—an unlucky contretemps involving a sausage and an awkwardly-placed member of the local constabulary—I won't bore you with the story—but my word, how uncomfortable it was! How do these criminal chappies put up with it?'

'They don't have much choice,' said Jameson politely.

'Well, I should revolt if I were in their position,' said Freddy. 'I believe I shall write a letter to the Home Secretary, to warn him of the danger of revolution within if standards of comfort and cleanliness are not improved in His Majesty's prisons very soon.'

'No doubt he will be very obliged to hear your thoughts on the matter,' said Jameson. 'Pardon me, but is this why you have come? To tell me your views on the British justice system and its operations?'

'Oh no,' said Freddy, 'although I'm quite sure you'd like to listen to them all day. No,' he went on, 'I have come to do my duty as a concerned citizen.'

'Oh yes?'

'Yes. You look doubtful, inspector,' he said. 'I can see you thinking, "When on earth will the fellow get to the point?"'

This was exactly what Jameson had been thinking, in fact, but he said nothing.

'Then I shall keep you in suspense no longer,' said Freddy. 'I understand from our mutual friend Mrs. M. that you have a certain interest in a fashionable establishment known as the Copernicus Club. Is that correct?'

'Perhaps,' said Jameson cautiously, wondering how much the boy knew.

'Oh, no need to be coy, inspector,' said Freddy. 'I can assure you I've promised Angela faithfully to keep the story out of the papers—for now, at least, although naturally I am hoping to get the scoop in return for my help, just as soon as you say the word. Very well, let us come to an understanding: I know that the woman whom Angela so carelessly almost ran over in her car was most likely a dance hostess named Lita de Marquez, and that she worked at the Copernicus until she went missing a few weeks ago. I also know that the staff at the Copernicus Club have been instructed not to say anything to the police, given the—let us say somewhat *precarious* existence of the club itself, and the very real possibility that talking to the Yard might land the whole boiling of them out on the street.'

'You seem to know all about it,' said the inspector dryly. 'But tell me, are you here to try and find out more—in which case, you needn't bother, or are you here to help?'

'Oh, the latter,' Freddy assured him.

'Then would you mind getting to the point?'

Freddy sat up. His affected carelessness was gone now, and he seemed rather pleased with himself.

'All right,' he said. 'I shall. I have done a little digging on my own account and found out all about the man Lita was seeing.'

'Oh yes?' said the inspector, suddenly alert. 'Who is he? Do you have a name?'

'Yes,' said Freddy, 'and it's one you know. His name is Johnny Chang.'

CHAPTER EIGHTEEN

H E SAT BACK to observe the effect of his words on the inspector. Jameson regarded him in some surprise.

'Are you sure of this?' he said.

'Oh yes,' replied Freddy. 'I can produce a witness, in fact. He worked at the club but was sacked a week or two before Lita disappeared, although he didn't say what for.'

'Hmm, he may be holding a grudge, then,' said Jameson. 'Who is this witness, and what exactly did he tell you?'

'His name is Cyril,' said Freddy, 'and he says that everybody most likely knew what was going on even if they pretended they didn't. Apparently it's not uncommon for young Master Chang to—er—avail himself of the services offered at his own club, although this one seemed a little more serious than the others.'

'How did you find this chap, exactly?' asked Jameson.

'I have my methods, Watson,' said Freddy mysteriously. Seeing Jameson's expression he went on quickly, 'I used to be rather an *habitué* of the Copernicus, and was pretty pally with most of the waiters. When I went to the club that night with Angela, I asked after Cyril and was told that he had left, so I tracked him down as I thought he might be prepared to talk, since he'd lost his job anyway. It turns out I was right.'

'Yes, well, that would have been our next step,' said Jameson with a cough, 'but you seem to have anticipated us.'

'Far be it from me to tell the police how to do their job,' said Freddy sententiously, then turned suddenly serious. 'I say, though, I do hope it's of some help. This is a nasty business. Murder is bad enough, but then deliberately to smash the poor woman's face in—it makes me feel rather sick, quite frankly.'

'Yes,' agreed the inspector, 'it does leave an unpleasant taste in one's mouth.' He found himself rather liking the young man despite his affectations. 'By the way, does Mrs. Marchmont know you are here?'

'No, although I dare say I shall tell her sooner or later,' said Freddy. 'I wanted her to introduce me to you, you know, but in the end I was too impatient and decided to shift for myself.'

'Why on earth did you want an introduction?' asked Jameson, surprised.

'Oh, well,' said Freddy uncomfortably. 'I don't like to say it, since Mother found me the job, and I secretly rather expected them to chuck me out after the first week, but I find myself unaccountably drawn to the work, and if I'm going to make a success of it, then I shall need a tame policeman or two to give me the official angle on things. A reciprocal arrangement, of course,' he went on hurriedly. 'I don't want you to think it would be all one way.'

'Well, we shall see,' said Inspector Jameson non-committally. 'I don't say we don't occasionally make use of reporters when it suits us. But to return to this fellow Cyril—what else did he tell you? Does he know anything about Lita's disappearance?'

'No, I told you—he left before she did,' said Freddy, 'but he said he had begun to wonder whether she wasn't rather tiring of Johnny. There was nothing definite, he said, but things did seem to have cooled a little between them. If you ask me, Cyril was sweet on Lita—at least, he certainly seems to have paid a good deal of attention to her personal affairs, but as it happens, that makes him rather a useful witness, don't you think?'

'Always assuming that he is telling the truth, and that his judgment has not been clouded by his feelings,' said Jameson practically. He saw Freddy's face fall, and said, 'We see it a lot in this line of work, I'm afraid. Very few people are able to give a completely objective account of things. Everyone has their own opinion, or their own view of an affair. That doesn't mean everything this chap says is wrong, but we will do well to take it with a grain of salt and seek confirmation elsewhere.'

'Oh, but I'm sure he was telling the truth,' said Freddy. 'I'm rather good at spotting when people are lying.'

'I don't doubt it for a moment,' said Jameson, 'but perspicacity is not enough when one has to make a case before a judge. It's not sufficient to say "I know he was telling the truth"—one has to demonstrate it beyond reasonable doubt, and that is not always so easy. I can't tell you the number of guilty men I have seen allowed to go free because their guilt could not be proved.'

'Well, I shall give you Cyril's address and you shall judge for yourself,' said Freddy, scribbling something down and handing it to the inspector. 'Perhaps you will find someone who can confirm what he says—I can't believe he is the only person ever to have been sacked by the Changs. Or perhaps someone who works there now can be persuaded to talk.'

'Hmph,' said Jameson. 'We haven't had much success so far. Even when Mrs. Marchmont spoke to one of the dance hostesses the girl denied all knowledge of any men-friends. They know how to keep their mouths shut in that world, right enough.'

'That's why you need me, inspector,' said Freddy. 'I can wriggle into confidences that would be denied to a mere policeman.'

'Well, then, let's see what you're made of,' said Jameson. 'I shall go and pay this Cyril chap a visit. If he really is prepared to give up the goods on Johnny Chang and can be shown to be a reliable witness, then this may well prove to be a big step forward in the case.'

'I should jolly well hope so,' said Freddy. 'I should hate to think I was wasting my efforts.' He stood up, seeing that the interview was over. 'You will let me know what comes of it, won't you, inspector? I should like to be the first to get the story—when I'm allowed to write it.'

'I'll see what I can do,' said Jameson, 'and thanks for the tip-off. If you find out any other information do give me a call.'

He got rid of Freddy and called for Sergeant Willis, and they went out in search of the sacked waiter, hoping that they might be getting somewhere at last. To Jameson's mild surprise, Freddy's witness turned out to be a good one. Cyril was a mischievous young man who had been sacked for larking about when he ought to have been working, as well as for being over-familiar with the customers. He freely admitted it was all his own fault, and insisted that he bore no grudge against the club or against the Changs. He was now engaged to be married, he said, and was working hard in his new job to save up for the wedding. He came across as honest enough, in Jameson's view.

According to Cyril, Johnny Chang was often seen out and about with one or other of the girls from the Copernicus Club, although he generally picked the prettiest ones. There was never anything serious in it—the girls were given generous gifts and Johnny got to display himself to advantage about the town, and everyone was happy. The thing with Lita had been going on for a bit longer, though, and Cyril had on occasion wondered whether Johnny hadn't been rather soft on her, although as far as Cyril could tell, it was never a big thing to Lita—as a matter of fact, he rather thought she had tired of Johnny. He'd heard them having a row once. No, he didn't know what it was about: he wasn't the type to eavesdrop on other people's arguments, but he did see her storm off, and heard Johnny shout after her that she would regret it.

Inspector Jameson made a note here.

'He said she would regret it?' he repeated. 'Did he say anything more specific than that? Did he say why she would regret it?'

'No,' said Cyril. 'It didn't sound like he meant anything much by it. It was just the kind of thing one might say during a row. I've probably said it myself, before.'

'Did anybody else see this argument?' asked Jameson.

'Oh yes,' said Cyril. 'There were other people there at the time. I can't remember who, though.'

The two policemen thanked him and returned to Scotland Yard.

'It looks as though the only thing for it is to go back to the Copernicus and its unhelpful staff,' said Jameson with an exasperated sigh. 'Are you ready to beat your head against a brick wall again, Willis?'

'I don't see why not,' said the sergeant. 'My head's taken enough knocks over the years. I'm sure it can take a few more.'

They were just about to leave when the telephone-bell rang. Jameson answered it. He spoke in short syllables, but his face gradually took on a look of excitement as he listened to the person at the other end, who evidently had something of interest to report. Eventually, he put down the phone and turned to Willis.

'They've found a witness who saw Lita at Charing Cross station on Wednesday the 7th of September—and she was with a young man of Chinese appearance who had an educated English accent.'

'Indeed?' remarked Willis. 'Who is this witness?'

'A commercial fellow,' said Jameson. 'He says he was standing behind a girl in a blue coat and hat in the queue for the cloak room. He remembers it as being that day in particular because it happened to be his birthday, and he was in a hurry to catch his train. However, as it turned out, he missed it because the girl in front of him was dithering with her luggage, and searching through her purse for spare change. Then the Chinese man turned up and spoke to her, and she looked at him in surprise and asked him what he was doing there. The commercial chap says she called him Jacky or Johnny, but he can't remember which. Then the two of them began arguing, at which point our witness lost patience and asked them to do it elsewhere as he wanted to deposit his bags and catch his train. They glared at him but went outside. He judged the pair of them to be no better than they ought to be and thought no more of the matter until he read the story in the newspapers.'

'Did he happen to hear what they were rowing about?'

Jameson shook his head.

'Apparently not,' he said. 'He just assumed it was a tiff between two people of a kind with whom he was not accustomed to mix. I gather those were his words—or something like them.'

'So, then,' said the sergeant. 'She was last seen alive on the afternoon of Wednesday the 7th of September at Charing Cross station.'

'And then was discovered dead in a ditch just outside Littlechurch two days later,' said Jameson. 'I wonder what exactly happened in those two days.'

'It looks as though we shall have to have another word with young Master Chang, then,' said Sergeant Willis.

'It does indeed,' said Jameson grimly. 'Let's go and see if he's at home, shall we?'

Chapter Nineteen

THE ARREST OF Johnny Chang on suspicion of murdering a dance hostess at the notorious Copernicus Club created a great sensation in the newspapers over the next few days. Johnny had denied everything vehemently, and had done his best to resist arrest. However, the incontrovertible fact of his having been seen with Lita at Charing Cross station on the date in question, together with his lack of an alibi for the two days following, gave the police quite sufficient grounds to overpower him and take him to the station for questioning. Further damning evidence was discovered when the club's premises were searched and the police found several packets of arsenic, which Johnny claimed had been bought for the purposes of getting rid of rats. Whether that were true or not, the presence of the poison was quite enough to keep him in prison for the present, and to allow the police to charge him formally with the murder of Lita de Marquez.

Meanwhile, the Copernicus Club was shut down until further notice, since there was nobody left to run it.

Angela put down her newspaper and stared thoughtfully out of the window, although she saw nothing of what was going on in the street below. Instead she was thinking about the case. It looked as though it had reached the most predictable of conclusions. Lita de Marquez had rejected her lover, and he had taken it badly and murdered her. It was an old, old story, but none the less pitiful for that. How many times had the same thing happened throughout the course of history? It was certainly the most obvious solution, and yet—and yet—Angela was uncomfortable. Several aspects of the case still puzzled her, and she wanted to talk about it with someone, but Inspector Jameson was very busy at present and could not be reached by telephone—even supposing he was willing to talk about it now that an arrest had been made.

Fortunately, she was rescued by Freddy Pilkington-Soames, who came to gloat over his cleverness at having solved the case, as he claimed.

'Oughtn't you to be reporting on the opening of a new civic building or something?' said Angela after they had exchanged greetings.

'No,' said Freddy airily. 'They sent me to listen to another speech by that old chump Rowbotham. Fortunately, having already attended one of his speeches I happen to know that he tends to drivel on interminably, so I took down his first few sentences just to be on the safe side, and then came out. No doubt he will still be prattling away when I get back and I can take down his closing remarks and applaud politely with the rest of the audience, without having to listen to all the rot in the middle.'

'But what shall you do if he's already finished by the time you get back?' said Angela.

'Then I shall just use my notes from the last speech of his that I attended,' said Freddy. 'Or perhaps I'll invent something of my own. Of course, there's always St. John,' he went on, as a thought struck him. 'He was there, listening avidly, and will probably be able to recite it word for word. Yes, I think I shall ask him.'

'Sit down and tell me all about what has been happening in the Lita de Marquez case,' said Angela, and poured him some coffee, which Marthe had just brought in. 'I gather you have wormed your way into Inspector Jameson's confidence by finding him a useful witness.'

'Yes, it was rather a *coup* on my part, wasn't it?' said Freddy, trying and failing to look modest. 'It was entirely thanks to me that the police found out about the liaison between Lita and Johnny Chang. I expect I'll get a medal of some sort.'

'But do you think they have got the right man?'

'Of course. Who else could it have been?'

'Why, I don't know,' said Angela, 'but I have been reading the story in the newspapers this morning and there is something that doesn't seem quite right to me.'

'What do you mean?'

'I'm not quite sure,' said Angela. 'It's just that—' she paused to consider, then went on, 'I'm not convinced by the method of the murder. She was poisoned with arsenic, the police said.'

'Yes,' put in Freddy, 'and they found enormous quantities of the stuff at the Copernicus Club.'

'Oh yes, I don't doubt for a moment that Johnny Chang was easily able to get hold of the poison, but the whole thing seems a bit—I don't know—awkward.'

'You're not explaining yourself very well,' said Freddy.

'I'm not, am I?' said Angela. 'Very well, then, let's think about it from Johnny's point of view. Let's say that Lita has tired of him and has decided to leave the club and go down to Kent for reasons of her own. She goes to Charing Cross and drops her suitcase in the cloak room, and prepares to catch her train. At that moment, she is accosted by Johnny, who has followed her to the station—'

'Just a minute,' interrupted Freddy. 'How do we know they weren't going to leave together?'

'Why, because of what the man behind them in the queue said. He said Lita was surprised to see Johnny and asked him what he was doing there. That doesn't sound as though they were planning to go away together, does it?'

'No,' admitted Freddy, 'but supposing they made it up after they left the cloak room, and decided to go down to Kent together. That's possible, isn't it?'

'It is, yes,' said Angela, 'but in that case why on earth was he carrying a packet of arsenic about with him? And why has nobody at the Kent end reported seeing an English woman in company with a Chinese man? It's unusual enough to attract attention in a place like that. And,' she went on, 'more importantly, where did he get the car?'

'Which car?'

'The car he used to get rid of her body, of course,' said Angela. 'Lita was found in a ditch in the middle of nowhere. Johnny certainly couldn't have carried her there by himself on foot.'

'Perhaps they walked there and then he killed her,' suggested Freddy, then corrected himself. 'No, of course that wouldn't work, not if he was planning to give her arsenic.'

'No,' agreed Angela. 'Surely the poisoning must have taken place in a house or a hotel. And there must have been a car, or a truck, or a wagon, or something that could carry a woman's body.'

'I see what you mean,' said Freddy thoughtfully. 'It is a little tricky.'

'Yes, it is,' said Angela. 'As I see it, if the police want the charges to stand up they will have to find convincing answers to the following questions—one: why was Johnny Chang carrying arsenic around with him? Two: where did he give Lita the poison, and how? And three: what kind of vehicle did he use to dispose of the body, and where did he get it? Remember, too, that when she was given the arsenic she would have been very sick indeed. Somebody will have had to clean that up.'

Freddy wrinkled his nose in distaste.

'I assume the Kent police have been dealing with the inquiries at that end,' he said. 'They will know what to look for.'

'Why was she going to Kent?' said Angela suddenly. 'We still don't know, but I have the feeling it might turn out to be rather important. And the police have still not tracked down the man Lew, who came looking for Lita after she disappeared.'

'Perhaps he has nothing to do with the case.'

'Perhaps. He said he needed to find her urgently, though.'

'He was probably from the Home and Colonial, coming to dun her for a back payment,' said Freddy. 'At any rate, if he has any connection with the case, he may come forward now that her name has been in all the papers.'

'He's not likely to do that if he's the one who killed her,' said Angela.

'I think you're making things too complicated, Angela,' said Freddy. 'I know you like a mystery, but I don't think there is one in this instance. I dare say that in the next few days the police will find all the evidence they need to hang Johnny Chang for the murder of Lita de Marquez.'

'I hope for his sake they do,' said Angela. 'I should hate them to hang him without it.'

'Yes,' agreed Freddy soberly. 'A jury isn't likely to look too kindly on his association with a white girl. People can be rather odd about things like that.'

He departed shortly afterwards, for he judged that Mr. Rowbotham would shortly be nearing the end of his speech and he wanted to catch his friend St. John and find out what had been said.

'I shall call again next time I have a *succès éclatant* to report,' he said. 'At the rate I am going it will probably be tomorrow,' he added, and left.

Angela returned to gazing out of the window. *Was* she making things too complicated, she wondered? The case certainly seemed straightforward enough, but it remained to be seen whether a jury would find Johnny Chang guilty even if there were no concrete evidence.

Unable to shake off her thoughts on the matter, Angela decided to go round to the mews where the Bentley was kept. William lived in a little room above the garage, and Angela happened to know that Alvie Berteau was staying with him at present while he and his band looked for a new engagement. Angela wanted to talk to the musician, but knew that he was unlikely to be very forthcoming if she summoned him to Mount Street, so instead she resolved to pay him a visit under the pretence of making some trivial inquiry of William about the car.

As she expected, she found William under the bonnet, tinkering idly, while Alvie sat on a packing-case and polished his trumpet. She dealt with the matter of the car first of all, and then said, 'Any luck in finding a new job yet, Alvie?'

The young man shook his head.

'No, ma'am,' he replied. 'I could find something for myself today if I wanted to, but you see, I'm looking for something for the whole orchestra, and that's not so easy to find at short notice.'

'I suppose not,' said Mrs. Marchmont. 'What a pity. I'm sorry it's come to this,' she went on. 'I had no idea this would happen when I asked you about Lita. I had no intention of putting you all out of a job.'

'No matter, ma'am,' said Alvie generously. 'You did the right thing. It's not fair that she should die and not get justice. I'm only sorry I didn't speak up sooner. That was wrong of me.'

'Do you think Johnny Chang is guilty, then?' asked Angela in curiosity.

Alvie shrugged.

'I don't know,' he said. 'The police seem to think he is.'

'But what is your feeling on the matter?'

Alvie, looking momentarily surprised that someone like Mrs. Marchmont should ask his feelings on anything, said after a pause, 'Well, I guess I never saw him as the type.'

'Why not?'

'He doesn't seem to have the hatred,' said Alvie. 'Whoever murdered Lita did it out of hatred, don't you think? I don't know who could have hated her that much but I don't think it was anybody at the club. Most people liked her well enough, as far as I could see.'

'That is very interesting,' said Angela thoughtfully. 'I hadn't thought of it like that. Yes, I think you are very likely right— there was real hatred behind this killing. I wonder what she did to inspire it?'

CHAPTER TWENTY

A DAY OR two after the arrest of Johnny Chang, Inspector Jameson received a telephone-call from the Suffolk police to say that they had found the mysterious Lew, who had come forward following the identification of the murder victim in the newspapers, claiming to be her brother. Jameson raised his eyebrows at this, but he and Willis duly went up to Felixstowe to speak to the man, who was unable to get time away from work to come and visit them in London.

They found him living in a cramped cottage in a dingy street not far from the docks. A man of about thirty answered the door to them in his shirt-sleeves, having evidently just returned from work. Jameson was struck by his dark looks; it was easy to see why Geraldine had thought he might be foreign when she had met him. He spoke with a perfectly normal English accent, however, which sat rather oddly upon him.

'You are Lewis Markham?' asked Inspector Jameson.

'Yes,' said the man, and stood back to let them in. He led them into a tiny but comfortable parlour, which was spotlessly clean.

'I believe you can tell us something about Lita de Marquez,' said Jameson.

'She was my sister,' said Lew Markham. 'My twin sister, as a matter of fact. And her real name wasn't Lita, it was Lily. Lily Markham, her maiden name was.' He hesitated for a second. 'Is she really dead? Can you be sure it's her?' he said.

'I'm afraid it's quite certain,' said Jameson gravely. 'She was identified by a birth-mark.'

'On her left arm? She had one there in the shape of a crescent-moon.'

Had there been any doubt in the inspector's mind that Lita de Marquez and Lily Markham were one and the same, it was now dispelled. He nodded.

'I'm afraid so. I'm very sorry, Mr. Markham.'

Markham bowed his head.

'I read that you've arrested the man who did it,' he said after a moment. 'When is the trial? I want to come and see it.'

'A date hasn't been set yet,' said Jameson. 'It's early days and there are still a few things we need to clear up.'

'Why did he do it?' demanded the young man. His face had darkened and his fists were clenched. 'What harm did she ever do to him?'

'As I said, we don't know the whole story yet,' said the inspector. 'We had enough evidence to arrest Chang but there's still a lot we don't know. Suppose you tell us about your sister. It might help us to build up a clearer picture of her last days.'

Lew Markham looked away.

'I can't say she lived a blameless life,' he said, 'but when you think about what she came from—well, it's hardly surprising.'

He sat on a shabby sofa, looking at the floor with his hands between his knees, and told them Lita—or Lily's story.

Their father had died when they were very young, and their mother had remarried shortly afterwards, to a drunkard and a bully who had hated the children and beat them often. The young Lew longed to protect his sister and mother from the violence, and felt shame that he was unable to do so. But over the years he grew, and eventually one day he was big enough to hit back. By that time it was too late to repair the damage, however. At fifteen, Lily ran away from home and went to London, vowing never to return as long as her stepfather remained. She had always liked singing and dancing, and very soon she began to get parts in the chorus of various productions.

Lew went to visit her whenever he could, but quickly became concerned about the company she was frequenting. She was a very pretty girl and, he felt, rather too free in her behaviour with some of the men she saw every day hanging about the theatre. He didn't like it, and tried to warn her of the dangers she was running, but Lily said there was no harm in it, and wasn't she entitled to a bit of fun at last, after having had such a miserable time of it? Lew went back home then, but not without misgivings, and not before warning her in no uncertain terms of what might happen if she were not more careful.

Eventually, their stepfather drank himself to death—much to everybody's relief, and then it was just Lew and his mother living in the little cottage together. Lew went away to fight in the war, but still he and Lily kept in touch, though infrequently. The war ended and he came back and was lucky enough to get his old job back at the docks. He was a good worker and had returned uninjured, thank God, and so they were only too pleased to take him, since many of the men from the area had died or been terribly wounded.

Shortly after the end of the war, Lily returned to their little cottage without warning, and to Lew it looked as though his worst fears had come true, since she brought with her an infant child. She would say nothing of its father—only that they had been honourably wed and that he had died. Whether it was true or not they never knew. Of course, there was gossip, and people in the neighbourhood said that there had been no wedding at all, but what could Lew and his mother do? Lily was theirs and they loved her, and they would never turn her away, child or no child.

For a few years they lived together comfortably enough in the cottage. He worked at the docks, and his mother earned a little money by taking in washing. Then, one day about three years ago Lily disappeared again. They soon received a letter from her. She was sorry she had run away and left the child, but she craved her freedom so very much, and wanted to return to her old career on the stage. As soon as she was settled and earning money she would send for her son, but in the meantime she was entrusting him to their care.

Lew doubted whether she would ever send for him. He knew she loved the boy, but she lacked the capacity to look after him—as a matter of fact, their mother had done most of the work in that regard. Still, they went on with their lives, and heard from Lily occasionally. She was unable to get any more work on the stage: her dreams of becoming a famous actress had been disappointed and she was becoming rather too old for the chorus, when there were girls coming up who were ten years younger than she. She wrote to him saying that she had taken a job as a dance hostess in a night-club, but did not mention which one. Lew was worried about her again: he was unfamiliar with the world of night-clubs and had no clear idea of what dance hostesses did, but surely the work would bring her into contact with all kinds of low company?

Then, two months ago the blow had fallen, and their mother had died suddenly. Now there was no-one to look after the child. He, Lew, was out at work for fourteen hours a day, and could not bear the responsibility alone. He had written to Lily, asking her to come home and claim her son, but had received no reply. He wrote once more, then gained the permission of his foreman to take some time away and went in search of her, leaving the boy in the care of a neighbour.

He spent a couple of weeks going from night-club to night-club, asking whether they had heard of a Lita de Marquez—since he knew that was the name she used. For some time he had no success, and was just about to give it up and go home when someone suggested he try the Copernicus Club. When he spoke to a waiter there who told him that yes, Lita worked at the club, Lew felt a huge sense of relief and thought that his search was over. He went to her lodgings, in the belief that the only difficulty that lay before him was how to persuade her to come home and be a mother to her son—only to find that she must somehow have got wind of his coming and had run away again. There was nothing to do but return home sorrowfully. At around the same time, he remembered reading about the dead woman in the ditch, but he made no connection between her and Lily, since the girl they found had had blonde hair and Lily was dark. It wasn't until the story of Johnny Chang's arrest for her murder got into all the newspapers that he finally realized the terrible truth. Hardly able to believe it and stricken with grief, he had gone to the police as soon as he could.

Inspector Jameson felt a great deal of sympathy for the young man, who had, after all, lost both his mother and his sister in the space of only a few weeks, and who now found himself having to care for a young boy alone. He was about to ask another question when they were interrupted by the entrance of the child in question, a boy of about eight or nine, who had just arrived home from school. Although he was older than he had been in the photograph found in Lita's suitcase, there was no doubt that it was the same child.

The boy stared at the two policemen curiously but said nothing.

'Go upstairs, Bertie,' said his uncle. 'I have something to talk about with these gentlemen.'

The boy gazed at them for another second, but then obeyed without question.

'Have you told him about his mother yet?' asked Jameson.

A spasm of pain passed across Lew's face.

'No,' he said. 'How can I tell him when he's only just lost his grandmother? What am I meant to say to him? That his mother was mixing with men she didn't ought to and that one of them murdered her? It's not right.' He fixed them with an intense stare. 'You will hang him, won't you?' he said. 'You won't let him get away with what he did to Lily?'

'If he did it, then he will get justice,' said Jameson. 'And all we need to do is to find some more evidence,' he said privately to Willis as the two of them left the little cottage and headed back to London. 'I'm not keen on the thought of putting Johnny Chang in front of a jury of typical Englishmen, with all their prejudices about Chinese men and white slavers, without something more concrete than we have already. Who knows what ridiculous ideas they will get into their heads?'

'Does it matter, if he did it?' said Sergeant Willis. 'We don't want him to get off scot-free if he really is a murderer.'

'You and I have made enough mistakes in the past to know that the evidence is the thing,' said Jameson. 'It's all very well saying that we're pretty sure he did it, but you can't hang a man on a hunch.'

'It sounds to me as though you're having doubts about his guilt, sir,' observed Willis.

'Oh no,' said Jameson. 'I can see clearly enough where the facts are pointing, but I won't be happy until the chaps down in Kent tell us that they've found the hotel where the two of them stayed and the motor-car they hired.'

'And what if they don't?' inquired Willis.

'Then they will have to look harder,' said Jameson.

CHAPTER TWENTY-ONE

DESPITE THEIR BEST efforts, however, the Kent police were unable to find any evidence that Johnny Chang had visited the area at all. When questioned, Johnny himself had finally admitted that he and Lita had been having an affair of sorts, that she had ended it and that he had followed her to Charing Cross in an attempt to persuade her to stay. Beyond that, though, he insisted that he knew nothing. She had refused to be won over, he said. It had never been anything serious on her part, and she was going away as she had bigger fish to fry now. She was sorry to throw him over, but that was how things were and he ought to take it like a man. He had seen then that she was firm in her purpose, and had finally stormed away angrily. He was sorry about that: he should have liked to part from her on better terms, but how was he to know that someone was going to kill her?

And that was all they could get out of him on the subject of Lita. He flatly denied ever having been to Littlechurch or

Hastings or the Romney Marsh, and was outraged that any-one could think him capable of murder. As for his lack of an alibi, he maintained that when he got home from Charing Cross he had been taken ill—perhaps it had been something he ate—and had remained in bed for two days. No, nobody had seen him. In the normal way of things his mother would have taken care of him, but she had been away visiting his sister and her new husband.

One morning, a day or two after they had returned from Felixstowe, Sergeant Willis looked up from a sheaf of reports which had just come in from Kent, and shook his head.

'Nothing,' he said with a sigh.

'What about that woman who says she saw a girl in a blue coat and hat getting into a motor-car at Hastings?' said James-on. 'Have they found out anything more about that?'

'No,' said Willis. 'No-one else seems to have seen it, and she can't give us a good description of the car except to say it was a big one. Not much use, really.'

'I suppose not,' agreed Jameson. 'Well, we shall just have to keep plugging away at it.'

He was not the only person feeling dissatisfied about the whole thing. Mrs. Marchmont had been reading the news-papers avidly since Johnny Chang's arrest, but now that the hue and cry had died down there was not much more to be told. Lily Markham's story had come out, and the papers—especially the *Clarion*—dwelt sentimentally on her poor but honest upbringing, her supposed dead husband (whom they imagined as having died tragically during the War) and her orphaned child. Meanwhile, there was little sympathy for the man who was supposed to have murdered her, and young women everywhere were warned to beware of foreigners who spoke with honeyed words yet hid evil in their hearts. Angela shook her head in disquiet. She hoped Freddy was not behind all this: she had not seen him for some time, and supposed that his recent piece on the police raid at the Copernicus Club and his experience in the cells (which he had written and published to great acclaim at Angela's suggestion), together with his coup in leading the police to Johnny Chang, had won him the respect of Mr. Bickerstaffe. The newspaper was keeping him busy, she imagined.

So the weeks passed, and soon enough it was time for Angela to return to Gipsy's Mile for the grand launch of Marguerite Harrison's sculpture exhibition in Littlechurch. The show had received a good deal of advance publicity—thanks no doubt to Freddy—and it was rumoured that some of the most important young artists of the moment had agreed to exhibit alongside Marguerite.

Accordingly, on a dull day in October Angela found herself once again sitting in the back seat of the Bentley as it motored powerfully along the Kent road. They drove in unaccustomed silence, since William seemed unusually absorbed in his own thoughts. By a sort of unspoken mutual consent, neither of them had mentioned the incident of the watch since that day a few weeks earlier, although Angela was longing to know what he had done with it. It had been foolish of Marguerite, who was used to dispensing generous gifts and largesse to all her protégés. She ought to have seen that William was a different case, owing to both his position and his character. Still,

Angela would not interfere. William was his own man and could quite well look after himself.

They arrived at Gipsy's Mile without incident—there was no fog to cause them to lose their way this time—and were greeted as effusively as ever by Marguerite. Miles came out too, and Angela was shocked at the change in him. His face had become thin and drawn, and deep frown lines had appeared on his forehead. She remembered what Marguerite had said about him, and deduced that he had not yet got over his 'queer fit,' although he saluted her in his usual laconic but friendly manner.

Cynthia and Freddy had already arrived and were laughing together about something in the sitting-room.

'Angela, *darling*,' cried Cynthia. 'Why, I haven't seen you for an age! Have you been hiding?'

Angela resisted the temptation to reply, 'Only from you,' and merely said, 'Hallo, Cynthia. Where is Herbert?'

Cynthia looked not a little vexed.

'*So* inconvenient, darling,' she said. 'You won't believe it, but just at the last moment he said that something had come up at the bank and that he couldn't come. So strange! I've never known him do that before.'

Freddy sidled up to Angela.

'Don't believe Mother,' he murmured. 'If you ask me, the work thing is all rot. I reckon the real story is that he couldn't bear the thought of having to find something original to say to the vicar's wife about forty heaps of bronze and marble fashioned roughly into the shape of something that would throw one's maiden aunt into a fainting fit.'

Angela had seen Marguerite's work before, and was inclined to agree, since it was rather modern and daring. She had herself been wondering how it would be received by the people of Littlechurch, in fact. It turned out, however, that Marguerite had invited so many of her London friends down that it would be a wonder if there were enough room in the gallery to accommodate many of the locals.

While the others talked of the exhibition, Angela took the opportunity to speak to Miles and inquire after his health.

'Marguerite said you have not been well,' she said. 'I hope you're quite recovered now.'

'Marguerite was talking bunk,' he said impatiently. 'There's nothing wrong with me—or at least nothing more than a touch of cold.' He saw Angela's surprise at his vehemence and looked a little sheepish. 'I can't bear fuss,' he explained, 'and Marguerite insisted on telling everybody that I was at death's door, when nothing could have been further from the truth.'

Angela apologized and said she was glad he wasn't ill, at any rate, and the conversation turned to other matters.

Meanwhile, Marguerite was holding forth with great enthusiasm about a young artist who was coming to the exhibition—indeed, was expected at Gipsy's Mile at any moment, since he apparently gloried in his poverty and was unable to afford to stay anywhere else for the event.

'I think you'll be *tremendously* impressed by Vassily's work, darlings,' she said. 'I feel that he has really captured the spirit of the age with his art. His *Eternity of the Damned* series in particular almost moved me to tears. So clever and witty, how he satirizes the way in which modern society is going. Just wait until you see it! But I shan't say any more, as I don't want to spoil it for you.'

Vassily, when he arrived, turned out to be a bulky young man with an intense and piercing stare and a lowering brow. He shook hands with everyone with great solemnity and declared himself honoured to meet them all.

'I am very glad you invite me,' he said in a deep voice to Marguerite, who was fluttering about him anxiously, 'although it is very painful for me to stop work even for moment. I do not like to interrupt creative force, but for you I make exception, Mrs. Harrison.'

'Oh, Marguerite, please,' said Marguerite. 'We're all terribly informal these days, you know. Now, if you'll just let me show you your room—'

She bore him away in triumph. The door to the sitting-room was open and William could be seen passing through the hall as they came out. Angela happened to be looking that way, and was entertained by the little scene that followed. The two men stopped and sized each other up for a second, then Vassily evidently dismissed William as being of no importance, for his face assumed a look of disdain. William glanced at Marguerite, who was clutching Vassily's arm, and she tossed her head and turned away. William's expression became impassive and he stepped back respectfully to allow them to pass. Angela noticed that the tips of his ears had turned pink, and felt a pang of sympathy for him.

Freddy had seen it too, clearly, for he threw her a look of malicious satisfaction, and shortly afterwards took the opportunity to sit down beside her on the large sofa.

'You see?' he murmured. 'What did I tell you? She flits here and there, just like a butterfly, and no man can hold her down. Apart from good old Miles, of course,' he added, looking over at the gentleman in question, who was pouring a drink for Cynthia and laughing at something she had said, having apparently missed what had just occurred.

Angela shook her head but did not reply. Instead, she said, 'So, Freddy, I gather your first month as a reporter has been a resounding success.'

'Oh, yes,' he said. 'Since that night at the Copernicus Club and the heartfelt piece I wrote about the unnecessary violence of the police and the appalling state of the prisons, I have become old Bickerstaffe's right-hand man. Why, the old man is as fond of me as of a son. I have a nose for the news, he says.' He lowered his voice confidentially. 'I don't mind telling you that some of the old hands there have begun looking rather askance upon me, but' (here he gave an exquisitely expressive shrug of the shoulders) 'how can I help it if I happen to be immoderately talented? It's something that was given to me by a sheer accident of birth. And are lesser men to be given opportunities over my head merely by dint of long service? No, I say: we must think of the greater good. If the future of the *Clarion* depends upon young upstarts such as myself, then I say long live the young upstarts, and down with the Old Guard!'

He sat back complacently and lit himself a cigarette.

'Quite,' said Angela, amused. 'So you have a "nose for the news," do you? That must be very useful.'

'Oh, yes,' Freddy assured her. 'You'd be quite astonished at the way things seem to happen whenever I chance to be on the spot. I have quickly learned never to leave the house without my notebook on me, since I never know when a story might suddenly present itself.'

'Indeed?' said Angela.

'Yes.' He paused to blow smoke into the air, then went on, 'As a matter of fact, I shouldn't be a bit surprised if something were to happen at Marguerite's exhibition.'

'What do you mean? What do you think is going to happen?'

'I don't know,' he said thoughtfully. 'But *something* will. I can feel it in my bones.'

CHAPTER TWENTY-TWO

MARGUERITE'S SCULPTURE EXHIBITION was to be held in the church hall in Littlechurch. There had been some grumbling among the locals that the hall was to be out of use for two whole weeks, but Marguerite had paid such a generous fee to the parish council to hire the place that their objections were overridden, and everyone except the few naysayers agreed what a good thing it was for the town to have such a renowned artist among their number. Some of the more excitable souls even predicted that as a result of the exhibition, Littlechurch would shortly become a centre of art and culture to rival London and Paris, and Mr. Culshaw, the local art teacher, suddenly began receiving dozens of requests for private lessons in painting and drawing, somewhat to his surprise.

Had Marguerite been worrying about whether there would be any interest in her exhibition, her fears were very quickly proved groundless. She and her guests had come along to the hall early to make sure that things were properly set up, and she had just declared herself satisfied when Freddy came in and said, 'I say, how many people will this hall hold, do you suppose? We appear to have the entire population of Littlechurch outside, waiting for the grand opening.'

'But of course,' said Vassily. 'They hear of the great talent of Marguerite and want to see her works.'

Marguerite gave a little trill of laughter.

'Oh, come now, Vassily,' she said. 'They may have *come* to see my poor little efforts, but it is your genius that will make them *stay*. I shouldn't be at all surprised if this exhibition were to be the start of a glorious career for you.'

Vassily looked as pleased with himself as was physically possible with his particular arrangement of facial features, and stepped across to move one of his sculptures a fraction of an inch. As far as Angela could see, his *Eternity of the Damned* series consisted of a row of half-formed human shapes carved roughly out of brown granite. They had a certain appeal, she supposed, although how the good people of Littlechurch would take art in such a modern style could only be conjectured. As for Marguerite's sculptures—Angela had to agree with Freddy in his view that they might well cause a certain amount of consternation among those of a more sensitive temperament.

'Do you think they'll arrest her for obscenity?' said Freddy as they gazed critically at one particularly suggestive piece.

'Oh, I shouldn't think so,' said Angela. 'Why, I shouldn't describe any of these sculptures as flagrant, even if they are a little daring. Is it time yet?'

But Freddy was staring into space thoughtfully, and did not seem to have heard.

'Let the fun begin!' declaimed Marguerite at last. 'Freddy, would you be a darling and open the door?'

An hour later the thing was in full swing and Angela was rather enjoying herself. She had made the acquaintance of the vicar's wife, Mrs. Henderson, a sensible, youngish woman who, glass of wine in hand, had gazed at Marguerite's sculptures and declared them to be 'awfully clever, although I probably oughtn't to admit that I can see what they're meant to be, ought I?' She lowered her voice confidentially. 'I'm fairly sure my husband has no idea what he has given his approval to, so it's probably best not to tell him, don't you agree?' The two of them laughed merrily, and Mrs. Henderson put a mischievous finger over her lips.

It looked as though the exhibition were a roaring success. Angela looked about her. Marguerite had introduced her to several people who were meant to be among the most important personages in London—at least, as far as the new art movements were concerned—but there were also one or two people she recognized from the local area, including Sergeant Spillett and P. C. Bass, who were both in uniform and, she guessed, there to see that the crowds did not get out of hand. She frowned as she spotted Freddy, who was whispering into the ear of a disreputable-looking old man. What was he up to?

'Hallo, Mrs. Marchmont—Angela,' said a voice at her shoulder, and she turned to see Lucy Syms standing next to her.

'Why, Lucy, how nice to see you again,' said Angela. 'Where is Gil?'

'Over there,' said Lucy, nodding towards the door. Angela turned and saw Gilbert Blakeney and his mother receiving an effusive greeting from Marguerite. Gil wore his usual slightly foolish expression, while Lady Alice was at her most gracious.

'Lucy, darling, come and see these sculptures and tell me what you think of them,' said Cynthia, who had just then approached them and put her hand on the girl's arm. 'I am trying to put together a little piece on this exhibition for the *Clarion*—the society column, you know—so tiresome, but necessary—and I'd simply adore to hear what you think of it all.'

She bore Lucy away, leaving Angela by herself for a few moments, until Gil and his mother came to speak to her. Mrs. Henderson soon joined them, and listened courteously to some minor complaint of Lady Alice's about the vicar's last sermon. The Blakeneys then turned away to talk to someone else, and Angela remained in conversation with the vicar's wife. Mrs. Henderson was a sympathetic listener and Angela, rather to her surprise, found herself telling the story of how she had discovered Lita's body several weeks earlier.

Mrs. Henderson shook her head soberly.

'Such a sad tale,' she said. 'I understand they have arrested the man who did it. Has he confessed?'

'No,' said Angela. 'I don't believe he has. As a matter of fact, I don't believe he did it,' she said suddenly, and she was surprised at the relief she felt at having finally said it aloud. The nagging doubt that had been sitting at the back of her mind for several weeks now was finally out in the open. She did *not* believe that Johnny Chang had murdered Lita de Marquez.

Mrs. Henderson raised her eyebrows.

'Oh?' she said. 'Why not?'

Angela remembered what Alvie Berteau had said to her, and thought back to that night at the Copernicus Club and her brief introduction to the calm, watchful Johnny Chang.

'He didn't hate her enough,' she said. 'Whoever killed her did so out of hatred.'

'Do you mean because he disfigured her face?' said Mrs. Henderson.

'Not only that,' said Angela. 'It's an awfully violent thing to do, I admit, but it's logical if you want to prevent the police from finding out who she was. But I was rather referring to the thing as a whole. It's almost incomprehensible: someone brought her down here and deliberately poisoned her to put her out of the way. Rather a lot of effort to go to for a girl who worked in a night-club and presumably gave no trouble to anybody, don't you think?'

'Then she must have given trouble to somebody,' said Mrs. Henderson. 'You might bash a girl over the head in a fit of anger, but you don't poison somebody on the spur of the moment.'

'Exactly,' said Angela eagerly. That was what she had been struggling to put into words herself. She glanced around and saw Lady Alice, who was still standing nearby, regarding her intently. The old woman caught Angela's eye and looked away.

'I wonder how they lured her down here,' said Mrs. Henderson. She was about to say something else, when their attention was arrested by the sound of a disturbance across the other side of the room, and they turned to see P. C. Bass, blushing furiously, throwing a coat over one of Marguerite's art-works, while people looked on with varying degrees of amusement or astonishment.

Marguerite pushed her way through the crowd and accosted the young constable.

'What on earth are you doing? Oh, *do* please be careful with that,' she said, as she saw Bass preparing to throw a jacket over another one of the sculptures. She turned to Sergeant Spillett, who was now approaching. 'What is going on?' she said.

The room had now fallen silent. Sergeant Spillett, also slightly pink in the face, said, 'We've just now received a formal complaint about these here statues from a member of the public, who considers them to be obscene and an affront to public decency. We are obliged to act on any such complaints, so it is my official duty to tell you that this exhibition is now closed.'

'What?' exclaimed Marguerite. She put her hand beseechingly on Spillett's arm. 'Why, sergeant, you can't mean it, surely?'

'I'm afraid I do,' said the sergeant. 'You must all leave immediately. Mr. Henderson, if you'll kindly give me the keys, I shall make sure the door is locked. P. C. Bass and I will come back tomorrow to examine these statues in greater detail—'

'I'll bet they will,' murmured Freddy at Angela's elbow.

'—to see if there are any grounds for prosecution.'

'Prosecution?' gasped Marguerite in horror. 'But my sculptures! What are you going to do with them? Surely nobody could find them offensive? Why, they are merely abstract representations of certain aspects of the human body in all its natural glory and beauty. What is offensive about that?'

'That's as may be,' said Spillett uncomfortably, 'but it's not for me to decide in the final instance. A judge may decide that they ought to be destroyed.'

As soon as he said that, Vassily gave a great roar of outrage.

'What?' he said. 'You would destroy our work? Are you mad? It is great crime to destroy art. Art does not answer to conventions of society but stands alone and speaks for itself. You are worse than Bolsheviks!'

'Now, we'll have none of that,' said the sergeant, who was not entirely sure what Bolsheviks meant but suspected that it might be rude from the sound of it. He stepped forward to throw his own coat over another sculpture, but Marguerite clung to his arm and let out a wail.

'Please, madam,' said Spillett. He shook her off, possibly more roughly than he had intended to. At this, Vassily gave another roar, threw his arms around the sergeant and wrestled him to the floor. There were screams and cries as everybody tried to get out of the way, and P. C. Bass flapped around uselessly, at a loss, as Sergeant Spillett curled up and tried to fend off the young sculptor's pummelling.

'I say, this won't do,' cried Freddy, alarmed. He rushed forward and began pulling at Vassily's jacket, in an attempt to get him off the policeman. Vassily resisted for a few moments, then stood up, causing Freddy to topple backwards and knock against a tall stand on which was displayed the final and most splendid piece in Vassily's *Eternity of the Damned* series, a tortured nude about eighteen inches high.

There was a collective gasp of dismay, followed by a dead silence as everybody watched the stand rock violently. Three times it swayed from side to side, then, just as it looked as though all might be safe, Freddy made a last-second grab to try and steady it—but instead caught the sculpture itself with his arm. The statue teetered dangerously for a second or two, then toppled off its perch. It seemed to take forever to hit the ground, but finally it landed with a great thud, and there was a loud 'Oh!' from the crowd as the head detached itself from the body and skittered off across the floor. Nobody spoke. Freddy looked fearfully at Vassily, whose expression was not unlike that on the face of the statue which had just been so rudely decapitated.

'I say, I'm most awfully sorry,' he said feebly.

Vassily, white in the face, put his hands to his hair and pulled at it as though not quite knowing what he did, then he turned slowly to face Freddy. The roar started low within his belly, but quickly gathered momentum and was finally given full vent as he opened his mouth to release it. Freddy cringed and then turned to run, but Vassily was too quick for him and, with a mighty leap, brought him down and began raining blows upon his head.

It was as though pandemonium had been let loose. People screamed and ran for the door, glasses were kicked over and crushed under-foot, and the vicar stood at the side of the room, wringing his hands. Miles and Gil hustled a shocked Lady Alice out of the way, while Marguerite fainted dead into the arms of William, who had just at that moment come in to find out whether he was wanted yet. He held onto her in astonishment; then, as nobody seemed inclined to tell him what to do with her, scooped her up and carried her outside.

Meanwhile, Sergeant Spillett had been pulled to his feet by P. C. Bass and was looking about him in confusion, wanting to restore order but not knowing where to begin. However, as most people had now made it out of the place, there was little left for him to do except to enlist one or two burly farmers to help him and Bass overpower Vassily. The young artist was finally borne away, struggling violently and swearing loudly in several languages, and Freddy was left lying on the floor, groaning. Angela picked her way through the mess and looked down at him.

'Are you still alive?' she said.

He squinted up at her.

'I'm not entirely sure,' he said weakly.

She held out a hand and helped him to his feet. He staggered a little, then tested his jaw gingerly to see whether Vassily had broken it. Apparently the investigation produced a satisfactory result, for he then bent down stiffly and began to brush himself off.

'No broken bones, as far as I can tell,' he remarked.

'Well, it would serve you jolly well right if there were,' said Angela severely.

Freddy assumed an injured expression.

'It was an accident!' he said. 'You must have seen that. I was trying to rescue poor old Spillett from that idiot Vassily. It wasn't my fault I lost my balance and knocked the dratted statue over.'

'You know very well that's not what I meant,' said Angela. 'I saw exactly what you did earlier. For shame, Freddy! How could you do it?'

Freddy opened his mouth to argue, but was forestalled by a commotion nearby. They turned and saw a little group of people, among them Miles, Gil and Lucy, fussing over Lady Alice, who had apparently been taken ill. She was led to a chair, clutching her heart, and given some water to drink.

'Somebody fetch a doctor immediately,' commanded Lucy, who was busy chafing the old lady's wrists.

'Oh, dear me,' said the vicar. 'Dr. Burns was here earlier. Perhaps he is still outside. I shall go and see.' He hurried off.

Gil was standing to one side, looking ashen-faced.

'Is there anything we can do to help?' said Angela in concern. 'Lady Alice, you must be cold. Let me bring you your coat.'

'Thank you, but there is really nothing wrong with me,' said Lady Alice, although she looked anything but well.

'I'll get it,' said Gil, relieved to be able to do something. He brought the coat and placed it tenderly over his mother's shoulders.

The doctor arrived, took one look at Lady Alice and pronounced that she must be put to bed immediately. Nobody was inclined to disagree, so the old lady was escorted out gently and taken home in the Blakeneys' stately old Wolseley, while the doctor followed in his own car, leaving Miles, Freddy and Angela to survey the damage wrought by the stampede.

'That was a little more eventful than I expected,' said Miles finally.

'I say, I hope Lady Alice is going to be all right,' said Freddy. He looked worried. 'Is it her heart, do you think? I hope the—er—fracas didn't set her off.'

'I couldn't say,' said Miles. 'Come on, we had better get home. There will be all kinds of hell to pay tomorrow if I'm not much mistaken.'

He strode out. Angela glanced at Freddy, who was still looking upset.

'I hope she's going to be all right,' he repeated.

CHAPTER TWENTY-THREE

THE NEXT DAY at breakfast, they had word from Blakeney Park that Lady Alice was seriously ill and unable to speak to anyone. Marguerite sent her sympathies and offers of help, although there did not seem to be much that they could do: the old woman's personal physician had been summoned from town, and she was receiving the best care that a healthy income could pay for. All they could do now was hope that she would somehow find the inner resources to pull through.

In reality, Marguerite had little attention to spare for the Blakeneys' plight, since she was more immediately concerned about the disastrous ending to her grand exhibition opening, and the possibility that her works would be destroyed—not to mention the effect the whole fiasco might be expected to have on her artistic reputation. Moreover, there was the awkward but unavoidable fact that her protégé, Vassily, was now sullenly enduring the hospitality of the local police, and must somehow be dealt with. The Littlechurch police seemed inclined to take a dim view of his unprovoked attack on one of their number—being perhaps less accustomed to this sort of high-spirited behaviour than the police in London—and were making noises about arraigning him on an assault and battery charge. Nothing could be done about him until Monday, but in the meantime the church hall needed clearing up, and so immediately after breakfast Marguerite prepared to set off and begin work.

'By the way, darling,' she said carelessly to Angela, 'would you mind awfully if I borrowed William? A strong young man will be just the thing to help me clear away all that mess.'

'By all means,' said Angela, smiling to herself. She looked across at Freddy to see his reaction, but he seemed absorbed in his own thoughts and had not heard the exchange. Shortly afterwards he got up and slunk out of the room. Angela decided it was time to have a word with him, and so rose and followed him into the parlour. She shut the door behind her and he looked up warily.

'Oh, it's you,' he said. 'Have you come to gloat?'

'Why on earth should I gloat?' said Angela. 'You got yourself into a mess and now you're worried that someone is going to die because of it. What is there to gloat about?'

'That ass, Vassily,' said Freddy crossly. 'It's because of him that the whole thing got out of hand. If he'd only kept his temper then everyone would have filed out calmly like good boys and girls and nobody would have had a heart attack.'

'But why did you do it?' said Angela.

'Why, because I wanted a story, of course,' said Freddy, as though the answer were perfectly obvious. 'They've come to expect it of me. After that article I wrote about the Copernicus, and the one about leading the police to Johnny Chang, I was the golden boy in old Bickerstaffe's view—why, I could do no wrong. I felt almost as though I could walk on water. Every time I went out to report on a story, something exciting happened and I got a scoop. But in the last week or two things have quietened down and I haven't had so much as a bite of a scandal, and then they sent me to write about a sculpture exhibition of all things, in a tiny town in the middle of nowhere, where there was absolutely no chance of anything interesting happening, so I thought I'd better try and—well—spice things up a bit. But I swear I never meant the thing to turn into a free-for-all. I only meant for the police to shut it down and for everyone to leave quietly, then I should have got a nice little story and stayed in Bickerstaffe's good books, while Marguerite would have got some first-rate publicity—you know how the man in the street loves an outrage to public decency.'

'So you got that man to make an official complaint to the police,' said Angela.

'Yes. The old fellow is a regular trouble-maker about these parts, as I understand it, and is always looking out for an opportunity to make money to fund his ten pints a day, so I slipped him a couple of quid on condition that he do the business. It was all going swimmingly, but then Vassily lost his head and set off a riot, and now you're going to tell everyone and if the old woman dies I suppose they'll all blame me for having given her heart failure,' he finished petulantly.

'Freddy, have you any morals at all?' said Angela, shaking her head in exasperation.

'Of course I have,' he returned indignantly. 'I'll admit that I'm not above taking a short-cut or two, but there is a line that I will not cross.'

'You wouldn't know it,' said Angela. 'So am I to understand that you deliberately arranged the fight at the Copernicus Club?'

'Oh, no, that was quite genuine,' Freddy assured her. 'If you'd known Gertie as long as I have you'd know that that sort of thing tends to follow her around.'

'And Johnny Chang?' said Angela, a horrid feeling stealing over her. 'I hope you didn't pay that waiter to make up stories about him.'

'Of course I didn't!' he said, outraged. 'How could you even suggest such a thing? Listen,' he went on, 'I really did start out well in the job, you know. But I had started to feel that I had to keep on delivering the goods if I were to prove myself worthy. Truly, Angela, I promise on my honour that last night was the first time I had ever tried something of this kind.'

'Well, it had better be the last, too,' said Angela. 'Look at how you ruined things for poor Marguerite.'

'Oh, she'll get over it,' said Freddy. 'She's not the type to dwell on her sorrows. And I'm sorry about Vassily's statue, but—well, it serves him right for being such a hot-headed ass. I do hope Lady Alice gets better soon, though. I don't mind admitting that I feel rather a worm about that. You won't tell anybody, will you, Angela?' he said suddenly. 'I've learned my lesson, and I promise I'll be a good boy from now on.'

'Very well,' said Angela reluctantly, seeing that he was genuinely contrite. 'But I shall be keeping an eye on you, and if

I find out that you have been getting up to any more tricks I shall tell Marguerite about what you did.'

'Thank you. Now that's two things you have to blackmail me about,' said Freddy, with a return to his usual good humour. 'Tell me—when do I get to blackmail *you*?'

'Never. I live a life of unparalleled virtue,' said Angela. 'Compared to you, at any rate,' she added.

Freddy pulled a face and went out. Angela followed him slowly, shaking her head. She was not at all sure that she had done the right thing in agreeing to keep quiet, but consoled herself when she saw Freddy making efforts to commiserate with Marguerite later, and heard him offer to write about the exhibition without mentioning either the possible prosecution for obscenity or the subsequent brawl. It was an empty gesture, she knew, since it would be difficult to prevent Cynthia from dwelling on it in gleeful detail in her society column; still, it showed that Freddy was sincere in his repentance—at least for the present.

Angela went back up to London on Monday, and on Tuesday dined with Inspector Jameson, who frankly admitted that the case against Johnny Chang was looking very weak, since they had been unable to find any evidence of his having ever gone to Kent; moreover, one of the waiters at the Copernicus Club was almost sure that he had seen Johnny on one of the days in question, coming downstairs from his mother's flat and into his own—although he would not swear to it.

'I don't like it at all,' he said, 'and I don't mind telling you that I should rather let a murderer go free than hang the wrong man.'

'Do you think you have got the wrong man, then?' said Angela, who had been wondering how to approach the subject.

The inspector sighed.

'It's a poser, I admit it,' he said. 'Of course, the affair between them means that he is far and away the most likely suspect, but there are so many things we still don't know. Was he the only man Lita was meeting, for example? Nobody has been willing to give us any other names, but she must have come into contact with lots of men in her job at the club. And then there is the fact that we have very little information about her last few hours. If only we knew why she had gone down to Kent, and what she did when she got there. However,' he went on, 'to answer your question—although logic says Johnny Chang must have done it, I myself am not convinced of it. I never rely on my intuition, but I have often found it to be correct in the past.'

'It's a pity no handbag was found,' said Angela, thinking. 'There might have been a clue there. I wonder what happened to it. She must have had one at one time, since she was carrying no money or anything in her pockets. But yes,' she went on. 'I'm afraid I agree with you, inspector. I don't think Johnny Chang did it either.'

'Well, it'll be a hell of a job trying to find out who *did* do it,' said Jameson glumly.

'What about her brother? Was he unable to help in any way? I assume she never told him about her men friends.'

'No,' said Jameson. 'I think he preferred to know as little as possible about what his sister was getting up to, and she certainly never volunteered the information.'

'What will happen to her son now?'

'Bertie? I don't know,' said Jameson. 'His grandmother and his mother are both dead, and his uncle is unable to spare the time to look after him. If he stays at home, I dare say he will have to learn to shift for himself—he must be eight or nine, and so is certainly old enough, although it is hard for a young lad to grow up without a mother.'

'Yes,' said Angela. 'Poor things. Both of them, I mean. Lew and the boy,' she explained in response to Inspector Jameson's inquiring look.

They finished dinner and left the restaurant, and the inspector escorted Angela to where William was waiting with the Bentley.

'Mrs. Marchmont!' came a call, and they turned to see a young woman wearing an enormous fur coat hurrying towards them.

'Why, it's Gertie!' said Angela, as she recognized the girl.

Gertie McAloon stopped somewhat breathlessly before her. She was looking very demure in comparison with the last time they had met, but this was easily explained when Angela saw the girl's companions, a rather smart and stiff-looking man and woman, who stood some distance away regarding the little group with suspicion.

'Oh, don't mind them,' said Gertie, when she saw Angela looking across at them. 'It's just Mother and Father. They brought me out this evening so I could show them that I can be trusted to behave myself. It's all gone swimmingly well—why, I haven't so much as smoked a cigarette or said "damn," once. With any luck, I'll be allowed out without them by

Christmas. Listen, Angela, I haven't had the chance to thank you for getting Walter and me out of prison the other week.'

'Oh, pray, don't mention it,' said Angela, trying not to laugh at Inspector Jameson's look of astonishment.

'Angela sprang us, you know,' said Gertie to the inspector, quite unabashed. 'Neither of us had any money, and if Angela hadn't come to the rescue we should still be in gaol now, quite probably.'

'Indeed—er—Miss?' said Jameson.

'This is Lady Gertrude McAloon,' said Angela. 'Gertie, this is Inspector Jameson of Scotland Yard. I should be careful what you say if I were you.'

'Oh, nonsense,' said Gertie briskly. 'Why, we're all paid-up and square. You've got nothing on me, inspector.'

'Ah,' said Jameson, understanding. 'You must be the young lady who had the little trouble at the Copernicus Club.'

'That's right,' said Gertie. 'All jolly good fun, except for the night in prison, of course. That was rather a bore, but I might have got away with it if the magistrate hadn't insisted on making me give my full name to all those reporters. I'd been rather hoping that Father wouldn't find out. I always knew it was a silly name, but it sounds even more ridiculous when recited out loud in court. Lucrèce, indeed! She was a great-aunt of mine, you know. Apparently she was a mistress of Napoleon the Third, although I don't know why they insisted on inflicting her name on me.'

'Come along, Gertie, dear, or we shall be late,' called the woman.

'Just coming, Mother,' said Gertie over her shoulder. 'Well, thank you, anyway, Angela. I shan't forget it.'

She flashed Angela and Jameson a wicked and unrepentant grin and ran off.

'Rather a lively young lady,' remarked the inspector. 'I shouldn't like to have the charge of her, I must say.'

Angela did not reply. She was staring after Gertie with a puzzled frown on her face.

'What is it?' said Jameson.

She turned back to him, and Jameson was struck by her odd expression. Then she returned to herself and smiled.

'It's nothing,' she said. 'I just had the most extraordinary and disturbing thought, that's all.'

'Oh? About what?'

She did not reply directly, but merely said, 'I was thinking of something you said earlier. I wonder, now—' she hesitated.

'Do you have an idea about the murder?' said Jameson.

She appeared to come to a decision.

'Look here, inspector,' she said. 'I should hate to waste your time by sending you on a ridiculous wild-goose chase. I'd like to do a little research on my own account first. May I call you tomorrow if anything turns up?'

'You're not going to put yourself in danger, I hope?' said the inspector in some alarm.

'Oh, no, nothing like that,' she assured him.

'I seem to remember your saying the same to me during the Underwood House case. You nearly got killed, then, don't you remember?' he said.

'I'd forgotten about that,' said Angela with a guilty laugh. 'But no—this time I shall just be taking a little trip to the Strand.'

'And you will call me tomorrow?'

'If I have anything to tell,' she replied. 'I'm almost certain I'm wrong, but there's no harm in making sure.'

CHAPTER TWENTY-FOUR

E ARLY THE NEXT morning Angela received a tele-phone-call from Cynthia Pilkington-Soames, who was still full of the events in Littlechurch and wanted to find out whether Angela could tell her anything more before she submitted her gossip column for that week to the *Clarion*. Angela wondered what Cynthia would say if she knew her own son had been behind the fiasco, but held her tongue.

'Vassily's been given thirty days,' said Cynthia breathlessly. 'Marguerite went along and pleaded his case, saying that they ought to make allowances for the artistic temperament, but the magistrate would have none of it. He merely said that if *that* was what the modern artistic temperament looked like, then perhaps a spell in prison would dampen it down a little; furthermore, if Mr. Constable was perfectly able to confine his artistic temperament to canvas without feeling the need to express it with his fists too, then he saw no reason why Vassily oughtn't to be held to the same standards.'

'Oh dear,' said Angela. 'How did Marguerite take it?'

'She was upset, naturally, but she seems to think that the sentence will furnish Vassily with plenty of new material and inspiration, and spur him on to further heights of creativity. At least, that's what she called out to him when they were leading him off to gaol. I'm not sure whether he was convinced, though.'

'Poor Marguerite,' said Angela. 'I know she wanted her exhibition to attract attention, but I don't suppose that was the sort she had in mind.'

'Oh, but I quite forgot the other news,' went on Cynthia excitedly. 'Did you know that Gil Blakeney has run off?'

'What?' said Angela in surprise. 'Are you sure?'

'Oh, yes. Nobody has seen him since Sunday. Lucy is tearing her hair out.'

Angela felt a chill at her heart.

'But are you quite sure he's run off, and not just gone away on business or something, and forgotten to tell anybody?' she said.

'Oh, quite sure,' said Cynthia. 'He left a note, saying that he had to get away and that he was sorry to leave them all in the lurch, especially with his mother being so ill and all that, but he had felt for some time that he wasn't good enough for Lucy and that he should bring her only misery. He said he was going away for a while to straighten things out in his mind, and that they shouldn't try to look for him.'

'I see. And don't Herbert or Miles have any idea where he might have gone?' said Angela.

'None that they will admit to,' said Cynthia in exasperation. 'They are as thick as thieves, those two, and it's no good trying to pry anything out of them when they want to keep it under their hats. Believe me, I've tried!'

Angela listened in silence, thinking hard. She got rid of Cynthia as soon as was decently possible and called William, who presented himself promptly.

'We are going to Somerset House this morning,' said Angela, 'although I have the feeling we may be too late.'

'Too late, ma'am?' inquired William.

'Yes. If I am right in my supposition, then we have missed our chance.' She saw the young man's blank look and said, 'Never mind. I shall explain all about it on the way, and you can help me look things up when we get there.'

Some time later, Angela sat in the back seat of the Bentley as they returned home, struggling with conflicting emotions. On the one hand, it was gratifying to have been proved right, and to feel that there was something she could usefully do to help Inspector Jameson with his investigation; on the other hand, though, there was the fact of the thing she had found out—a fact that could only cause hurt to several, if not many people.

'It's a very unpleasant situation, William,' she remarked. 'I almost wish I hadn't poked my nose into it now.'

'No,' said William emphatically, somewhat to her surprise. 'You were right to do it, ma'am. Nobody deserves to die like she did—thrown aside like a piece of garbage as though she were of no importance. Don't you think she deserved better? From what we found out this morning, it looks as though all she wanted to do was to try and make a comfortable life for herself and her son. Surely she had the right to do that? And then to be killed just because she was an inconvenience—it's not fair.'

'You are quite right,' said Angela. 'I oughtn't to let myself be influenced by social conventions, but—well, one can't help it at times. I shall telephone Inspector Jameson as soon as we get back.'

She was as good as her word. Jameson listened to what she had to say in astonishment, then let out a long whistle at the other end of the line.

'Good Lord!' he exclaimed. 'Why, that changes everything! But pardon me—are you quite sure?'

'Oh yes,' said Angela. 'There's no doubt of it. Lily Markham married Gilbert Blakeney in April 1918 at the Westminster Register Office.'

'Then the boy is presumably his son,' said Jameson.

'According to his birth certificate, yes he is,' said Angela. 'His name is also Gilbert Blakeney.'

'Bertie! Of course,' said the inspector. 'I wonder it didn't occur to me at the time.'

'But why should it?' said Angela. 'Gil was never a suspect as far as I am aware. But I have met him several times, as he is a friend of some friends of mine, and so it was easier for me to make the connection—at least once I knew that the little boy was known as Bertie. It always seemed strange to me that Lita should have been found down in Kent, where she had apparently no connections, especially since no evidence has ever been found of her having gone down there in company with Johnny Chang. But now, you see, we have a perfectly good reason for her having been in the area. She must have come to see Gil—it can't possibly be a coincidence, surely.'

'And so this Blakeney fellow is engaged to be married to another young lady?'

'Yes, a Lucy Syms. It is considered by everybody concerned to be an eminently suitable match.'

'Which naturally gives Blakeney a thumping motive to put his wife out of the way and try to pretend that the inconvenient first marriage never took place at all.'

'I'm afraid so,' said Angela soberly.

'I wonder why they parted so soon after the wedding,' said Jameson.

'I don't know,' said Angela. 'At any rate, for some reason she must have decided to communicate with him again quite recently.'

'That must be what she meant when she talked about her prospects,' said Jameson. 'She must have gone down to Kent to claim her rightful position as his wife—or perhaps even to blackmail him. We may never know which. And so he killed her.'

'That's very much what it looks like,' agreed Angela.

'I shall call the Kent police immediately and have them issue a warrant for Gilbert Blakeney's arrest,' said the inspector. 'We must act as quickly as possible.'

'Ah,' said Angela. 'That was another thing I wanted to tell you. Apparently he's gone missing.'

'What?'

She told him of the telephone-call she had received from Cynthia Pilkington-Soames that morning.

'Naturally, there was no sense at all in reporting it to you until I was sure that it was something that you need worry about,' she said hurriedly, 'so I went to Somerset House to look at the documents as quickly as I could, and—well—I'm sorry to say I was right.'

'Don't be sorry,' he said. 'You must remember that none of this is your fault, and that you may well have saved an innocent man from the noose. That is the most important thing.'

This was true, but Angela felt it to be scant comfort just then in comparison with the blow that was about to fall on the Blakeneys, Lucy, and even Miles and Herbert.

'I'm most awfully grateful to you for this,' Jameson went on. 'I must go now, but I shall let you know how things turn out. In the meantime, if you have any idea where Gilbert Blakeney might have gone—but perhaps it's not fair to ask that of you, since he is by way of being a friend of yours.'

But Angela was having none of it.

'Don't be silly,' she said firmly. 'If I can report someone I know as a possible murderer, I'm hardly likely to baulk at telling you where he is if I happen to find it out.'

'Thank you,' said Jameson sincerely, and rang off, leaving Angela to her own uncomfortable thoughts. She went over to the window and looked out. It was a grey, gloomy day and the clouds were lowering, a state of affairs which matched her mood to perfection. There was no doubt that things looked very bad for Gilbert Blakeney, but she had enjoyed his hospitality at lunch only a few weeks ago, and it seemed terribly ungrateful to repay it with an arrest for murder. How would Lucy take it? Would she hide her feelings as usual, and arrange for the finest defence counsels in the land to plead his case? Or would the fact of his having been married and presumably kept it a secret from her prove too much and induce her to abandon him to his fate? Angela did not know. And what about Lady Alice? According to Cynthia, she was still very ill and barely even conscious half the time. Would they tell her what had befallen her only son, or would they deem it more of a kindness to keep it from her?

Angela sighed and turned away from the window. She had no desire to spend the rest of the afternoon cooped up at home in company with her own reflections. Perhaps a turn in the fresh air would do her good. Accordingly, she went out and set off for the Park, intending to shake off her grim mood and guilty feelings with a brisk walk. It was chilly, so she walked quickly to warm up, and then slowed down so that she could observe what was going on around her. The place was busy with its usual complement of nursemaids, children, servants on their day out, flirting sweethearts and delivery-boys taking short-cuts, and Angela found some entertainment in watching their activities as she passed. Soon enough, she reached the Serpentine, and here her pace faltered, for to her surprise she spotted a figure she recognized: a large man with a bald head and a moustache, who was standing by the edge of the lake and gazing absently into the water.

After a moment's thought, she approached him.

'Why, Herbert,' she said, 'whatever are you doing here?'

Herbert Pilkington-Soames jumped when he heard her voice, but then turned and recovered when he saw her.

'Hallo, Angela,' he said, in something like his usual jocular manner. 'Have you recovered from the scrimmage down in Littlechurch yet? I hear there was quite a to-do.'

'Yes,' said Angela, but that was not what she wanted to talk about, and she went on quickly, 'Herbert, did you know that Gil has gone missing?'

His smile faded and a look of surprise passed briefly across his face, to be replaced by an expression that Angela could not read.

'Gone missing? What do you mean?' he said.

'Just what I say. He ran off on Sunday, leaving a note.'

'Oh? And what did the note say?' said Herbert warily.

'It said that he felt he wasn't good enough for Lucy, and that he wanted to go and think about things for a while, and that nobody should go and look for him.'

Herbert let out a breath.

'Really? Just that?' he said.

'You sound surprised. What else did you expect?' said Angela, regarding him closely.

'Oh, nothing,' he said. 'I just meant—I thought—it's just a shock, that's all.'

'You weren't expecting a confession, perhaps?'

Again the look of surprise passed fleetingly across his face, but then he turned away.

'A confession? Of what?' he said.

'Murder,' said Angela.

He turned back towards her and his face was white, but he said nothing and only gazed at her questioningly.

'How much do you know, Herbert?' said Angela.

CHAPTER TWENTY-FIVE

I HOPE YOU don't think I'm happy about all this,' said Herbert at last. 'It's a rotten business. Rotten, I tell you. But—well—Gil saved my life once, and it doesn't do to let a fellow down when he's done that for you. So you know it all, do you? I suppose you've told the police.'

'I had to, Herbert,' said Angela. 'You must see that.'

'Oh, quite, quite,' he said. 'You're not to blame. You know your duty. I only wish I knew *mine*.'

Angela regarded him sympathetically.

'I suppose the police will be out combing the country for him now,' he went on.

'I imagine so,' said Angela.

'And then they'll catch him and hang him like a dog. A fine end for him.'

'Don't!' cried Angela. A wave of horror flooded over her. What had she done?

He saw her face and hastened to apologize.

'I'm sorry, old girl. Please don't suppose I blame you. Gil must face up to what he has done—and besides, it wouldn't have been right of him to let that Chinese chappie hang in his place. Damn' bad show, what?'

Angela pulled herself together.

'Suppose you tell me the whole story,' she said. 'Perhaps there are circumstances that will cause the judge to look upon him sympathetically.'

'I hope so,' he said soberly. 'Very well, what do you want to know?'

'Did you know he was already married before he got engaged to Lucy?'

'No!' he said emphatically. 'I swear I knew nothing about it.'

'But you had met Lita?'

He nodded.

'If it's the girl I think it is, then yes.'

Little by little, Angela drew the tale out of him. In the spring of 1918 he, Miles and Gil had managed to wangle a few days' leave from the Front and had decided to spend them in London. Herbert was the only one of the three who was married then, but Cynthia and Freddy were staying with her parents in the North of England, since her father was gravely ill, so it was not possible for him to see them in the time available, and he had therefore remained with his friends. Things had been pretty grim in Belgium up until then, and so they were determined to celebrate their brief time of freedom. They had a riotous time of it, all told, and did one or two things which— here he coughed—it was not strictly necessary for Angela to know about. During the course of those few days, however, they had gone to the theatre to see a musical production, and went around to wait by the stage door afterwards. As a result of that, Gil took up with a girl who danced in the chorus and called herself Lita. At a certain point, Gil had abandoned them and disappeared with Lita, and they had not seen him again until they returned to duty. He had said nothing about the girl, and they assumed that things had finished there and then.

'But they hadn't,' said Angela.

'No,' said Herbert.

'When did you find out about the marriage?'

'Not until the other week, when we were all down at Gipsy's Mile,' said Herbert grimly. 'It was Miles who told me.'

'Miles? How did he know about it?'

'Why, because he helped Gil dispose of the body, of course.'

Angela stared at him, thunderstruck.

'What?' she cried, hardly able to believe her ears.

'But I thought you knew,' said Herbert. 'I thought Miles must have told you everything.'

'No, he didn't,' said Angela. She felt suddenly as though she had been pitched from an unpleasant dream into the most frightful nightmare. 'I didn't know anything about it.'

'Then how did you find out about Gil and Lita?'

'I've seen a copy of their marriage certificate,' said Angela.

Herbert nodded in comprehension, but did not ask why or how.

'I see,' he said. 'And so you realized immediately that he must have done it. Of course.'

'Tell me what happened,' said Angela, although she was not at all sure that she wanted to hear. Poor Marguerite! What would happen to them now? This was far worse than she had imagined.

'I don't know, exactly,' said Herbert. 'It was all over by the time I arrived, but Miles confided to me the next day that Gil had got himself into the most tremendous scrape and he'd somehow found himself helping and was feeling terrible about it.'

According to Herbert, Gil had telephoned Miles on the Thursday afternoon—the day before the party arrived at Gipsy's Mile—in a great state, saying confusedly that something awful had happened and he didn't know what to do about it. To Miles it sounded very much as though Gil had plunged into another nervous episode similar to the one he'd had years ago, so he hastened to his friend's assistance, thinking that perhaps he just needed bucking up a bit. Never in his wildest imaginings had he expected what he found when he arrived at Blakeney Park and discovered that Gil had a dead body on his hands and couldn't quite explain where it had come from, but needed to get rid of it in a hurry.

Of course, Miles wanted to know who she was, and Gil confessed that it was Lita, the girl he'd met in London that time, and that he had rather stupidly married her without mentioning it. They had both realized immediately that it was a mistake, and had parted, and Gil had more or less forgotten about her, or at least had succeeded in blocking her out of his mind (here Angela shook her head in astonishment), but then years later she turned up out of the blue, and although he was engaged to Lucy there was no getting away from the fact that he was already married. And now Lita was dead and it was all his fault, although he couldn't quite say how it had happened, and now what was he to do? Miles, naturally, was completely shocked and taken aback by the whole thing, and in the tumult of his thoughts the one idea that came to the fore was the need to get rid of the body as soon as possible, so that's what they did.

'Whose idea was it to disfigure her face?' said Angela.

'I don't know,' said Herbert, looking rather sick. 'I didn't ask, because I didn't want to know anything more about it. The whole thing has been weighing on my mind for weeks now. I wish Miles hadn't told me.'

'Is that why you didn't come to the sculpture exhibition?'

'Yes,' he said. 'I didn't think I could play the part any more. I managed it that first weekend at Gipsy's Mile, but I expect that's because it hadn't really sunk in then.'

They both fell silent, deep in thought. If it had been difficult for Angela to report Gil to the police, it was a real wrench to the heart now that she knew Miles was mixed up in the thing, and she heartily wished that she had kept on walking when she spotted Herbert standing by the Serpentine. But a thing once known could never be unknown, and now she had to decide what to do. Miles was her friend's husband; could she give him away to the police?

She glanced up and saw Herbert regarding her sympathetically.

'I know, old girl, it's hard,' he said. 'Now you know how I have felt these past few weeks.'

'I almost wish I hadn't asked,' said Angela.

'So the police know nothing about Miles, then?'

'No—or at least, not from me,' said Angela.

'They will find out soon enough, though.'

Angela said nothing, uncomfortably aware that the only way they were likely to find out was if she told them, since she doubted that Gil would want to betray the friend who had helped him out.

'What are you going to do now?' said Herbert.

'I don't know,' said Angela.

'Your friend in the police will want to know about Miles.'

'Yes, I suppose he will.'

'Well, I won't blame you if you tell him,' said Herbert. 'I'm in rather a muddle about the whole thing myself.'

'Herbert, do you know where Gil has gone?'

'I didn't even know he'd gone missing until you told me,' he said. 'I hope he's not going to do anything silly, though. He can't have been in his right mind when he—he did it. Gil's not like that. He's a good fellow, Angela,' he went on firmly, 'and I can't help thinking that there must be more to this than meets the eye. I can't and won't believe he killed a woman in cold blood. We went through a lot together, the three of us, and had the kind of experiences that really test the mettle of a man, and I know he's not that sort.'

Angela did not know what to reply. She had no doubt that what Herbert said about his friend was true; but even the best of men had their weak moments, and who knew what had occurred between Gil and Lita to cause him to kill her? It was not hard to imagine a situation in which the pressure put upon him by his mother to make a suitable marriage had built up gradually inside him until it became intolerable and finally found vent in violence following the arrival of his long-forgotten and wholly *un*suitable wife.

'I must go,' said Angela at last.

'Yes, you'd better go and telephone your tame inspector,' said Herbert with a sad smile. 'Try not to feel too bad about it.'

They shook hands and Angela returned to Mount Street and her flat. As an exercise in shaking off the gloom, she reflected, the walk had failed badly.

As soon as she got home, she picked up the telephone-receiver, determined to get the unpleasant business over and done with as soon as possible. To her great relief, however, the voice on the other end of the line informed her that Inspector Jameson was out and not expected back for some time. Would Mrs. Marchmont like to leave a message? No, said Angela, feeling as though she had been given a reprieve; she would call back later.

She replaced the receiver and stood staring at her reflection in a glass that hung on the wall next to the telephone-table. She lifted her hands and attempted to smooth out the furrows that seemed to have appeared on her brow overnight, but as soon as she took her hands away the frown re-formed itself. She sighed. It was no good: what was done was done, and they should all have to live with the consequences, whatever they may be.

CHAPTER TWENTY-SIX

A NGELA SLEPT BADLY that night and rose the next morning with her head still full of the revelations of the day before. She knew she would have to telephone Scotland Yard again, but decided to put off doing it until later. Fortunately for her, shortly after breakfast she received an unexpected visit from some friends who had come up to London for a few days, and she was able to forget her troubles for a little while. The friends stayed for lunch and then departed, and Angela reluctantly decided that she must put off the telephone-call no longer. She was just about to lift the receiver when the instrument rang shrilly and she jumped. She picked it up. It was a trunk call.

'Angela, is that you?' came Marguerite's voice at the other end of the line, then, without waiting for a reply, she went on, 'Oh, Angela, Miles has been arrested!'

'What?' said Angela.

'Yes. Oh, I hardly know where I am or what I'm doing, darling. We've had one shock after another down here. Yesterday afternoon we were thrown all into confusion when the police came and said that they had a warrant to arrest Gil for the murder of that woman—you know, the one you found in the ditch. I couldn't believe it! Gil, of all people! It turns out that he'd *married* this girl secretly years ago, and thought she was dead, or something, but then she turned up and was threatening to ruin the wedding—well, of course, there wouldn't have been a wedding, would there? You can't go marrying someone when you're already married to someone else. Apparently Gil got into the most awful fright and killed her in a panic, but didn't know what to do next so he called Miles, who went along and gave him a hand to dump the body and has now gone and confessed it to the police, the silly old fool. Did you ever hear anything so ridiculous in all your life? What on earth was he thinking? And now he's been arrested and they're going to charge him with having been an accessory after the fact, and I just *know* they'll give him twenty years in prison, and then what shall I do, darling?' The last few words came out as sobs.

Angela felt a mixture of shock and relief. Now that Miles had spoken up of his own accord, his arrest was one thing at least for which she need not blame herself.

'But why did he confess?' she said.

'Herbert knew all about it, and persuaded him to do it,' sniffed Marguerite. 'He telephoned yesterday to say that he'd heard the police were after Gil, and that the fat was in the fire now, so he'd better go and tell all.'

'I see,' said Angela. Good old Herbert—he had saved her some sleepless nights, at least. 'And where is Miles now?'

'At the police station,' said Marguerite. 'Scotland Yard are there, questioning him. He must be feeling dreadful, the poor darling. I don't suppose he'd have done it had he not felt there was a jolly good reason for it.'

Angela marvelled at Marguerite's unfailing ability to sympathize with people and see the best in them. Never mind the fact that her husband had helped cover up a murder; she was concerned only with the effect on him of his presumed guilty conscience.

'What will you do now?' she asked.

'That's why I called you,' said Marguerite. 'I can't bear the thought of being all alone at home. Freddy is here, of course, and he's sympathetic enough, but he's only really come because the *Clarion* have sent him and they want to bags the story. Will you come down and stay for a few days? Please say you will, darling. Cynthia would be no good to me at all, but you are always such a comforting presence.'

'Of course I will,' said Angela. She rang off and instructed Marthe to pack some things, as she was going away for a few days. Then she called William and told him to get the Bentley ready, as they were going back down to Kent.

He saw her serious expression and said, 'Has something happened, ma'am?'

'Several things have happened,' said Angela. 'Gilbert Blakeney is being hunted by the police for the murder of Lita de Marquez, and Mr. Harrison has been arrested on suspicion of helping to dispose of the body. The good news, such as it is, is that Johnny Chang is in the clear, and it looks likely that your friend Alvie will shortly get his job back.'

William digested this information in silence, then went off to do as he was bid.

They made good time on the journey down to Kent. Marguerite was looking out for them, and ran outside as soon as she saw the motor-car arrive.

'Darling!' she cried, throwing herself on Angela. 'I'm so glad you've come. I couldn't bear being all alone here for a moment longer.'

She was exaggerating somewhat, for when Angela entered the house she found Freddy in the sitting-room, lounging glumly in a window-seat and staring out into the garden. To her surprise, Lucy Syms was also there.

'Oh, Lucy!' said Angela.

'Hallo, Angela,' replied the girl. 'I expect you've heard that we've had a bit of a sticky time of it here lately.' Her self-possession was as complete as ever.

'Do—do the police have any idea where Gil has gone?' said Angela, uncomfortably conscious that she had been the one to set them on to him in the first place.

'No,' said Lucy. 'He left suddenly on Sunday afternoon and hasn't been seen since. Of course, I was terribly concerned at first because Lady Alice was so ill, and it really was a most inconvenient time for him to have a nervous episode, but it wasn't until yesterday that the police came and told me the whole story. I must say, it came as rather a surprise.'

This seemed such an enormous understatement that Angela's face must have shown her astonishment, and Lucy blushed slightly.

'You must think me terribly unfeeling,' she said, 'but I'm not, truly. This has hit me as hard as anyone, I assure you. It's just that—well, I was on my own for such a long time, and I got used to shifting for myself and shaking things off as best I could. One doesn't get on in life if one takes every little adversity too much to heart.'

'Then you didn't know anything about the marriage?' said Angela, feeling the greatest curiosity towards a woman who could describe the events of the past few days as a 'little adversity.' 'Had Gil never even mentioned having been married before and perhaps widowed?'

'Never,' she replied. 'I knew nothing of the existence of this woman or her son. It came as a complete shock to me.'

'Does Lady Alice know?'

'No,' said Lucy. 'She is very weak, and we have been warned not to do anything to upset her, although it has been difficult to explain to her why her own son has kept away from her bedside.'

'Yes, I can imagine,' said Angela. 'Is she going to recover, do you think?'

'It's difficult to say. You know doctors—they never like to commit themselves, but I have the feeling that she may be close to the end.'

Angela glanced across and saw that Freddy had turned towards them, and had presumably been listening. His face was pale.

'I hope for all our sakes that you're wrong,' he said.

Marguerite fluttered in.

'I don't know about you, but I'm simply gasping for a drink,' she said. 'Freddy, darling, would you mind?'

Freddy dragged himself up from his seat and poured strong drinks for them all, including Lucy. Marguerite took hers and drank it in two gulps.

'That's better,' she said. 'Well, my dears, we have managed to put two of our number in gaol so far this week. Let's see if we can make it three by Sunday.' She saw Lucy's face and was immediately contrite. 'I'm sorry, darling, I didn't mean it,' she said. 'It's just my silly humour getting the better of me again. How does one get through this, otherwise?'

'I wish—I wish I knew where Gil had gone,' said Lucy suddenly. 'He must be dreadfully scared, and he can't possibly be in his right mind. We need to find him, or I'm terribly worried that he will do something silly—harm himself, perhaps.'

Angela's first thought was that perhaps it would be better for everyone concerned if he did, but she said nothing. Lucy was not a stupid girl, and must surely realize it for herself sooner or later.

'But do you think you could persuade him to come back, if you knew where he was?' said Freddy. 'He seems to have disappeared fairly thoroughly. It doesn't look as though he were intending to come back, in fact.'

'I know I could convince him,' said Lucy. 'You see, I am certain he didn't do it.'

Freddy looked at her in pity.

'But all the evidence is against him,' he said. 'You must see that.'

'Perhaps,' said Lucy. 'But I know Gil. He's not a murderer. Oh, I know he can be weak, and he's hardly an intellectual, but he's a good man. Why, he saved your father's life, Freddy, all those years ago. How could someone like that kill a woman in cold blood? He didn't do it, I tell you, and I shall find a way to prove it.'

It was the most passionate speech Angela had ever heard her make, and she looked at Lucy in some surprise. It was clear that whatever Gil's past sins had been, Lucy was determined to forget them and concentrate her efforts on assisting him as far as she could.

'Gil is very lucky to have you,' she could not help saying.

Lucy set her jaw.

'Some might say I'm being stupid,' she said. 'There can't be many women who would find out that the man they were about to marry already had a wife and yet still be determined to stand by him. But I'm sure the worst thing he's done is to be very, very foolish. The world wants to think him guilty of murder, I know, but—' she broke off and looked at the floor, as though embarrassed at her vehemence. Marguerite went over to her and gave her a hug.

'Now, don't be downhearted,' she said. 'I'm sure everything will be quite all right in the end. Why, we have Angela on our side! If anybody can find out the truth, she can.'

'Oh,' said Angela in dismay, thinking of the harm she had done to her friends already through her inquisitiveness. 'I can't do anything. It's all in the hands of the police now. Inspector Jameson and Sergeant Willis are very capable men, though, and I'm sure they will be absolutely scrupulous in seeking the truth.'

'Yes,' said Lucy with a small sigh, and Angela could almost hear in that sigh the words, 'but what if the truth is something I don't want to hear?'

Soon after that Lucy rose and said she must get back to Blakeney Park, where she had been staying ever since Lady Alice had been taken ill.

'But I shall come back again tomorrow,' she said. 'In the meantime, please do try and think of anything that might help us find him.'

'We will,' promised Marguerite.

Lucy went out, and the remaining three were left to spend the evening as best they could in the circumstances.

CHAPTER TWENTY-SEVEN

LUCY ARRIVED BRIGHT and early the next morning—so early, in fact, that Marguerite was convinced
something must have happened.

'What is it?' she cried when Lucy entered. 'Have they found
Gil?'

'No,' said Lucy. 'I've come to deliver a message from Lady
Alice. She would like to speak to Angela.'

'To me?' said Angela in astonishment. 'Whatever for?'

'I don't know,' said Lucy, 'but she was most insistent in asking for you.'

'Why, of course I shall speak to her if she wants me to,' said
Angela. 'Shall I go now?'

'If it wouldn't be too much trouble,' said Lucy. 'She is quite
awake now, but if you wait until the afternoon then she might
be asleep again.'

Angela took her advice and set off as soon as she could,
and shortly afterwards found herself being admitted into the

gloomy entrance hall of the old house. A starched maid informed her that Lady Alice was expecting her, and led her up the grand staircase and along to a door at the end of a passage.

Angela entered. The curtains were drawn partly shut, but in the dim light she could see that she was in a large bed-chamber with wood-panelled walls and an ornately-carved ceiling. In the centre of the room was an old-fashioned four-post bed, and on the wall behind the bed a series of rich tapestries hung. The effect was all very opulent and imposing, although it lacked the personal touch and Angela wondered how comfortable it could be.

She moved closer to the bed and saw Lady Alice Blakeney lying back against a mountain of pillows. She was wearing a ruffled nightgown, and her hair fanned out loosely around her head. Angela looked at her face. Her skin was as smooth as ever, but it appeared to have taken on a grey hue. Her mouth turned down at the corners and she gazed straight ahead, seemingly at nothing.

'Lady Alice?' said Angela softly, fearing to disturb her.

There was a rustle and a sharp movement as the old woman raised her head to look at her.

'Mrs. Marchmont,' she said. Her voice was weak, but still held a trace of her old imperious manner. 'Ah, yes, I wanted to see you, didn't I? Lucy must have fetched you, I suppose.'

'Yes,' said Angela. 'I hope you are feeling better.'

Lady Alice wafted a hand.

'Not particularly,' she said. 'I am very tired. They tell me it's my heart. No doubt it is wearing out, like the rest of me. One cannot go on forever, no matter how much one might wish to. I don't suppose I've much time left.' Angela had no reply to that, and Lady Alice went on after a moment, 'I expect you were surprised to hear that I wished to speak to you.'

'I was, rather,' said Angela.

Lady Alice sighed.

'Lucy and I don't get on, you know,' she said, 'but I expect you know that.'

'I had heard something of the sort,' admitted Angela cautiously.

'Had I been able to find anyone else as suitable as she then I should never have forwarded the marriage, but—well, the fact is that she is the perfect match for him, and for the estate. Most women would not be capable of placing themselves above such personal considerations, Mrs. Marchmont, but I am not most women. Lucy will be an excellent wife for Gilbert, and I shall do everything in my power to make sure that the wedding goes ahead—even if that means removing myself from Blakeney Park.'

'I'm sure that won't be necessary,' said Angela. 'And, anyway, I doubt Gil would hear of it given your current state of health. You must allow that he is capable of making his own decisions too.'

'You know nothing of the matter,' snapped Lady Alice. 'Gilbert is my only child, and on him rests the future of the Blakeney Park estate. I love him dearly, but unfortunately he is somewhat weak in the head, as you must have noticed. He wholly lacks the capacity to manage the Park on his own. That is why I selected Lucy for him.'

'Did Lucy have nothing to say about it?'

'Lucy knows a good thing when she sees it,' said Lady Alice contemptuously. 'Her family have been closely allied to the Blakeneys for centuries and I am certain that she has intended to marry my son since she was quite a child.'

'I see,' said Angela. This was all very interesting, but surely Lady Alice had not called her to Blakeney simply to explain her feelings towards her future daughter-in-law?

Lady Alice seemed to have realized the same thing, for she said, 'But of course you will not be interested in our petty family squabbles, although I'm afraid I called you here precisely because of one of them.'

'Oh?' said Angela.

The old woman turned her face with difficulty towards her.

'Where is my son?' she said suddenly.

Angela hesitated, not knowing what to say. The fact of Gil's disappearance had been deliberately kept from his mother on the instructions of her physician, who feared that the news would be too much for her heart to bear.

'Why, I—' she began.

'Oh, you need not pretend, Mrs. Marchmont,' said Lady Alice. 'I am not stupid. Gilbert has not come to see me since I was taken ill on Sunday. They told me that he was keeping away so as not to disturb me, and yet Lucy has been here several times. He has gone off somewhere, and I want to know where.'

'I think perhaps you had better ask Lucy,' said Angela. 'I'm not sure it's my place to talk about it.'

'I have already spoken to Lucy and heard what she has to say,' said Lady Alice, 'but I want to know whether she was speaking the truth. I understand you are a trusted friend of the police, Mrs. Marchmont, so perhaps you can tell me: is my son wanted for murder?'

Here she grew agitated and began to breathe with difficulty.

'Oh!' exclaimed Angela in alarm, looking about her for the bell.

'My medicine,' whispered the old lady, gesturing feebly towards a little bottle that rested on a side-table. 'Two drops.'

Angela administered the medicine as requested, and after a minute or two Lady Alice began to breathe more easily.

'Perhaps I ought to go,' said Angela. 'Shall I summon your maid?'

'Would you be so kind as to pour me a glass of water?' said Lady Alice. Angela filled a glass from a jug that stood near at hand, and gave it to her. She took a sip and handed it back. 'Thank you. I am quite well now, but I have been warned not to allow myself to become agitated.'

'Then perhaps this is not the best moment to have this conversation,' said Angela reasonably.

'I must know, Mrs. Marchmont. Where is Gilbert? I am his mother and I have a right to know. Is he on the run?'

Angela saw that she was determined to pursue the matter. She nodded slowly.

'It appears he is,' she said. 'He has not been seen since Sunday. Pardon me, but what exactly did Lucy tell you?'

'She told me that the dead woman you found the other week was a chorus-girl who married my son many years ago, and that he killed her in order to avoid becoming a bigamist. Is that known to be true?'

'I'm afraid it is true that he was married,' said Angela, 'and the fact of Lita's body having been found near his home makes it look rather as though he were responsible for her death. That is certainly what the police would like to find out. However, as Gil is not here to answer their questions they are choosing to interpret that as confirmation of his guilt, and are anxious to find him so they can question him.'

'I understand Miles Harrison has confessed to having helped Gilbert dispose of this woman's body,' said Lady Alice. 'Did he see Gilbert kill her?'

'No,' said Angela. 'Gil telephoned him after she was dead, to ask for his assistance.'

'Then there is no evidence that my son committed the murder. Tell me, Mrs. Marchmont—do you believe him to be guilty?'

'He has certainly behaved as though he were, by hiding her body and then running away,' said Angela cautiously. 'And even if he is not, I don't suppose the police will be looking for anyone else. They have ample evidence to send him to trial, assuming they can find him.'

'That is no answer at all,' said Lady Alice. 'I want to know what *you* think.'

Angela hesitated, then said, 'I don't like the poison. It doesn't seem to fit the facts as we know them. And as for motive, he is not the only one—' She was about to go on, but thought better of it.

Lady Alice nodded.

Very well,' she said, 'now I must decide what to do to bring him back.'

'I don't think you ought to be doing anything at present,' said Angela.

'Don't be absurd,' said Lady Alice. 'My son is innocent, and I must prove it. You are a sensible woman, Mrs. Marchmont,' she went on, 'and, it appears, to be trusted. Can I rely on you to let me know when Gilbert is found? I dare not depend on Lucy, who has already tried to keep the news of his disappearance from me for several days.'

'She kept it from you because the doctor told her to, not out of spite,' said Angela. 'I believe you do Lucy an injustice, Lady Alice. Perhaps she is not to your taste but I don't think she is deliberately plotting against you. I believe she is very fond of Gil and would hate to see him come to harm—indeed, she has said as much to me—so she is hardly likely to try and hurt you, since to do that would be to hurt him too.'

'I'm afraid you don't know what you're talking about,' said Lady Alice. 'We understand each other very well, she and I,' she went on somewhat obliquely. Angela saw there would be no convincing her and determined to waste no more breath in defence of Lucy.

'Very well, I shall see to it that you are informed when your son has been found,' she said.

'Thank you,' said Lady Alice. 'And now if you would have the goodness to ring for my maid, I shall bid you good day.'

Angela left the house, thinking about what Lady Alice had said to her. Did she really trust Lucy so little that she believed her to be lying about Gil? Angela found the relationship between the two women unfathomable.

'Well, William, it looks as though the cat is out of the bag now, and Lady Alice knows all,' she remarked as they drove back along the narrow lanes to Gipsy's Mile. 'She must have got wind of what was happening and asked Lucy about it. I wonder Lucy didn't say anything when I saw her this morning. It's a pity she couldn't have kept the secret.'

'From what I've heard, the two ladies don't exactly get along,' said William, 'and now that Lady Alice is so ill maybe Miss Syms thought that if she told her about Mr. Blakeney it might hurry her along a little, so to speak.'

'Do you mean Lucy was hoping to give Lady Alice another heart attack? Surely not!' said Angela, half-laughing.

William cocked his head and looked expressively as though to say, 'Stranger things have happened,' and Angela paused for a moment to wonder whether it was true. Gil's troubles aside, it would certainly make their lives a little easier to have Lady Alice out of the way. But then she thought of Lucy's open, sensible face and rejected the thought.

'I believe you are becoming a cynic, William,' she said.

'Maybe I am, ma'am,' he replied. 'But after hearing about all these people who hate each other, who could blame me?'

Angela glanced at him curiously. There was that word again: 'hate.' Alvie Berteau had said that someone must have hated Lita to have murdered her, and now William was using the same word in connection with Lucy and Lady Alice. Was hatred really what this case was all about?

CHAPTER TWENTY-EIGHT

ANGELA ARRIVED BACK at Gipsy's Mile to find that Lucy had just left—which was something of a relief—and that Marguerite had been along to Littlechurch and stood bail for Miles, who had been released, with instructions not to leave the area. He was sitting in his usual easy-chair, looking even more white and drawn than usual, while Marguerite danced attendance on him, but he managed a smile when Angela came in, and spoke to her in much his usual manner.

'I expect you've heard I've been rather an idiot,' he said.

'I've heard something of the sort, yes,' replied Angela with a smile.

'Of course, it's nothing to the trouble Gil's got himself into, but it's bad enough,' he went on. 'The police are talking about ten years.'

'Oh, don't, darling,' cried Marguerite in distress. 'You mustn't think like that. You did it with the best of intentions, to help a friend.'

'It was very wrong of me,' said Miles, 'but poor Gil was in such a state I rather lost my head, I think.'

'But what happened, exactly?' said Angela. 'I mean, I know what you did, but how did Gil explain the fact of having a dead body to get rid of?'

'Why, the fellow was barely coherent,' said Miles. 'All I understood from him was that this was some girl he had married years ago, and she'd turned up and given him a terrible shock, and now he was terrified that his mother and Lucy would find out and cancel the wedding, when everything had been so neatly organized between them.'

'But where was the body when you arrived at Blakeney Park?'

'In the boot of the Wolseley. He'd put her there while he tried to decide what to do. I saw her face and remembered her immediately—she had the sort of face one does remember. It was the girl he'd taken up with all those years ago in London. I don't know which gave me the bigger shock: the fact that he was married or the fact that he'd apparently killed her, but I can't have been thinking straight or I never should have helped him.'

'Was it you who disfigured her face?' said Angela.

Miles winced and shook his head.

'No,' he said, 'but I think it might have been my fault. You see, I said we should have to make sure that nobody could identify her if she was found. I meant that we ought to remove all possessions that could be easily traced, but Gil took it rather more literally than that and decided to—well, you know what he did. I'm afraid he took a golf club to her. He was dreadfully sick afterwards.'

'This was on the Thursday, was it? That is, the day before we all arrived?'

'Yes. He called me in the afternoon, and I went along and found him shivering on the ground by the car. He was in a bad way, as a matter of fact. I finally got him to calm down and tell me what had happened, and he opened the boot and showed me the body.'

'But he couldn't tell you how he'd killed her?'

'No. He didn't seem to know,' said Miles.

'How odd,' said Angela, half to herself.

'He just kept saying that there would be hell to pay when his mother and Lucy found out. The police appeared to be merely a secondary consideration. At any rate, once we'd established that we needed to get rid of Lita, we sat and waited until later, when darkness had fallen, and did the deed then.'

'Was it your idea to hide her in the undergrowth?'

'Yes,' he said. 'It was such a beautiful hiding-place. I thought no-one would ever find her there.'

'But I did—the very next day, in fact,' said Angela wryly, feeling once again as though she had been responsible for unleashing chaos where previously there had been order.

Freddy now spoke up.

'It was just your bad luck that the darling of Scotland Yard happened to be passing, Miles,' he said.

'Freddy,' said Angela reproachfully, and he looked a little ashamed of himself.

'Sorry,' he said. 'It's a rotten affair, this whole thing, and I don't mind telling you I'm not nearly so fond of this reporting business as I was. It's all very well writing stories about the weddings of fatuous aristocrats one's never met before and never shall again, but this—well, this feels all wrong. Old Bickerstaffe has sent me down here because of my close connection to the case, and he's expecting me to get a nice, juicy story out of it, but it sticks in my throat to profit from the misery of friends, especially since it turns out that my own father knew about it all along. I never thought I'd find myself in this sort of position.'

'You aren't going to put what's been said just now in the paper, I hope?' said Angela, alarmed.

'No, of course not,' he said. 'But I shall have to produce *something* for them, since I'm on the inside, so to speak. However, at present the well of inspiration seems to have run dry. Really, it would be better for all concerned if Gil would do the decent thing and turn himself in. But where the devil can he be? Miles, are you sure you don't have an idea?'

Miles sighed.

'No, none at all,' he said, 'as I've already told the police several times. They seemed to think I might know where he went—as a matter of fact, it was touch and go as to whether or not they charged me with having helped him do the deed—but I assure you I haven't the faintest idea. He might be in Bournemouth or Bulawayo as far as I know.'

'I wonder, now,' murmured Freddy. 'Marguerite, might I use the telephone?'

'Why, certainly,' said Marguerite.

Freddy wandered out and was gone for a few minutes, then he returned and said that he was going into Littlechurch, to try and speak to the police.

'Perhaps they will have something to tell me that's tame enough for me to use and yet still worth publishing,' he said glumly. 'I'm sure I saw Corky Beckwith of the *Herald* on the road on my way down here. I shouldn't be surprised if he's stolen a march on me. I warn you all now—on no account must you speak to him if you happen to meet him, or if he comes here. He has the morals of a snake and the sting of a wasp, and he'll leave you smarting for weeks if he decides to do a story on you. I shan't be back for lunch, so do go ahead without me.'

He went out, looking more serious than Angela had ever seen him, and returned at about half-past two, having succeeded in speaking to Inspector Jameson for a short while.

'Well? Have you found out anything new?' said Angela.

Freddy grimaced.

'It's not looking good for old Gil, I'm afraid,' he said. 'The police have been nosing around at Blakeney Park, and they seem to have come up with the goods, all right.'

'Oh?' said Angela.

'Yes,' went on Freddy. 'I don't suppose you know the estate well, but in the grounds there are three or four little cottages which were originally built to house faithful old retainers, gamekeepers, secret mistresses and suchlike. Most of them are inhabited by tenants, but one of them is presently vacant, and it was there that the police directed their search. You see, it occurred to them that in a grand house such as Blakeney, with its many servants, it would be rather difficult to poison a visitor with arsenic without drawing unwelcome and pointed attention from a passing abigail.'

'That is very true,' said Angela.

'Their theory is that Lita wrote to Gil to tell him she was coming, and that he went to meet her at Hastings station on the Wednesday afternoon, and brought her back to Blakeney, but not to the great house—the idea being that he slipped her the poison and put her somewhere out of the way while it did its work. So, yesterday they went to this cottage, which is situated in some woods not far from the house, and searched it thoroughly. According to Jameson, the house has only two rooms and is small but smartly and comfortably furnished, and there is no reason why a guest of the Blakeneys might not be put up there for a night or two.'

He paused.

'Go on,' said Angela.

'Well, the police did their stuff in the usual fashion and searched the place from top to bottom. The cottage was almost immaculate—but not quite. The linen on the bed was fresh, and the place had evidently been scrubbed clean fairly recently, so for a good while they thought they wouldn't be able to find anything useful—or perhaps that there was nothing to find. However, when they examined the bed more closely, they discovered several blonde hairs with dark roots trapped in a crack in the wooden headboard.'

'Did they, now?' said Angela thoughtfully.

'Now, those hairs may have a quite innocent explanation, but then there is the fact of the poison. I suppose you are aware that poisoning by arsenic tends to give one something of an upset stomach, to say the very least, so in theory, if Lita did indeed spend the night in that cottage as the police were assuming, then she ought to have left plenty of traces of it.'

'And did she?'

'It looks like it,' said Freddy. 'As I said, the place had been scrubbed clean, especially the floor around the bed, but whoever did the cleaning had evidently missed a section or two over by the door, and the police found unmistakable signs that someone had been very ill there.'

'I see,' said Angela. 'And can they link all this to Lita?'

'They are doing tests on the substances they have found, to see if they can find traces of arsenic,' said Freddy. 'If they do, I imagine all doubt will be at an end.'

'Poor Lucy,' said Angela. 'If it looked bad for Gil before, it looks even worse for him now.'

'Yes,' said Freddy. 'If I were he I'd have tried to get away with it by claiming I killed her in a fit of passion, and then I'd have thrown myself upon the mercy of the jury. But arsenic is a cold, deliberate method of killing someone—you can't claim you did it without thinking good and hard about it beforehand.'

'I wonder why she came down here,' said Angela. 'Was it to blackmail him, do you think? Or do you suppose she had some idea of patching things up for the sake of the boy? I suppose it depends on whether or not she knew about Gil's engagement to Lucy.'

'There's no reason she shouldn't have known,' said Freddy. 'After all, the notice was in the papers—Lucy told us herself, don't you remember?'

'Perhaps that's what spurred her on to come down here in the first place,' said Angela. 'Presumably Gil will be able to confirm whether or not that is the case, though—that is, assuming he is ever found, and that he is willing to talk when he is.'

'Hmm,' said Freddy. 'It's a mess, all right.' He wandered over to the window and stared out into the garden. The day was grey and overcast, and it looked as though rain were threatening. 'I say, Angela,' he said suddenly. 'I'm feeling cooped up and in need of a little fresh air. Why don't we go out for a while?'

'Out?' said Angela. 'Where do you want to go?'

'Oh, I don't know,' he said vaguely. 'Perhaps we might take a little drive down to the coast. It's quite nearby and I understand there are many natural beauties to be seen on the way.'

'I didn't know you were an admirer of nature, Freddy,' said Angela in surprise.

'Oh yes,' he assured her. 'There is a pleasure in the pathless woods, and a rapture on the lonely shore, and all that. I like nothing better than to feel the grass under my feet and hear the cry of the birds as they sing their joyful song. It brings a tear to my eye and a flutter to my jaded heart. We who live in the grim, grimy city would do well to think about what lies beyond its walls, and make room in our lives now and again for a little freshness and purity.'

'I see,' said Angela, who was not fooled for an instant. 'I suppose I had better fetch my coat, then. And perhaps an umbrella, since it looks as though it might rain at any moment.'

'What is a little rain, when set against the unalloyed ecstasy that can be felt only at the first glimpse of the unspoilt English countryside?' said Freddy sententiously.

Angela saw that she should get no sense out of him, at least for the present, and went to fetch her outdoor things.

Chapter Twenty-Nine

T HEY SAT IN silence for a while as Freddy steered his little motor-car carefully through the narrow streets of Littlechurch, and out onto the open road. Here, the scenery was as stark as anything Angela had seen in the area, but there was a sort of desolate beauty to the flat, dull green landscape, which stretched for miles in every direction until it reached the point where the sky bent close to the earth and they merged into one.

It was cold, and Angela was glad of her warm coat and gloves. She pulled the fur collar of her coat more tightly about her and huddled down into her seat. There was a slight tang of salt in the air, and she guessed that they were not far from the sea, although there was little joy in the prospect given the dismal skies, which spoke of imminent rain.

'Where are we going?' she said at last to Freddy, who had been lost in his own thoughts.

'Dungeness,' he replied. 'I have a fancy to see the place.'

'No you don't,' said Angela. 'You have some plan of your own, I can tell.'

'Well, perhaps I do,' he said. He fell silent for a few moments, then said, 'I telephoned Father this morning. I thought he might be able to tell me where Gil had gone, since Miles was determined to give nothing away.'

'Do you think Miles and your father know where he is, then?' said Angela.

'I think they have a jolly good idea,' he said, 'but of course they didn't want to say. Poor Father is feeling rotten about the whole business—he's not a bad old stick, you know—so I suspected he'd be easier to work on than Miles, and I was right. I laid the guilt on thick and he came up with the goods, as they say.'

'How can you be so cool about it?' said Angela curiously.

'I'm not cool at all,' said Freddy. 'A murder has been committed and I want to see the man who did it brought to justice. It's easier for me than it is for Father, that's all, because Gil's not a personal friend of mine. Somebody has to bite on the bullet and bring the chap in.'

'So that's where we're going, is it?' said Angela. 'To find Gil? Can you be certain he is where your father said he'd be?'

'No, not at all,' said Freddy, 'but we may as well give it a try. If he's not there then there's no harm done, is there?'

'What is this place?'

'It's a fisherman's cottage on the headland that the three of them used to visit years ago. Father said that Gil had run off and hidden there once or twice when he first came back from the war and needed time to think.'

'And you think he might be there now? I suppose it's possible. But if he is, how do you intend to persuade him to come back?'

'I don't know,' said Freddy. 'I'm sure we'll think of something, though.' Despite his careless tone he was not as indifferent as he pretended to be, for once or twice Angela saw an uncertain look flicker across his face.

'Don't you think that perhaps you ought to have let Inspector Jameson know of your suspicions?' said Angela. 'After all, this is none of our business, really.'

'Oh, come now,' said Freddy. 'Don't tell me you're not simply dying to see how it all turns out! Why, you were in at the very beginning—it was *your* corpse, so to speak. Surely you want to be in at the finish, too. Look at it this way—if he's there and we find him, we can simply say we were out on a little jaunt and happened to run across him. If he's not—well, then, we can just enjoy the day, can't we?'

Angela opened her mouth to reply, but then shut it again. Freddy—damn his perspicacity—was right: she *did* want to be in at the finish. She had been the one to start this whole thing off with her unlucky plunge into the ditch, and now she felt it was her responsibility to make sure the thing ended properly. Quite apart from anything else, she had unwittingly caused an innocent man to be wrongly imprisoned and many people to be thrown out of work. Of course, none of that was her fault, as such, but she felt vaguely as though the matter must be resolved, and that she must be the one to do it. How their presence would help bring Gil back she did not know, but as Freddy said, there was no harm in trying it.

They came to a point where the road turned sharply left and curved back on itself and along the coast. Straight ahead of them was a narrow track that led seemingly to nowhere, for all that could be seen in the distance was a never-ending stretch of stone, shingle and sea-grass, dotted with a few battered and weather-beaten huts which could hardly be dignified with the name cottage, but which presumably belonged to local fishermen. Down this track Freddy guided the motor-car until the bumps became too much for it, and he jolted to a stop.

'I think we'd better get out here,' he said.

Angela stepped out and looked about her. The sky was more overcast than ever, and there was a fine, grey mist in the air that swirled around them and was almost as wet as rain. The only sound to be heard was the infrequent cry of a seagull and the rush of the wind and the distant waves. It was almost impossible to imagine a more bleak and desolate spot.

'Do you really think he has come here?' she said. 'It's not exactly hospitable, is it?'

'Not in this weather,' said Freddy, 'although I understand it can be rather pleasant on a warm summer's day, for those who want a little peace and quiet.'

They set off across the beach, walking at a brisk pace to keep warm. The shingle crunched under their feet as they went. It was so quiet that Angela felt as though they were the only people for miles around, although here and there a fisherman must surely be sitting in his little hut, smoking his pipe and waiting for a favourable tide.

'Where is the cottage?' she said at last.

'It's that one, I think,' said Freddy, pointing. Angela looked and saw a small, weather-beaten building that stood some way apart from the others. Perhaps it had once been painted in cheery colours, but the wind and the rain had long since stripped it of its greens and blues and rendered it a dull, stone-grey. 'I gather it belongs to the Blakeneys,' he said.

As they approached, Angela's heart began to beat faster, and she pulled her coat more closely around her—for warmth, she told herself. She suddenly noticed that the sound of their footsteps seemed very loud in that barren place and her pace faltered. Freddy seemed to have realized the same thing, for he put his hand on her arm and then placed a finger across his lips. They walked, quietly and warily, up to the hut. It had a little window but no door on this side, and so they crept as silently as they could around to the front of the dwelling. Then they were brought up short.

'You needn't have bothered to be so sneaky about it,' said Gilbert Blakeney. 'I saw you coming from miles away.'

He was sitting on the wooden doorstep of the fisherman's hut, smoking a cigarette and staring out to sea. His clothes were dirty, and damp from the drizzle, and he had several days' growth of beard.

'You look ghastly, old chap,' said Freddy not unsympathetically. Gil turned a pair of red-rimmed eyes towards them and Angela was appalled at the change in him. His once round, jolly face was now sunken and hollow-cheeked, and he looked thin and exhausted.

'Well, it's not exactly the Ritz, this place, what?' he replied with grim humour.

'When did you last have anything to eat?' said Angela in concern.

He shrugged.

'A few days ago, I think,' he said. 'There's not much to eat around here unless one has a boat and a fishing-net.'

'We ought to have brought some food with us,' said Angela, 'but I didn't think of it, I'm afraid.'

'No matter,' said Gil. He seemed perfectly unconcerned about their arrival and went on with his cigarette. 'I found this on the beach over there,' he said. 'Somebody must have dropped it. I smoked my last one days ago, of course. Luckily, this one wasn't too damp. I suppose the police are looking for me, are they?'

Angela nodded.

'I thought so. I knew it was only a matter of time before it all came out. They know about the marriage, I take it.'

'Yes,' said Angela.

'It seemed rather a laugh at the time, you see. I'd had too much to drink, and—' he hesitated. 'It's rather uncivil to claim that one only married a woman because one was drunk, don't you think? No, I shan't try and take that way out. Lita was a good, kind girl, but we were both mad. People did crazy things like that during the war. I was about to return to the Front, and it must have seemed like a good idea then to have a girl waiting for me when I came back. Of course, we realized almost immediately that it had been a mistake, and agreed to part. I returned to Belgium, and I suppose she went back to her old life in the theatre.'

'Did you never hear from her again?' asked Angela.

'No,' he said, then looked uncomfortable. 'To be perfectly truthful, I'm not sure I ever gave her an address to write to. She certainly didn't give one to me. I tell you, we had both realized that the marriage was a mistake.'

'But you couldn't just pretend it never happened,' said Angela, with a certain amount of exasperation.

'I know,' he said. 'And yet, that's exactly what I tried to do. Silly, isn't it, how one can convince oneself of certain things? I'd practically forgotten Lita, and when Lucy came along and Mother was so keen on my marrying her I told myself that the first marriage didn't matter—probably wasn't even legal, in fact. I thought that if the story did come to light then we could have the thing annulled, or something.'

'But you couldn't,' said Angela. 'She had a son.'

He stared down at the shingle.

'Yes,' he said. 'So she told me. That made things rather awkward.'

'She wrote to you, then?' said Freddy.

'Yes,' said Gil. 'It was shortly after I got engaged to Lucy. I got a letter from Lita, out of the blue, saying that she'd seen the announcement in the newspaper, and was I the same Gilbert Blakeney who had been in such-and-such a place at such-and-such a time? If I was, then presumably I would remember her. She had never tried to find me before as she'd somehow got the idea that I died in the war, but obviously if I were the same Gilbert Blakeney then the situation with respect to my current engagement was rather awkward.'

'How did you reply?' said Freddy.

'I'm sorry to say I didn't,' replied Gil. 'It was rotten of me, I know, but the letter gave me the most frightful shock when I read it, and I didn't know what to do, so the safest course of action seemed to be to do nothing. But of course she wrote again a few weeks later, saying that she was now sure I was the same man, and did I know I had a son and heir for Blakeney Park?'

'Had she known about the Park when you got married?' asked Angela. 'I mean, did she know you were a wealthy man?'

'I don't know,' he said. 'Probably not. I mean, it's not the sort of thing one talks about with strangers, is it?' He gave a grim laugh. 'And she *was* a stranger—even though we were man and wife.'

'And did you reply to her the second time?'

He looked down again and shook his head.

'You must think me an awful bounder,' he said, 'but I've never been good at dealing with tricky situations of that sort. It's the kind of thing that I should normally let Lucy take care of—except of course, that's the one thing I simply couldn't do in this case.'

'So you ignored the thing and hoped it would go away,' said Angela, not unkindly.

'That's about the size of it,' he agreed. 'I'm not proud of it, but—well, the thing's done now and I can't go back.'

'Did you receive any more letters from her?' asked Freddy.

'No.'

'Then how did you know she was coming to Blakeney?'

'I didn't,' he said, staring at them.

'Are you quite sure?' said Angela. 'You didn't go and meet her at Hastings in the car?'

'Of course I'm sure,' he said. 'She just turned up. She must have come by herself.'

'When was this?' said Angela.

'In the morning—the Thursday morning, it must have been. I'd been away until late on Wednesday—as a matter of fact I wasn't supposed to return until the Friday but I finished my business more quickly than I'd expected—and went to bed as soon as I got back at around midnight. Then the next morning I saw her.'

'Do you mean she came to the door of the big house?'

'Oh no,' he said. 'I'd been out with the dogs early, and I was just on my way back when I saw her coming towards me through the woods. Of course, I didn't recognize her to start with, because I wasn't expecting her and, to be quite honest, I'd forgotten all about the letters by that time, since they'd come weeks ago and I thought she must have given it up.'

He paused and rubbed his chin.

'What happened then?' asked Freddy quietly.

'I'm not entirely sure,' said Gil, and there was a puzzled expression on his face. 'I only wish I could remember the whole thing, but I can't. I do remember her walking towards me slowly. She was carrying her coat and hat—I don't know why—and then she stretched out her arm and sort of gasped my name. That's when I realized who she was. She was blonde, but I could have sworn she'd had black hair when I married her. That's how little I knew her.'

'She was naturally dark, but she had recently dyed her hair,' said Angela.

'Ah,' said Gil. 'That explains it.'

'What did you do then?'

There was a pause, broken only by the shriek of a seagull overhead.

'I killed her,' he whispered at last.

CHAPTER THIRTY

THERE WAS ANOTHER silence.

'How did you do it?' said Angela.

He looked up at her.

'Does it matter?' he said. 'Isn't it enough that I did it?'

'The police will want to know,' said Angela.

'Well, they can ask all they like but they needn't bother, because I can't remember a thing about it.'

'What *do* you remember, then?' asked Freddy, with a glance at Angela.

'I don't know,' he said impatiently. 'I've had spells before where I've sort of blacked out and couldn't tell you what I've been doing. They began after the war. This must have been another one of them. All I remember is coming to myself and seeing her there, lying on the ground at my feet. I looked at my watch and saw that I'd been out for more than three hours and that the dogs must have run off home by themselves. And then I looked at her and it was all terribly clear. I knew I'd done it—knew it was my fault.'

'How could you have known that if you don't remember what you did?' said Freddy.

'Who else could it have been? There she was, dead, and there was no-one else nearby, and I had every reason to kill her. Of course I did it.'

Angela and Freddy exchanged glances again.

'What did you do with her then?'

'I put her coat and hat on her and hid her behind a tree. Then I brought the Wolseley up as close as I could, and put her in the boot. After it was dark I went out and disposed of the body where Angela found it,' he said.

'Alone?' said Freddy.

'Yes,' he said firmly.

'I see,' said Freddy. It was evident that Gil had no idea about Miles's confession. 'And then you went back home and behaved as though nothing had happened?'

'Yes.'

'You didn't—er—tidy up at all?'

'Tidy up? Not that I remember. No,' he went on bitterly, 'I went home and pretended that everything was perfectly all right, and that I hadn't just killed my long-lost wife in cold blood. Then the next day Lucy and I went over to Gipsy's Mile, and we all smiled and laughed and drank sherry as we talked about finding the body of some woman, whom none of us knew or cared about, dumped in a ditch.'

Angela and Freddy gazed at Gil and then at each other. However terrible his crime, it was impossible not to feel some sympathy for him.

'As a matter of fact, you've got here just in time,' Gil went on.

'In time? For what?' said Freddy.

'I don't much like saying goodbye myself, but I understand some people are rather fond of that kind of thing,' said Gil. 'I had intended to slip off without a word, but now I come to think of it, your arrival is quite convenient, really.'

'What do you mean?' said Angela sharply.

'Why, you can be witnesses,' he said. 'That way it's all safe and above-board, don't you know, and no-one can possibly say that instead of clearing things up in the end, I went and confused things even more. I must say, though,' he went on, 'I'm glad it's you two who turned up, and not Lucy or Miles. I should have hated either of them to see it—not, of course, that I'm especially keen to inflict the thing on you either. I don't want to upset anybody, but—well, there you have it.'

'Gil,' said Angela slowly, 'I don't think—'

'How is Mother, by the way?' he said, ignoring Angela. 'I ought to have asked before. Poor thing—she's a tough old bird, but I don't know how her heart will bear the shock of her son's having been unmasked as a murderer.'

'She is very poorly, but is being well cared for by the doctor and Lucy,' said Angela.

He looked relieved.

'Good,' he said. 'I half-thought you were going to tell me she was dead.'

'No,' said Angela, 'she's not dead—but she is very worried about you, naturally.'

'I expect she is,' he said. 'Well, she won't need to worry about me any longer after today.'

'Why not?' said Freddy.

'Why, because I'm going to end it all, of course,' said Gil impatiently. 'I thought I'd made myself quite clear. I want you two as witnesses, just to make sure there's no mistake. Oh, don't worry—I shan't make you watch. I shall merely go into the hut and do the thing while you stand outside. There's nobody else here, so there can be no doubt that I did it myself. I'll even leave a note, if you think it will help. Then you two can toddle off to the police and they'll come and get me, and that will resolve the case nicely and save money on a trial. And Lucy won't have to sit there in court and congratulate herself on having made a lucky escape from a marriage to a coward,' he finished. His face crumpled a little but he recovered himself quickly.

'But—look here,' said Freddy in dismay. 'You can't do that! I refuse to be part of it, d'you hear? And Angela—how can you do it in front of a woman?'

'I told you, I'm not going to do it in front of you. I shall go inside. Angela needn't see anything if she doesn't like it.'

'That's very kind of you,' said Angela dryly, 'but I should far rather you didn't do it at all.'

'Why not? What reason have I to return to Blakeney? The police will arrest me, and then I shall be tried and hanged, and there's not a thing anyone can do about it. At least this way I am sparing those I love from having to watch the whole sorry spectacle.'

'But what about Miles?' said Angela. 'Are you going to leave him to face up to the charges against him alone?'

'What charges?' said Gil.

'I'm afraid Miles has confessed to the police that he helped you get rid of the body,' said Angela.

'What?' exclaimed Gil. 'Are you joking?'

'Of course not,' said Angela. 'This is hardly the moment.'

He stared at her in consternation.

'But why on earth did the silly ass have to do that?' he said. 'I never should have told anyone. He knew that. Has—has he been arrested?'

'Yes,' said Angela, 'The police have released him for now, but I'm rather afraid they want to give him the whole book.'

She paused, to allow Gil to digest this information. Would it make him change his mind?

'Perhaps if you were to put in a good word for him, the judge might be a little more lenient,' hinted Freddy.

'Yes, I really ought to do that for him,' said Gil as though to himself. 'I can't let the poor chap down, after all he's done for me. Very well,' he went on, 'I shall write in my note that he was not to blame in any way, and that I forced him to help me. Will that do, do you think?'

'Oh, no, I don't think that will do at all,' said Angela. 'They will want to speak to you in person.'

Gil regarded them both with suspicion.

'I believe you are talking nonsense, to try and get me to come along quietly,' he said. 'Why, I'll bet you invented the story about Miles confessing.'

'We didn't,' said Freddy. 'It's perfectly true.'

But Gil had made up his mind that they were lying. It looked as though their little ruse had failed.

'Look here,' he said. 'I've had enough of this. Whether you like it or not, I'm going to do it now and you two shall be witnesses. It's the best way, I tell you. Look.' He brought out a revolver from his pocket and showed it to them. 'This will do the job cleanly. One shot straight through the roof of the mouth and it'll be over and done with.'

He raised the pistol to his lips with a shaking hand.

'Don't!' cried Angela.

'Give me one good reason not to,' he said. 'I'm sorry, Angela, but it's all over.'

Freddy was looking about him desperately, and she heard him let out a little breath as his attention was caught by something.

'Ah,' he said. 'Here comes the cavalry at last. Where *has* she been? Look, Gil—your lady love has come to rescue you.'

Angela glanced up and to her astonishment saw, a short distance away, a chestnut horse approaching along the deserted beach at a gallop, with a young woman on its back.

'It's Lucy!' she said.

Gil stared and lowered the revolver as the horse drew closer.

'Gil!' cried Lucy as soon as she could make herself heard. Castana covered the last twenty yards to the hut in a few seconds, and Lucy pulled her up and jumped down. 'Gil!' she said again. 'What are you doing?'

Her eyes were wide and there was real terror in her tone. Angela had never seen her self-possession so thoroughly shattered.

'Why did you come, Lucy?' said Gil, with a break in his voice. 'You oughtn't to have come.' The revolver sat loosely in his hand and they all gazed at it warily.

'Of course I had to come,' said Lucy. She stood a little way away from him. 'I couldn't leave you to face this all alone. Why, we are going to be married soon. A good wife ought to stand by her husband and help him get through things, and that is what I mean to do.'

'But I am not a good husband,' he said in despair. 'Lita found that out to her cost. And we shall never be married now, Lucy, you must have realized that. How could you even begin to think of it, knowing what I have done?'

'Nonsense,' she said briskly. 'I don't believe for a second that you did it, even if you believe it yourself. You're simply not capable.' She moved slowly towards him and knelt on the damp shingle at his feet. Her hair and clothes were wet, and her boots muddy, but despite all that there was a kind of beauty about her at that moment, born of her sense of purpose and her determination to put things right. In all Angela's encounters with the two of them, she had always seen Lucy as the one in charge, but now it was Lucy who was kneeling in an attitude of supplication, begging him not to do what he was threatening to do, but instead to hold his head up high and face the battle with her.

'I believe she really does love him,' thought Angela.

'Gil, darling,' said Lucy, putting a hand on his knee. 'You ought to have told me about Lita.'

'I know that now,' said Gil. 'But I was so anxious to do the right thing and please you and Mother, that I'm afraid it rather slipped to the back of my mind. I'm so desperately sorry, Lucy. We ought never to have got engaged. And what a beastly thing for you to have to face now. It was *my* mistake in marrying Lita that got me into this awful mess in the first place, and now the poor girl is dead and her son has been left an orphan—'

'*Your* son, Gil,' said Lucy gently. 'He's yours too, you know.'

'How can I claim him?' he said. 'What son would want anything to do with the man who killed his mother?'

'Stop saying that!' cried Lucy. 'You didn't kill her, and I shall prove it.'

'How?' said Gil. 'How, Lucy? It's impossible. Even I know in my heart that I did it, although I can't remember it. I *must* have done it.'

'Come back to Blakeney with me, Gil,' she said. 'We shall find a way through this—I know we shall. But there's no use in trying to solve things here, in this God-forsaken place. Look at you—you're filthy, and you haven't eaten for days, and probably haven't slept either. How can anyone think properly in those circumstances? Come back with me, and I'll take care of you and make sure that nobody harms you. I promise you I'll do it,' she went on softly.

'But they'll arrest me,' he said.

'Yes, they will,' she replied, 'and you shall just have to bear it. But I won't let them arrest you before you've had something to eat, and a bath, and a good night's sleep. After that, we'll go to the police together and you'll have to face up to it. But I swear I won't let you hang. You do trust me, Gil, don't you?' she said.

He looked at her, a broken man, and swallowed. Then he nodded.

'Yes,' he said. 'I trust you.'

'Never forget that we belong to each other, and it is my job to protect you and look after you,' she said. 'Just as it is your job to look after me.'

'I'm not making much of a fist of it at the moment, am I?' he said.

'I'm happy to have found you at last, and that is all that matters at present,' she said. She reached out and took the revolver from his unresisting hand, then gave it to Freddy. 'Now,' she went on, 'there's no room in Freddy's car so you must come back with me on Castana. I shall take you home to Blakeney and then tomorrow we will go into Littlechurch together.'

She held out her hand, and he took it and got to his feet.

'I'd offer to take the horse and give you my car, but I'm afraid we're not exactly dressed for riding,' said Freddy.

Lucy smiled.

'Don't worry,' she said. 'We shall be back in no time.'

'Might I suggest that you go and see Lady Alice as soon as you return?' said Angela. 'I fear she thinks that you are plotting to keep her son away from her, and she made me promise to let her know when Gil was found.'

'Of course,' said Lucy serenely. She had won the battle with Lady Alice, and she knew it and was prepared to be generous.

Gil mounted the chestnut mare with some difficulty, since he was weak from lack of food. Lucy climbed up in front of him.

'Thank you,' she said to Angela and Freddy. 'I shan't forget this.'

She nudged Castana and they set off slowly along the beach.

'How did she know to come here?' said Angela.

'I telephoned her just before we set off,' said Freddy. 'I—er—thought she might be able to do something with him. It appears I was right.'

'Yes,' said Angela thoughtfully. 'I'm glad she gave you the gun, though.'

'Why, do you think he might have got it back off her and done something stupid?'

'Not exactly. I was thinking more on the lines of her putting him out of his misery, as she might a sick horse,' she replied. Freddy gazed at her in astonishment, and she went on hurriedly, 'I know, it's a ridiculous idea. Why on earth should she have persuaded him not to kill himself in that case?'

'Well, quite.'

'All the same,' said Angela. 'I'm glad we have the gun and not them.'

They watched as the horse with its two riders disappeared into the mist, then Freddy shivered.

'I'm drenched, and it's starting to get dark,' he said. 'Let's go home and have some hot chocolate.'

CHAPTER THIRTY-ONE

'WHY, DARLINGS, WHEREVER have you been?' exclaimed Marguerite when they returned, cold and damp. 'You look freezing. Go and change, and then you can come and warm yourselves by the fire and I shall get you hot drinks.'

Shortly afterwards, dry and warm and fortified with hot chocolate, Angela and Freddy recounted the events of that afternoon, much to the astonishment of Miles and Marguerite.

'Do you mean he was at the old cottage all the time?' said Miles. 'Why, that's where we used to go years ago when Herbert and I used to visit Gil at the Park. It never occurred to me that he might be there.' Freddy looked disbelieving, but said nothing, and Miles said, 'It's true, Freddy—I swear it. Perhaps I ought to have known, but it never crossed my mind.'

'What will happen now?' said Marguerite fearfully.

'Lucy has promised to take him in tomorrow, after he's had a square meal and a good night's sleep,' said Freddy.

'But do you think she will? Mightn't she spirit him away somewhere else?'

'Where could she take him, without getting herself into trouble too? No,' said Freddy, 'I think she'll do it all right. You didn't see him, Marguerite. He looked in a bad way, and anyone with a heart would have done the same—taken him home and fed him up, I mean. I'm sure she'll do as she promised, though.'

'I almost wish you hadn't found him,' said Miles soberly. 'Perhaps it would have been better had he been allowed to do what he wanted to do without interference. It might have been easier for everybody.'

'That's what Gil said,' said Angela, 'but Lucy wouldn't hear of it.'

'But now there will have to be a trial, and he's bound to be found guilty,' said Miles. 'Perhaps he may be able to plead temporary insanity and avoid the hangman, but he will still have to spend many years in prison. No,' he went on, 'the more I think about it, the more I see that it would have been better for everybody had he ended it all today.'

'I am not sure I agree with you,' said Angela. 'First of all, you must remember that you yourself have a charge laid against you, which must be dealt with. Perhaps things will go easier for you if Gil is there to explain himself in person. I don't suppose you particularly *want* to go to prison for ten years, do you? You wouldn't have done what you did had Gil not asked you to, so it seems only reasonable that he should be there to help you get out of the scrape if he can. I'm sure he never intended to get you into trouble.'

'I suppose not,' conceded Miles.

'And quite apart from that,' said Angela, 'Lucy seems to think she can get him off the murder charge. I've seen enough of her to know that if anybody can arrange that, then she can.'

'Get him off?' said Miles, staring. 'How in heaven's name is she going to do that?'

'She says she knows he didn't do it,' said Angela. 'Perhaps that is true.'

'But you forget, Angela, I was there that day. I helped him hide Lita's body. Why, he's even confessed to the thing. Of course he did it.'

'Oh yes, he certainly *believes* he did it,' said Angela. 'There's no doubt about that.'

Miles looked at her oddly.

'I believe there's something you're not telling us,' he said. 'Do you know something?'

'I just have great faith in Lucy, that's all,' said Angela. 'I think that if she is determined to do something, then it shall be done. And she has promised to get Gil off.'

Miles shook his head.

'I am going to telephone the Park,' he said.

'Do,' said Freddy. 'And make sure you speak to Gil in person if Lucy will let you. We—er—had some doubts as to whether he would reach home safely. He wasn't well, and they were doubled up on a horse, which can be slow going,' he said in explanation to Miles's inquiring look.

Miles went out and returned a few minutes later to say that he had managed to snatch a few moments' conversation with Gil, and that he sounded very tired and confused.

'They are going to the police station in Littlechurch tomorrow morning,' he said. 'I offered to go along with him but he wouldn't hear of it. He said he was sorry that I'd got into trouble, and that he'd do his best to clear me as far as possible. Poor chap—how I wish none of this had ever happened.'

Angela could not help but agree with him.

The next day, they received word that Gil had, true to his promise, handed himself in to the police in Littlechurch, who had arrested him on suspicion of the murder of Lily Markham, also known as Lita de Marquez. Lucy had said goodbye to him and then gone back to Blakeney to see to Lady Alice and to summon the family's London solicitor, who had already started to prepare a defence.

They heard nothing more until Monday, when Angela happened to run into Inspector Jameson in Littlechurch. He was peering through the window of an antique shop, apparently admiring a pair of decorative silver-handled duelling pistols that were on display there.

'Good morning, inspector,' she said. 'Do your superiors at the Yard expect you to buy your own weapons these days? I'm not sure those will be much use to you.'

He laughed.

'No,' he replied, 'but they are rather splendid, don't you think? I was just wondering whether to buy them and put them on my wall at home, but I see the shop is shut at present.'

'So it is. You shall have to come back later,' said Angela. She prepared to pass on. 'Anyway, I won't stop you, as I'm sure you're very busy at present.'

'As a matter of fact, I had just come out for a little fresh air,' he said. 'Suppose we walk for a few minutes. I should like to stretch my legs—and, furthermore, I still haven't thanked you for finding Gilbert Blakeney for us.'

'Oh, don't thank me,' said Angela. 'I had very little to do with it. It's Freddy you ought to thank for finding him, and it was Lucy who persuaded him to give himself up. I just stood there and nodded in the right places.'

'I see,' said the inspector. 'Young Freddy was mixed up in it, was he? I can't say I'm surprised.'

'Is Gil all right?' she said anxiously. 'He was in rather a bad way when we found him.'

'Don't worry,' said Jameson. 'We have been very gentle with him—for practical reasons more than anything else, since we'd never get anything out of him if we were too hard, given the state of him.'

'Have you actually charged him with the murder?'

He nodded.

'Yes. He has a solicitor with him now—some young whizz from London, who will no doubt find all kinds of reasons why we ought to let him off with a hand-shake and a pat on the back, and then send him on his way with a rousing chorus of "For he's a jolly good fellow".'

Angela laughed.

'I imagine Lucy was responsible for that,' she said. 'She is rather a remarkable young woman.'

'Yes,' he agreed. 'She certainly seems to have great strength of character.'

Angela looked down.

'She believes he is innocent, you know,' she said.

'Of course she does,' said Jameson. 'I should think the less of her if she didn't.'

She stopped, and looked him directly in the eye.

'What do you believe?' she said.

He returned her gaze steadily.

'It's not my job to believe anything,' he said. 'It's my job to deal with the evidence we have—and the evidence we have says he is guilty. We certainly have enough of it to proceed with a trial, at any rate.'

'I understand,' said Angela.

He regarded her suspiciously.

'What are you plotting?' he said. 'I know that wicked look of yours.'

'Do I have a wicked look?' she said in surprise.

'Only when you have something up your sleeve.'

'Good gracious! I had no idea of it. But to answer your rather ungenerous question,' she went on, 'I am not plotting anything.'

'Then what do you know?' he said. 'Come on, out with it.'

'I don't know anything. As a matter of fact, I prefer to deal with solid evidence too,' she said. 'Let us just say I have the feeling that something is going to happen soon.'

'Such as what?'

'I don't know exactly. But whatever it is, we won't have to wait long.'

'Why not?' said Jameson.

'Why, because Gil is in prison, of course,' said Angela.

CHAPTER THIRTY-TWO

SOMETHING DID INDEED happen soon, although it was not exactly what Angela had foreseen, for the very next day Lady Alice Blakeney died. She drew her last breath on Tuesday evening, with Gil by her side—since Lucy had sent an urgent summons to Littlechurch police station to say that the old lady was not expected to last until morning, and he had therefore been granted special permission to visit her bedside. Two burly policemen accompanied him, and stood in stolid embarrassment at the side of the room as Gil wept over his mother's body and kissed her hand. After a decent interval, they coughed and took him away again.

'At least she won't have the pain of seeing her poor son put on trial,' said Marguerite, when she heard the news after breakfast on Wednesday. 'Now there's just Lucy left to take care of him. Why, Angela, darling, what's wrong? You look worried.'

Angela hesitated.

'It's nothing,' she said. 'Lady Alice's death caught me by surprise, that's all. I had thought perhaps—' she stopped.

'What?'

'I don't know,' murmured Angela. 'I'm just a little concerned about Gil.'

She stood up and went out of the room to begin packing her things. She was planning to return to London that day, since Miles was home now and Marguerite did not need her any longer. In the hall she ran into Miles himself.

'Letter for you, Angela,' he said. He handed her an envelope and went off, frowning absently over his own post.

'A letter? For me?' said Angela in surprise. She looked at the envelope. It was made of thick, creamy paper and was closed with a rather ornate seal bearing the initial B. Her heart began to beat rapidly. Devoured with curiosity, she went into the empty parlour, sat down and ripped it open. The letter was written in a faint, shaky hand which was difficult to decipher, but as far as Angela could make out, it read as follows:

> *Blakeney Park*
> *Friday, 28th October*

Dear Mrs. Marchmont,

You will no doubt wonder why I am writing to you, given that we have met only once or twice and can hardly be said to be close acquaintances. Indeed, I am not entirely sure of the answer myself. I can only say that, having met you, I believe that you are the most suitable person to entrust with this con-fidence—not, you understand, because I feel any particular sympathy between us, but because from objective observation, you strike me as reasonably sensible and trustworthy—two qualities which are, unfortunately, not often found together in a wom-an. Lucy, for example, while being eminently prac-tical and intelligent, I consider to be underhanded and duplicitous (as you know), while Mrs. Harri-son, whom I believe to be a most honest and truthful woman, can hardly be described as wholly rational by any right-thinking person. In addition, I under-stand that you are well thought of at Scotland Yard, having helped them solve a number of difficult cases in recent times. I have no doubt, therefore, that you will know how to act when you receive this. I do not send it to the police directly, since they are men and I do not expect them to understand my motive in doing what I have done. As a woman you, perhaps, will be able to explain it to them.

Very well, then, since circumstances appear to have forced me to explain myself, I shall begin. You know, of course, that Gilbert is my only son, and that, following the death of his father some years ago he inherited the Blakeney estate in its entirety. In addition, you cannot have failed to observe that Gil-bert, while a decent and honourable man in many respects, is not gifted by nature with an abundance of intellectual capacity. Delightful though he is (and please believe that as his mother, I am exceedingly fond of him), he is undoubtedly somewhat weak in the head. As such, he was admirably suited to a life in the army, which he embraced with great enthusiasm when given the opportunity, but much less so to the responsibility of running a great estate such as Blakeney Park. I had seen and understood this when he was quite a child, and so I always intended that when he grew up, he should marry a woman who would be capable of compensating for his mental failings with a first-rate brain of her own, since the future of the estate was at stake.

I knew Lucy Syms from a girl, and suspected that she might have the qualities I required, so I watched her progress closely as she grew up, and she did not disappoint me in that respect, since she grew up to be a most capable young woman. I disliked her personally, but never saw anyone else who seemed to possess the particular abilities that were necessary, and so I swallowed my antipathy and encouraged the friendship between her and my son as far as possible. Fortunately, they had known each other since childhood—although she is a few years younger than he—so there was no awkwardness between them to overcome, and I had no doubt that they would do as I wished and marry once she was old enough, since Lucy could hardly object to a man of his position and wealth.

Then the war came, and Gilbert went off to fight. I feared that in the meantime Lucy might be tempted by one of the other young men who passed through the area, but I need not have worried: she knew what she wanted and was prepared to wait for it. Sure enough, when Gilbert returned, they became reacquainted—but much to my annoyance, it seemed only a friendly feeling on Gilbert's part. The situation was not helped by the fact that my son had a series of nervous episodes in the first few years after his return, but eventually he seemed to recover, and he and Lucy began to grow closer.

Eventually, after some prompting on my part, he acceded to my wishes and asked Lucy to marry him. (Please do not suppose, by the way, that I forced him into an engagement against his inclination: I knew he was very fond of her and that they would be happy together, but suspected that without a little encouragement nothing would ever come of it.) All that was left for me to do then was to swallow my dislike of Lucy and wish them well, although that proved a little more difficult than I expected, given that I was forced to spend more time in company with her than I liked. Nonetheless, I regarded the arrangement with satisfaction and firmly believed that the Blakeney estate was now in safe hands.

You will, therefore, readily comprehend my shock and dismay when I received a letter last August from a woman calling herself Lily Blakeney, who claimed *to be Gilbert's wife. She hoped I would forgive the intrusion, but she had no choice, she said, since she had written to Gilbert twice without receiving a reply, and so, as the matter was an urgent one, she was taking the liberty of writing to me instead. She explained the circumstances of the marriage, and said that they had parted shortly afterwards. A month or two later, she had discovered herself to be in a delicate condition and had tried to find him, but without success, and in some way or other had got the impression that he had died. She therefore returned to her family to bring up her son alone, and had done so until July of this year, when she happened to read the announcement of Gilbert's engagement in the* Times *and discovered to her surprise that her husband was still alive. At first, she did not believe that Gilbert was deliberately contemplating bigamy; rather, she supposed that he had thought her dead too and therefore considered himself free to marry again. However, after having written to him twice without receiving a reply, she was now wondering whether it might not be a deliberate act, since it was hardly likely that both the letters she sent to Blakeney Park had gone astray, and if Gilbert had read them there was no excuse at all for ignoring them.*

The letter finished by requesting that I take steps to prevent the marriage from going ahead, at least until arrangements could be made for the first marriage to be legally dissolved—she had no idea how this might be done, although of course an annulment was out of the question since the marriage had resulted in legitimate issue with the birth of her son. She had no claims to make in regard to herself, she said, but she was anxious to secure her son's future and see to it that he was admitted to the family as the rightful heir of Blakeney Park. Of course, she did not expect me to believe her story without evidence, and if I—or better still, Gilbert—would only agree to meet her, she would furnish us with copies of her marriage certificate and her son's birth certificate, which would attest that the date of his birth tallied with the date of the marriage, and that everything was perfectly in order.

This letter, as you will imagine, caused me no little consternation and alarm for a day or two. My first reaction, on reading it, was immediately to reject its contents as untrue and to throw the thing in the fire. I cannot say that it surprised me to discover that Gilbert had entangled himself with a woman of low reputation who was now attempting to make some money out of the association—as I have said, he is not the brightest of men and is rather easily taken advantage of—but that they were legally wed I had no doubt was a lie. However, she claimed to have a son, and seemed to think that he would fall heir to the Blakeney estate one day. This was something that could not be easily dismissed: a son, whether legitimate or not, presents a solid obstacle that a money-grabbing chorus-girl does not. This woman might put forward a legal claim and make things very awkward for us if she chose, and with such a cause hanging over our heads the wedding would be spoilt, which would be an inauspicious beginning to the marriage that I had been desiring for so many years.

I hesitated as I considered how to act, and after pondering the matter for some time I wrote back to the girl as politely as I could. I made no secret of the fact that I had been surprised by her letter, since I had known nothing of the marriage, and that I had no idea why my son should have kept such a thing from me, or why he had not replied to her letters: perhaps they had gone astray. Moreover, I agreed that Gilbert must have believed her to be dead, and that the situation was indeed rather awkward in view of his current engagement to another woman. Given the circumstances, however, and since there was much to be decided upon, I had no hesitation in inviting her to Blakeney Park to talk about the matter in person, and to consider together how to proceed if she and Gilbert wished to dissolve the marriage. I said that I was sure she would not object to bringing with her the certificates in question, since it was as well to be certain that all was in order. As a precaution, I also asked that she bring with her my letter, as I had no wish for it to fall into the wrong hands and perhaps cause a scandal: natural-

ly, it would be better for all concerned if the matter could be resolved privately without becoming public knowledge. If everything proved to be as she said it was, then she was very welcome to stay at Blakeney for a week or two while the affair was settled.

She wrote back, expressing her relief that I had taken the news so kindly, and said that she was sure something could be arranged without any publicity. She said that if it were not inconvenient to me, she would come down to Hastings on the 7th of September, but would stay only one night: she was anxious to return home and tell her son the news about his change of circumstances, since he presently knew very little about his father. Perhaps afterwards she would come to Blakeney again, and this time bring the boy. Until then, however, she would say nothing to anyone.

This suited me perfectly since, as you will no doubt have guessed by now, I had plans of my own. First, I had to ensure that Gilbert would not be there when Lily arrived, and so I arranged to send him away on business for a few days. He went off obediently, leaving the way clear for me to act. On the afternoon of the 7th of September I sent our chauffeur, who is fortunately a taciturn fellow with little interest in the goings-on of his betters, to meet the girl at Hastings and bring her back to Blakeney. She arrived, and finally I saw her in person and could judge her for myself. I had not believed in her sin-

cerity for a second when I read her letter: I assumed that her story of wronged innocence and anxiety to resolve the matter discreetly was a lie, and that in reality she was out for anything she could get. When I met her, of course I knew immediately that I was right. She was even more common than I had supposed, and there was a shrewd, calculating air about her that spoke of her real intentions. She was not interested in her son's claims: what she wanted was money.

I hid my feelings, naturally, and met her with reserved politeness, since too effusive a greeting would have looked suspicious, and she could hardly expect me to be overjoyed at her existence. We sat down to tea, and she immediately handed me some documents which, she said, ought to allay any uncertainty I might have had as to the legitimacy of her claims. One of them was a marriage certificate, which immediately proved beyond all doubt that she had been telling the truth in that respect, at least. The other was her son's birth certificate, which appeared to show the correct date, given the short time she and my son had spent together—although, of course, with that type of person nothing can be taken for granted. Still, her claim was a strong one, as was that of her son.

I confess my heart sank at that moment, at the thought of the task which lay before me. Had she been telling lies I might have sent her about her business and given no further thought to the matter, but this could not so easily be got over. I should wish you to understand, Mrs. Marchmont, that I am not an evil woman, and that I feel the same distaste for wickedness as anyone might be supposed to do. Nonetheless, I felt myself forced to act given what was at stake. If I failed to do so, then Blakeney Park would eventually pass into the hands of this boy, a usurper, and there would be nothing we could do about it—even supposing Gilbert and Lucy produced a son of their own, as I had long hoped.

And so I acted. I invited her to stay to dinner, and said that she was most welcome to stay the night, as I had already mentioned—although, for the purposes of discretion I had arranged for comfortable accommodation to be prepared for her in a cottage in the grounds. She quite understood, she said, and was perfectly happy to do as I thought best.

We ate in my private apartment, rather than in the dining-room, and maintained all appearances of being on polite and friendly terms. I must say that she kept it up very well, and never for a second gave the slightest hint that she was anything other than a devoted mother who wished only the best for her son. I knew better, of course, and it only strengthened my determination to resolve the problem as soon as possible.

I had, before her arrival, provided myself with a small amount of arsenic from the stores we keep around the place as a matter of course, taking care that nobody should notice that any of it had gone missing. Our first course was soup, and I was tempted to put the arsenic in that, but I resisted since I did not want her to be taken ill before I had had the chance to get her out of the house. She therefore enjoyed her dinner in unadulterated form, and I waited for my opportunity. At last, she asked if she might be shown to her accommodation as she was rather tired. I acquiesced, but urged her to take a cup of hot chocolate with me before she went, and she agreed. The chocolate arrived and I put the arsenic into it under the pretence of adding some sugar. Nothing could have been easier. She drank it greedily, and then I escorted her myself out of the house and to the cottage—since it was a fine night, and I should like a little fresh air, I said. I then went to bed, with the intention of returning the next day. I knew nobody would pass near the place, and was certain that everything had gone according to plan, and so I slept well, confident that I had resolved the matter to everyone's satisfaction.

Of course, I was wrong. The next morning I returned to the cottage, expecting to find a dead body to be disposed of. Instead, I discovered to my great consternation that Lily was no longer there, although the arsenic had evidently taken effect, to judge by the state of the room. I am not often moved to fright, Mrs. Marchmont, but you will no doubt

appreciate the agitation of my mind on this particular occasion. For a few minutes, indeed, I had no
idea how to act. I soon gathered my faculties, however, and set out to look for her. I assumed that in the
throes of her illness she had attempted to fetch help,
and thought it likely that I should find her collapsed
in the grounds somewhere. I searched for some time
but could find no trace of her, and eventually decided that I had better return to the house, lest my un-
characteristic activity draw notice and suspicion.

That was the Thursday morning. At that time, I
had no idea that Gilbert had returned unexpected-
ly the night before and was even then weeping over
the girl's body, believing, in his muddle-headed way,
that he had killed her himself. I went inside and sat
in dreadful apprehension, waiting for the inevitable moment when a servant would come and tell me
that the body of a woman had been found in the
Park—or, worse still, that she had been found alive
and had somehow been able to accuse me. The moment never came, however, and I began to breathe
more easily. I even began to hope that she had escaped Blakeney altogether and had died elsewhere.
Later that evening, Gilbert came in and said only
that he was back early as he had finished his business sooner than he expected. I assumed he had just
returned at that moment, and was relieved that he
had not been there to witness the incident. As a mat-

ter of fact, of course, he had returned the day before
without telling me and had been the one to find her.

You know the rest. On the Friday you rather in-
conveniently stumbled upon the body that my son
and Miles Harrison had so thoughtfully hidden,
and set in train the series of events which led to Gilbert's being arrested for the murder of his wife. I do
not blame you for this, naturally. You were only doing your duty, and under any other circumstances I
should applaud it. In this instance, however—well,
there is nothing to be said. What is done is done,
and it is useless to wish things otherwise.

Now to business. I saw, when you came to visit
me the other day, that you suspected the truth about
what had happened. You also had the good sense not
to say anything—realizing, I suppose, that I should
never dream of allowing my son to be hanged for
murder in my stead and that a full confession on my
part would be a more efficient way of going about
things. I do not wish to go to the gallows either, of
course, but in my case the matter is more easily resolved, since I am already weak and have to hand a
bottle of medicine which can easily be taken in over-
dose if necessary—although a cold feeling has begun
to creep through my body lately which tells me that
it will probably not be needed. If the police require
proof, they will find it in the closet nearest to my
bed, where I have hidden the remains of the arse-

nic, together with the little bag in which Lily carried her night-things and personal effects. It is of leather, and ought to be easy to test for finger-prints, which will show that my son never touched it. I should like to state quite clearly that he had nothing whatsoever to do with Lily's death—indeed, I imagine it will come as quite a shock to him to discover that his own mother is a murderer. I understand he is likely to be prosecuted for tampering with the body, but that cannot be helped. I am sure that Lucy will arrange an admirable defence for him, and that any sentence will be a light one.

I told you, Mrs. Marchmont, that I was prepared to remove myself from Blakeney Park in order to secure its future and that of my son, and now you will see that I spoke only the truth. I have instructed my maid to send this letter to you after my death, and am placing the utmost faith in you to do what is right and ensure that Gilbert is released as soon as possible. There will, no doubt, be many legal matters to settle—not least the question of what is to become of the boy who, it now appears, is the legitimate heir to the estate. Since the problem is unlikely to be got over, perhaps the best thing will be for Gilbert and Lucy to take him in after they are married, since I understand he is presently very poor and neglected. He will certainly need to be educated in the ways of Blakeney before he can be trusted to run the place. However, that will be for them to decide.

It has taken me several days to write this letter, and I feel myself growing weak now, so I shall finish here. I am leaving this whole business in your hands, Mrs. Marchmont: since you were, in a manner of speaking, the person who began the thing, I think it only fair that you be the one to end it. If you feel inclined to judge me harshly, please remember that throughout all this my only thought has been to protect the Blakeney estate and to ensure the happiness and comfort of my son. Can any mother truly say that they would not do the same?

I trust that everything has now been explained to your satisfaction and that of the police, and remain,

Yours sincerely,

A. Blakeney

CHAPTER THIRTY-THREE

'THEN YOU NEVER believed that Gil did it?' said Freddy Pilkington-Soames, as he prodded at an oyster with his fork and then regarded it, frowning.

'I wouldn't say that, exactly,' said Angela, 'but the fact of the arsenic did rather point in another direction, since it required a certain amount of planning. I could easily imagine that Gil might have strangled Lita or hit her over the head in a moment of panic, but the poison didn't seem to fit his character at all. Once he was arrested, though, I had the feeling that the real murderer would confess.'

Freddy decided he did not like the look of the first oyster and picked up another one.

'Did you find the evidence, as she said?' he asked Inspector Jameson. 'You can tell us, can't you, now that the whole thing is over and done with? Old Bickerstaffe has been simply dying for me to get the low-down from you, but you've been as silent as the grave. Surely, now that Gilbert has been sent on his way with a rap over the knuckles, you can speak up and tell all? Do have pity, inspector—my reputation as the new boy wonder of Fleet Street is at stake, especially since the—er—little disagreement at Marguerite's exhibition.'

'I suppose there's no harm in telling you now,' said Jameson. 'Yes, we found Lita's bag in the cupboard as she said, together with Lady Alice's letter to her. She had brought it with her, as instructed. We also found Lita's letters to Lady Alice hidden away in a writing-desk, which confirm the whole thing.'

'Then there is no suggestion that Gil had anything at all to do with it?'

'None that we can find. He appears to have been caught up in it completely unwittingly—although, of course, that's no excuse for what he did. The Littlechurch police are still planning to prosecute him and Mr. Harrison for preventing the lawful and decent burial of a body.'

'It was very foolish of him,' said Angela, 'but it's difficult not to feel some sympathy towards him. He must have suffered torments, believing that he had killed Lita.'

'It serves him right for ignoring her letters,' said Freddy severely. 'That's a rotter's trick. He married the woman and she was his responsibility. He ought to have faced up to it like a man. You're too soft-hearted, Angela. By the way, how did Gil take the news of his mother's crime, inspector? It must have hit him pretty hard.'

'I'm not sure he quite took it in,' said Jameson. 'Not after everything else that had happened. The whole experience has completely shaken him up. Lucy is looking after him now, though, and I've no doubt is doing it with admirable competence.'

'Oh, by the way,' said Angela, 'did you know that they've decided to bring the wedding forward? It's to be at Christmas now.'

'No,' said Jameson. 'I can't say I'm surprised, though. Now that Lady Alice has gone, young Blakeney has no doubt decided that he needs Lucy to take care of him and the estate.'

'Rot,' said Freddy. 'I'll bet it's all Lucy's doing. She wants to pin him down and make it all legal before he runs off and marries another chorus-girl then forgets about it.'

'I imagine she'll be keeping a close eye on him from now on,' agreed the inspector. 'She's an odd one, Lucy Syms. I don't mind confessing that I find her a puzzle in many ways.'

'Do you think she was shocked to discover that the whole thing was Lady Alice's doing?' said Freddy.

'I imagine so,' said Jameson.

Angela said nothing. She had her own ideas about exactly how much Lucy had known of the plan to kill Lita de Marquez, but there was no proof and it seemed useless to bring it all up again. Lady Alice had taken all the blame upon herself and the affair was considered closed. Nonetheless, Angela could not help but remember the first time she had seen Lucy, sitting there on Castana by the side of the road on that misty afternoon. What was she doing out in the fog? Had she perhaps been looking for something—or someone? Lita had gone missing from the cottage in the Park and it was a matter of urgency to find out what had happened to her. Despite their mutual dislike, had Lady Alice taken Lucy into her confidence, knowing that Lucy would do anything to save Gil and the estate? Angela supposed they would never know.

'I see the Copernicus Club has reopened,' said Freddy. 'I don't expect Johnny Chang is feeling particularly well-disposed towards you chaps—although I suppose he ought to be relieved that you didn't hang him.'

'Yes,' said Jameson. 'As a matter of fact, I was thinking of having a quiet word with the powers that be at the licensing office about issuing a later licence for the club.'

'I shouldn't if I were you,' said Freddy. 'If you do that, then the place will lose all its cachet. Why, the only reason most people go is for the thrill of being raided by the police. Mrs. Chang and young Johnny know that very well, and I'm pretty sure they wouldn't thank you.'

'But Mrs. Chang is in prison. She can't possibly have planned that.'

'It's a hazard of the job, I assure you,' said Freddy.

'How odd,' said Inspector Jameson, as though the idea had never struck him before.

'Oh yes,' said Freddy. 'You wouldn't want the place to become unfashionable and go out of business, would you? Not now that all the staff have got their jobs back.'

'I suppose not,' said the inspector.

'Well, then, there you have it,' said Freddy. 'I say, why don't you go there one night yourself? It's rather good fun. They have an awfully good orchestra. You could take Angela—you're more her age than I am.'

'Thank you,' said Angela dryly.

'I shall—er—think about it,' said Jameson, 'although I'm not *entirely* sure the superintendent would approve.'

Freddy looked at his watch.

'I'd better go,' he said. 'Mr. Rowbotham is speaking in Brixton this afternoon, and I have it on good authority that trouble is expected from a group known as the Young Bolshevists. They are planning to let off fireworks and smoke-bombs, apparently. I should hate to miss that.'

'Freddy,' said Angela suspiciously, and he had the grace to blush.

'It's nothing to do with me, I promise,' he said hurriedly. 'As a matter of fact, it was all thought up by my friend St. John, who seems to have become rather—er—militant lately. I don't suppose the Labour Party will select him as a candidate after this. Still, it ought to be worth seeing, don't you think?'

He saluted them and sauntered off.

'Will there really be fireworks and smoke-bombs?' said Jameson in some concern.

'One never knows with Freddy,' she replied, 'but I shouldn't be a bit surprised.'

It was late in November when Angela returned to Littlechurch. Vassily had been released from prison and Marguerite was making a second attempt to stage her exhibition, this time without interference. When Angela arrived at the crowded church hall a little later than she had planned, she found the young Russian striking a dramatic attitude next to his work and holding forth to Mrs. Henderson, the vicar's wife, on the state of modern art and the exceptional talents of his hostess. He was in no way chastened by his spell in gaol, which he dismissed as a mere inconvenience; he was much more upset at the destruction of his statue by that criminal Freddy, or Teddy, or whatever his name was. It was a good thing, he said darkly, that the young man had not dared to show himself this time: otherwise he, Vassily, might have been forced to act.

'Fortunately, I have been able to mend statue,' he said, indicating the last in the *Eternity of the Damned* series, which to Angela's eye looked as good as new, 'and for that, I shall not kill him. But he had better keep away in future.'

He waved expressively, and Angela started slightly as she noticed on his wrist something that she recognized immediately.

'I rather like your watch,' she said. He glanced at it complacently.

'Thank you,' he said. 'It is present from Mrs. Harrison. She is very kind lady. I owe to her everything.'

He blew an extravagant kiss towards Marguerite, who preened a little. Angela suppressed a laugh.

'I'm *so* glad you decided to come, darling,' said Marguerite to Angela. 'Cynthia tried to invite herself, you know, but I still haven't forgiven her for that horrid piece she wrote after the last exhibition, so I said she couldn't come. She was terribly contrite, so I suppose I shall forgive her eventually, but I couldn't bear the thought of something going wrong again and her giving me that malicious look, as she did last time, then running off to twist the knife in her silly society column.'

'Where is Miles?' said Angela, looking about her.

'At home,' said Marguerite. 'You shall see him later—you are staying with us tonight, aren't you? Of course you are.'

'How is he?'

'Better, I think,' said Marguerite. 'This whole thing with Gil's chorus-girl has hit him rather hard, although at least there's no danger of him being put in prison now—Sergeant Spillett seems to think that he and Gil will be let off with a fine.'

'Oh, good,' said Angela.

'Yes, it's *such* a relief, darling. I don't know what on earth I should have done without him. He is my rock, you know—simply my rock.'

She fluttered off, and Angela shortly afterwards saw her flirting openly with Vassily. She shook her head with a smile.

'Hallo, Angela,' said a familiar voice. It was Lucy Syms. She appeared to be alone.

'Lucy!' said Angela. 'Where is Gil?'

'At home,' she replied. 'He didn't feel quite up to coming this evening, but I thought I ought to make the effort myself.'

'How is he?'

'Oh, very much better,' said Lucy, 'but he didn't want to steal Marguerite's thunder by making an appearance. He is still rather the talk of the place, you see.'

'I imagine he is,' said Angela. 'And how are you? I hear you are getting married very soon.'

'Yes,' said Lucy with a little blush. 'We thought it best, after all that has happened. The sooner we can return to normal life the better, I think.'

'I think you are quite right,' said Angela. 'The whole affair has been very unfortunate. Poor Gil—first of all he is arrested for murder, and then finds out that his mother was behind it! It must have been a blow.'

'Yes, it was. It came as a complete shock to both of us, in fact.'

Angela looked directly at Lucy, whose face was as bland and impassive as ever.

'I see,' she said. 'I had thought perhaps—'

'Yes?' said Lucy.

'Lady Alice was an old woman,' said Angela carefully, 'and it had occurred to me to wonder how exactly she was planning to get rid of Lita's body. She could hardly lift it by herself, could she?'

'I suppose not,' said Lucy.

'She would have needed help from someone, don't you think?'

'Perhaps,' said Lucy. 'Or perhaps she hadn't taken it into account. After all, Lita disappeared, and fortunately for Lady Alice she never had to dispose of the body in the end, did she?'

She returned Angela's gaze steadily.

'Do you think she cleaned the cottage herself?' said Angela.

'Why, she must have, I suppose,' said Lucy.

'And yet I can't see her doing it, somehow.'

'No, but you must remember she was desperate,' said Lucy. She went on briskly, 'At any rate, the case has been closed now to everybody's satisfaction, and even if she did have someone to help her—'

'A servant, perhaps?' said Angela, still holding Lucy's gaze.

'Perhaps,' said Lucy. 'Even if she did have an accomplice, whoever it was, there's no proof. And what use would there be in dragging it all up again?'

'None at all,' said Angela, 'were it not for the little boy who is now heir to Blakeney Park. I understand he is to visit you.'

'Yes, he is. His uncle was very reluctant at first, after all that happened, but Gil is anxious to acknowledge his son and provide for him. What of it?' She was defiant now.

'Oh, nothing. I just thought that there might be some members of the Blakeney household—' Angela paused delicately.

'Servants, perhaps?'

'—servants, perhaps—who are very loyal to the family and would consider him an obstacle. After all, he is in line to inherit the estate, and any children of your marriage are bound to be disadvantaged.'

Lucy shook her head.

'Nobody considers him an obstacle,' she said firmly. 'Bertie is Gil's son, and as such will be welcomed by everyone—including myself. I very much look forward to meeting him.'

'I am glad to hear it,' said Angela, smiling. 'With you as his mother I need not worry that he will come to any harm.' She paused, and went on with emphasis, 'I shall be watching his progress with interest.'

'I don't doubt it,' said Lucy. Angela was satisfied that they understood each other, and excused herself. How much of the plan had been Lucy's they should never know, but Angela strongly suspected that she had persuaded—or challenged—Lady Alice to confess to the whole thing after Gil disappeared. After all, Lady Alice herself had promised not to stand in the way of the marriage. Had Lucy held her to that promise by forcing her to take all the blame onto herself? Angela shivered slightly. She was certain that Blakeney Park was in safe hands with Lucy, but pitied anyone who decided to cross her. Lucy Syms was a remarkable girl.

'Well, William,' said Angela the next morning as they drove away from Gipsy's Mile, 'it looks as though Mrs. Harrison's exhibition has been a roaring success this time. I must say, it was quite refreshing to spend the evening contemplating the higher forms of art without risking a punch in the face from the artist.'

'Art, do you call it?' said William. 'I can't say it's to my taste, but I dare say you know better, ma'am.'

'Oh, no,' said Angela. 'Beauty is in the eye of the beholder, as they say. You're quite welcome to dislike it, if you prefer.'

'I didn't mind some of it,' he said awkwardly. 'Mrs. Harrison's work is kind of interesting, I guess.'

'It is, isn't it? Some people find it rather too daring, but I believe I am a modern woman and I must say I quite like it. Now, then, do you suppose we shall arrive back in London in time for lunch? We set off a little late—by the way, William, you really must stop disappearing like that.'

'I'm sorry, ma'am,' said the young man, going pink. 'It won't happen again.'

Angela glanced at him.

'Your face, William,' she said.

William scrubbed at his cheek.

New Releases

If you'd like to receive news of further releases by Clara Benson, you can sign up to my mailing list here: smarturl.it/ClaraBenson.

We take data confidentiality very seriously and will not pass your details on to anybody else or send you any spam.

ClaraBenson.com